PRAISE FOR *DOWNTOWN OWL*

"Klosterman roams around in [his characters'] heads, turning out great line after great line. He's an entertaining guy, but also capable of real insight and artistry."

—*Entertainment Weekly*

"An astonishingly moving book, a minor masterpiece in the genre we might call small-town quirkiana. Klosterman is a real writer, it turns out, full of pathos and wisdom, ultimately determined to place his cleverness in the service of his readers. . . . He's doing the honest labor of a novelist, exposing the terrifying confusions that live within his characters. His ability to see past their evasions, and his determination to lay them bare with stabbing insights, calls to mind another famous American satirist, Kurt Vonnegut."

—*The Boston Globe*

"It's tempting to compare this novel with Sherwood Anderson's classic portrait of small-town American life, *Winesburg, Ohio*. But no one in Winesburg listened to Ozzy Osbourne. And Klosterman is much funnier than Anderson."

—*The Washington Post*

"Gifted with a superb ear for dialogue, a kind of perfect pitch for the way ordinary people talk, Klosterman is also capable of fine word-portraits of the three principal [characters]. Think of this as a literary relative of the movies *Fargo* and *American Graffiti*."

—*Booklist* (starred review)

"Chuck Klosterman is no doubt intimately familiar with characters like those who populate his debut novel. . . . He may now be a New York writer with a cult following, but these characters, that dialogue—he knows it all, inside out."

—*Minneapolis Star-Tribune*

"Klosterman is adept at thinking up bizarre, somehow plausible scenarios that hook readers while pushing the story along . . . [his] prose is a joy to read."

—*Paste*

"*Downtown Owl* is a virtuoso effort. . . . It is always clever, and often outright brilliant."

—Blogcritics.org

"He has a talent for infusing everyday situations with unorthodox detail and unexpected imagery."

—*National Post* (Canada)

"Four books of nonfiction and a steady magazine presence have established Klosterman as a pop culture writer known for his air-quotes wit. There's plenty of that sensibility in his first novel. . . . Klosterman creates a satisfying character study and strikes a perfect balance between the funny and the profound."

—*Publishers Weekly*

ALSO BY CHUCK KLOSTERMAN

Fargo Rock City:
A Heavy Metal Odyssey in Rural Nörth Dakota

Sex, Drugs, and Cocoa Puffs:
A Low Culture Manifesto

Killing Yourself to Live:
85% of a True Story

Chuck Klosterman IV:
A Decade of Curious People and Dangerous Ideas

DOWNTOWN OWL

A Novel

CHUCK KLOSTERMAN

SCRIBNER
New York London Toronto Sydney

SCRIBNER
A Division of Simon & Schuster
1230 Avenue of the Americas
New York, NY 10020

First Scribner trade paperback edition June 2009

DESIGNED BY ERICH HOBBING

Manufactured in the United States of America

1 3 5 7 9 10 8 6 4 2

Library of Congress Cataloging-in-Publication Data

Klosterman, Chuck, 1972–
Downtown Owl : a novel / by Chuck Klosterman.—1st Scribner hardcover ed.
p. cm.
1. North Dakota—Fiction. I. Title.

PS3611.L67D69 2008
813'.6—dc22
2007047088
ISBN 978-1-4165-4418-0
ISBN 978-1-4165-4419-7 (pbk)
ISBN 978-1-4165-8065-2 (ebook)

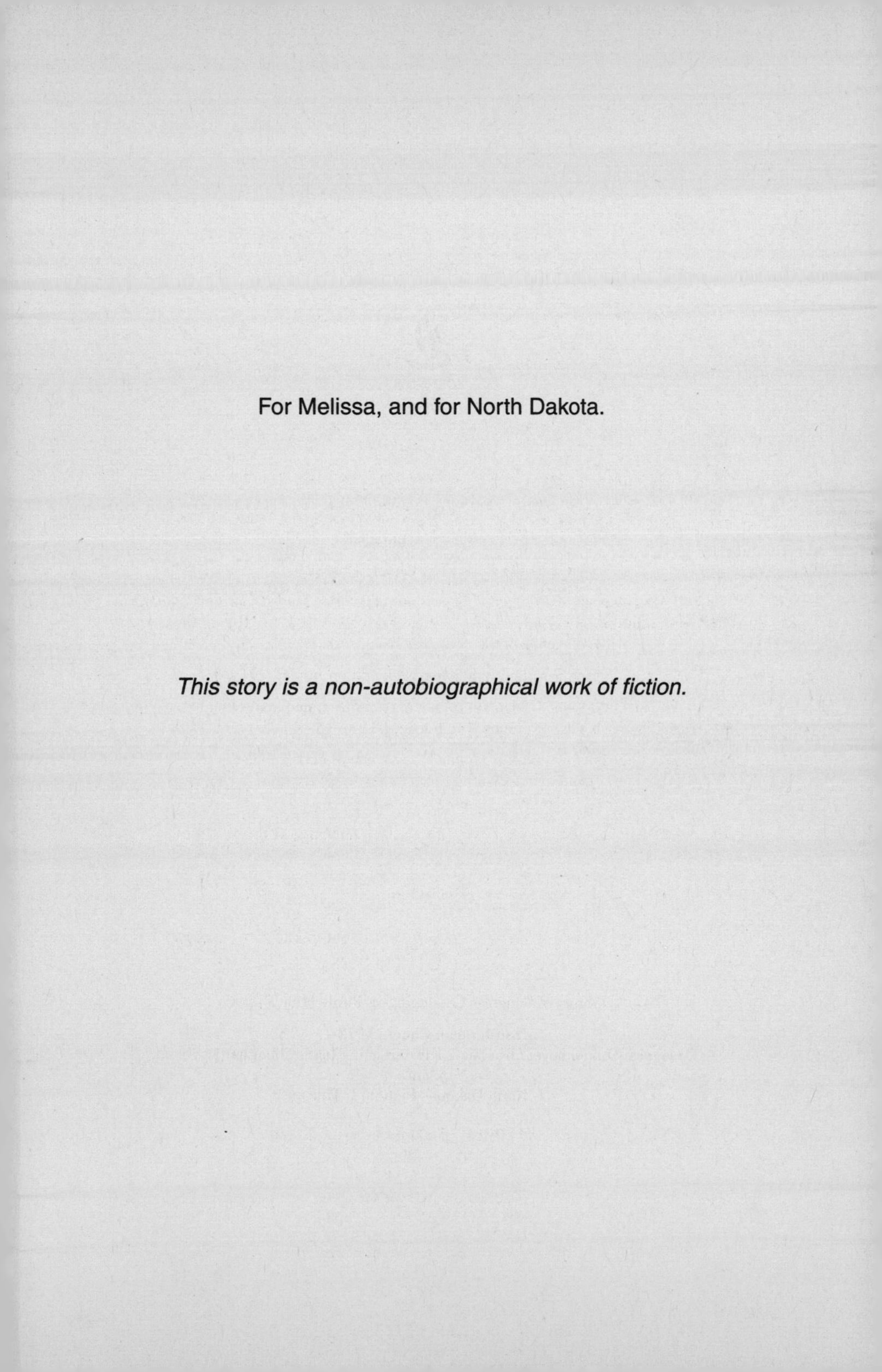

For Melissa, and for North Dakota.

This story is a non-autobiographical work of fiction.

DOWNTOWN OWL

FEBRUARY 5, 1984

Killer blizzard paralyzes region

FARGO, N.D. (UPI)—At least 11 people are dead and dozens more remain missing in the wake of the Red River Valley's most cataclysmic winter storm in more than a decade.

"This has been beyond a nightmare scenario," Lyle Condon of the National Weather Service said. "The speed with which this particular storm system moved across the region was almost unprecedented. By the time the reality of this blizzard became obvious, it was already too late for a whole lot of people."

Surprisingly, snow accumulations from the killer storm only measure between one and two inches. The intensity of the disaster was solely a product of its wind. Pushed by an "Alberta Clipper" that formed over British Columbia, Saturday's storm was punctuated by gusts of between 55 and 80 m.p.h., dropping visibility in open areas to less than a foot. At 6 p.m., the windchill factor at Fargo's Hector Internal Airport was measured at 74 degrees below zero. This falls in stark contrast with the local meteorological conditions just three hours prior, which NWS officials described as "calm, sunny, and unseasonably warm" (39 degrees).

The storm's initial northerly blast knocked numerous moving vehicles off of roadways and into ditches, particularly those cars and trucks moving along an east-west trajectory. Carbon monoxide killed four people on Fargo's 19th Avenue when their trapped vehicle was covered by drifting snow. The extent of the casualties remains less clear in rural areas, where many of the blizzard's victims are still classified as missing.

AUGUST 15, 1983

(Mitch)

When Mitch Hrlicka heard that his high school football coach had gotten another teenage girl pregnant, he was forty bushels beyond bamboozled. He could not understand what so many females saw in Mr. Laidlaw. He was inhumane, and also sarcastic. Whenever Mitch made the slightest mental error, Laidlaw would rhetorically scream, "Vanna? *Vanna?* Are you *drowsy*, Vanna? Wake up! You can sleep when you are dead, Vanna!" Mr. Laidlaw seemed unnaturally proud that he had nicknamed Mitch "Vanna White" last winter, solely based on one semifunny joke about how the surname "Hrlicka" needed more vowels. Mitch did not mind when other kids called him Vanna, because almost everyone he knew had a nickname; as far as he could tell, there was nothing remotely humiliating about being called "Vanna," assuming everyone understood that the name had been assigned arbitrarily. It symbolized nothing. But Mitch hated when John Laidlaw called him "Vanna," because Laidlaw *assumed* it was humiliating. And that, clearly, was his goal.

Christ, it was humid. When Mitch and his teenage associates had practiced that morning at 7:30 a.m., it was almost cool; the ground had been wet with dew and the clouds hovered fourteen feet off the ground. But now—eleven hours later—the sun was burning and falling like the Hindenburg. The air was damp wool. Mitch limped toward the practice field for the evening's upcoming death session; he could already feel sweat forming on his back and above his nose and under his crotch. His quadriceps stored enough lactic acid to turn a triceratops into limestone.

"God damn," he thought. "Why do I want this?" In two days the team would begin practicing in full pads. It would feel like being wrapped in cellophane while hauling bricks in a backpack. "God damn," he thought again. "This must be what it's like to live in Africa." Football was not designed for the summer, even if Herschel Walker believed otherwise.

When Mitch made it to the field, the other two Owl quarterbacks were already there, facing each other twelve yards apart, each standing next to a freshman. They were playing catch, but not directly; one QB would rifle the ball to the opposite freshman, who would (in theory) catch it and immediately flip it over to the second QB who was waiting at his side. The other quarterback would then throw the ball back to the other freshman, and the process would continue. This was how NFL quarterbacks warmed up on NFL sidelines. The process would have looked impressive to most objective onlookers, except for the fact that both freshman receivers dropped 30 percent of the passes that struck them in the hands. This detracted from the fake professionalism.

Mitch had no one to throw to, so he served as the holder while the kickers practiced field goals. This duty required him to crouch on one knee and remain motionless, which (of course) is not an ideal way to get one's throwing arm loose and relaxed. Which (of course) did not really matter, since Coach Laidlaw did not view Mitch's attempts at quarterbacking with any degree of seriousness. Mitch was not clutch. Nobody said this, but everybody knew. It was the biggest problem in his life.

At 7:01, John Laidlaw blew into a steel whistle and instructed everyone to *bring it in*. They did so posthaste.

"Okay," Laidlaw began. "This is the situation. The situation is this: We will not waste any light tonight, because we have a beautiful evening with not many mosquitoes and a first-class opportunity to start implementing some of the offense. I realize this is only the fourth practice, but we're already way behind on everything. It's obvious that most of you didn't put five goddamn minutes into thinking about football all goddamn summer, so now we're *all* behind. And I don't like being behind. I've never been a follower. I'm not that kind of person. Maybe you are, but I am not.

"Classes start in two weeks. Our first game is in three weeks. We need to have *the entire offense* ready by the day we begin classes, and we need to have all of the defensive sets memorized *before* we begin classes. And right now, I must be honest: I don't even know who the hell is going to play for us. So this is the situation. The situation is this: Right now, everybody here is equally useless. This is going to be an important, crucial, important, critical, important two weeks for everyone here, and it's going to be a real kick in the face to any of you who still want to be home watching *The Price Is Right.* And I know there's going to be a lot of people in this town talking about a lot of bull crap that doesn't have anything to do with football, and you're going to hear about certain things that happened or didn't happen or that supposedly happened or that supposedly allegedly didn't happen to somebody that probably doesn't even exist. These are what we call *distractions.* These distractions will come from all the people who don't want you to think about Owl Lobo football. So if I hear anyone on this team perpetuating those kinds of bullshit stories, everyone is going to pay for those distractions. Everyone. *Because we are here to think about Owl Lobo football.* And if you are not thinking exclusively—*exclusively*—about Owl Lobo football, go home and turn on *The Price Is Right.* Try to win yourself a washing machine."

It remains unclear why John Laidlaw carried such a specific, all-encompassing hatred for viewers of *The Price Is Right.* No one will ever know why this was. Almost as confusing was the explanation as to why Owl High School was nicknamed the Lobos, particularly since they had been the Owl Owls up until 1964. During the summer of '64, the citizens of Owl suddenly concluded that being called the Owl Owls was somewhat embarrassing, urging the school board to change the nickname to something "less repetitive." This proposal was deeply polarizing to much of the community. The motion didn't pass until the third vote. And because most of the existing Owl High School athletic gear still featured its long-standing logo of a feathered wing, it was decided that the new nickname should remain ornithological. As such, the program was known as the Owl Eagles for all of the 1964–1965 school year. Contrary to community hopes, this change dramatically increased the degree to which its sports teams were mocked by opposing schools. During the especially oppressive summer of 1969, they decided to change the nickname again, this time becoming the Owl High Screaming Satans. (New uniforms were immediately purchased.) Two games into the '69 football season, the local Lutheran and Methodist churches jointly petitioned the school board, arguing that the nickname "Satan" glorified the occult and needed to be changed on religious grounds; oddly (or perhaps predictably), the local Catholic church responded by aggressively supporting the new moniker, thereby initiating a bitter feud among the various congregations. (This was punctuated by a now infamous street fight that involved the punching of a horse.) When the Lutheran minister ultimately decreed that all Protestant athletes would have to quit all extracurricular activities if the name "Satan" remained in place, the school was forced to change nicknames midseason. Nobody knew how to handle this unprecedented turn of events. Eventually, one of the cheerleaders noticed that the existing satanic logo actually resembled an angry humanoid wolf, a realization that seemed brilliant at the time. (The cheerleader, Janelle Fluto, is now a lesbian living in Thunder Bay, Ontario.) The Screaming Satans subsequently became the Screaming Lobos, a name that was edited down to Lobos upon the recognition that wolves do not scream. This nickname still causes mild confusion, as strangers sometimes assume the existence of a mythological creature called the "Owl Lobo," which would (indeed) be a terrifying (and potentially winged) carnivore hailing from western Mexico. But—nonetheless, and more importantly—there has not been any major community controversy since the late sixties. Things have been perfect ever since, if by "perfect" you mean "exactly the same."

Mitch and the rest of the Lobos clapped their hands simultaneously and started to jog one lap around the practice field, ostensibly preparing to perform a variety of calisthenics while thinking exclusively about Owl Lobo football and not fantasizing about *The Price Is Right.* But such a goal was always impossible. It was still summer. As Mitch loped along the sidelines, his mind drifted to other subjects, most notably a) Gordon Kahl, b) the Georgetown Hoyas, c) how John Laidlaw managed to seduce and impregnate Tina McAndrew, and d) how awful it must feel to be John Laidlaw's wife.

AUGUST 25, 1983

(Julia)

"You're going to like it here," said Walter Valentine. He said this from behind a nine-hundred-pound cherrywood desk, hands interlocked behind his head while his eyes looked toward the ceiling, focusing on nothing. "I have no doubt about that. I mean, it's not like this is some kind of wonderland. This isn't anyone's destination city. It's not Las Vegas. It's not Monaco. It's not like you'll be phoning your gal pals every night and saying, 'I'm living in Owl, North Dakota, and it's a dream come true.' *But you will like it here.* It's a good place to live. The kids are great, in their own way. The people are friendly, by and large. You will be popular. You will be very, very popular."

Julia did not know what most of those sentences meant.

"I will be popular," she said, almost as if she was posing a question (but not quite).

"Oh, absolutely," Valentine continued, now rifling through documents that did not appear particularly official. "I know that you are scheduled to teach seventh-grade history, eighth-grade geography, U.S. History, World History, and something else. Are you teaching Our State? I think you're scheduled to teach Our State. Yes. Yes, you are. 'Our State.' But that's just an unfancy name for North Dakota history, so that's simple enough: Teddy Roosevelt, Angie Dickinson, lignite coal, that sort of thing. The Gordon Kahl incident, I suppose. Of course, the fact that you're not *from* North Dakota might make that a tad trickier, but only during the first year. After that, history just repeats itself. But I suppose the first thing we should talk about is volleyball."

"Pardon?"

"What do you know about volleyball?"

Julia had been in downtown Owl for less than forty-eight hours. The land here was so relentlessly flat; it was the flattest place she'd ever seen. She had driven from Madison, Wisconsin, in nine hours, easily packing her entire existence into the hatchback of a Honda Civic. There was only one apartment building in the entire town and it was on the edge of the city limits; it was a two-story four-plex, and the top two apartments were empty. She took the bigger one, which rented for fifty-five dollars a month. When she looked out her bedroom window, she could see for ten miles to the north. Maybe for twenty miles. Maybe she was seeing Manitoba. It was like the earth had been pounded with a rolling pin. The landlord told her that Owl was supposedly getting cable television services next spring, but he admitted some skepticism about the rumor; he had heard such rumors before.

Julia was now sitting in the office of the Owl High principal. He resumed looking at the ceiling, appreciating its flatness.

"I've never played volleyball," Julia replied. "I don't know the rules. I don't even know how the players keep score of the volley balling."

"Oh. Oh. Well, that's unfortunate," Valentine said. "No worries, but that's too bad. I only ask because it looks like we're going to have to add volleyball to the extracurricular schedule in two years, or maybe even as soon as next year. It's one of those idiotic Title IX situations—apparently, we can't offer three boys' sports unless we offer three girls' sports. So now we have to figure out who in the hell is going to coach girls' volleyball, which is proving to be damn near impossible. Are you sure that isn't something you might *eventually* be interested in? Just as a thought? You would be paid an additional three hundred dollars per season. You'd have a full year to get familiar with the sport. We'd pay for any books on the subject you might need. I'm sure there are some wonderful books out there on the nature of volleyball."

"I really, really cannot coach volleyball," Julia said. "I'm not coordinated."

"Oh. Oh! Okay, no problem. I just thought I'd ask." Mr. Valentine looked at her for a few moments before his pupils returned to the ceiling. "Obviously, it would be appreciated if you thought about it, but—ultimately—volleyball doesn't matter. We just want you to do all the things that you do, whatever those things may be. I'm sure you bring a lot to the table. Do you have any questions for me?"

Julia had 140,000 questions. She asked only one.

"What's it like to live here?"

This was not supposed to sound flip, but that's how it came out. Julia always came across as cocky whenever she felt nervous.

"It's like living anywhere, I suppose." Valentine unlocked his fingers and crossed his arms, glancing momentarily at Julia's face. He then proceeded to stare at the mallard duck that was painted on his coffee cup, half filled with cherry Kool-Aid. "Owl's population used to be around twelve hundred during the height of the 1970s, but now it's more like eight hundred. Maybe eight fifty. I don't know where all the people went. It's a down town, Owl. We still have a decent grocery store, which is important, but—these days—it seems like a lot of folks will drive to Jamestown, or even all the way to Valley City, just to do their food shopping. Americans are crazy. There's a hardware store, but I wonder how much longer that will last. We have a first-rate Chevrolet dealership. We have two gas stations. We have seven bars, although you can hardly count the Oasis Wheel. You probably don't want to spend your nights at the Oasis Wheel, unless you're not the kind of woman I think you are. Heh! And you've probably heard that the movie theater is going to close, and I'm afraid that's true: It *is* closing. But the bowling alley is thriving. It's probably the best bowling alley in the region. I honestly believe that."

By chance, Julia did enjoy bowling. However, when the most positive detail about your new home is that the bowling alley is thriving, you have to like bowling *a lot* in order to stave off depression. And—right now, in the middle of this conversation—Julia was more depressed than she had ever been in her entire twenty-three-year existence. As she sat in Walter Valentine's office, she felt herself wanting to take a nap on the floor. But she (of course) did not do this; she just looked at him, nodding and half smiling. She could always sleep later, after she finished crying.

"The thing that you have to realize about a place like Owl is that everyone is aware of all the same things. There's a lot of shared knowledge," Valentine said. He was now leaning forward in his chair, looking at Julia and casually pointing at her chest with both his index fingers. "Take this year's senior class, for example. There are twenty-six kids in that class. Fifteen of them started kindergarten together. That means that a lot of those students have sat next to each other—in just about every single class—for thirteen straight years. They've shared every single experience. You said you grew up in Milwaukee, correct?"

"Yes."

"How big was your graduating class?"

"Oh, man. I have no idea," Julia said. "Around seven hundred, I think. It was a normal public school."

"Exactly. *Normal.* But your normal class was almost as big as our whole town. And the thing is, when those twenty-six seniors graduate, the majority will go to college, at least for two years. But almost all the farm kids—or at least all the farm *boys*—inevitably come back here when they're done with school, and they start farming with their fathers. In other words, the same kids who spent thirteen years in class with each other start going to the same bars and they bowl together and they go to the same church and pretty much live an adult version of their high school life. You know, people always say that nothing changes in a small town, but—whenever they say that—they usually mean that nothing changes *figuratively.* The truth is that nothing changes *literally*: It's always all the same people, doing all the same things."

Upon hearing this description, the one singular phrase that went through Julia's head was "Jesus fucking Christ." However, those were not the words that she spoke.

"Wow," she said. "That sounds kind of . . . unmodern."

"It is," Valentine said. Then he chuckled. Then he re-interlocked his fingers behind his skull and refocused his gaze on the ceiling. "Except that it's not. It's actually not abnormal at all. Look: I came here as a math teacher twenty years ago, and I thought I would be bored out of my trousers. I had grown up in Minot and I went to college in Grand Forks, so I considered myself urban. I always imagined I'd end up in Minneapolis, or even maybe Chicago; I have a friend from college who lives just outside of Chicago, so I've eaten in restaurants in that area and I have an understanding of that life. But once I really settled in Owl, I never tried to leave. I mean . . . sure, sometimes you think, 'Hey, maybe there's something else out there.' But there really isn't. This is what being alive feels like, you know? The place doesn't matter. You just live."

Julia could feel hydrochloric acid inside her tear ducts. There was an especially fuzzy tennis ball in her esophagus, and she wanted to be high.

But she remained cool.

Julia told Mr. Valentine she was extremely excited to be working at Owl High, and she thanked him for giving her the opportunity to start a career in teaching, which she claimed was her lifelong dream. "Everybody only has one first job," he said in response. "No matter what you do in life, you'll always remember your first job. So welcome aboard and good luck, although you won't need it. You'll be extremely popular here. And if you change your mind about that excellent volleyball opportunity, do not hesitate to call. Keep me in the loop. I'm always here, obviously."

Julia exited Valentine's office and walked toward the school's main entrance, faster and more violent with every step. She was virtually running when she got to the door and sprinted to her car, which was one of only three vehicles in the parking lot. Ten days from now, school would officially start. This building would be the totality of her life. She already hated it. The overtly idyllic nature of Owl seemed paradoxically menacing; it was like a Burmese tiger trap for apolitical strangers who needed uninteresting jobs. She didn't know anyone and had no idea how she ever would. Her apartment was on the far side of town, which meant it was a three-minute drive. She passed two cars and two pickup trucks; all four drivers waved hello as she passed. The waving scared her. She soon arrived in her apartment, where she had no furniture (and no idea how to acquire any, as there were apparently no furniture stores within a thirty-mile radius). She cut open the cardboard box that held her cassettes and found a dubbed copy of Foreigner's *4*, which she robotically placed into a boom box sitting on the floor. She fast-forwarded to "Juke Box Hero" and pushed play; the emptiness of the room produced a slight echo behind Lou Gramm's voice. Her apartment was like a bank vault with a refrigerator. Julia reached into the same cardboard box and found her copy of *The Random House Thesaurus (College Edition)*, which contained drugs. The day before leaving Madison, Julia and her college roommates meticulously rolled four perfect joints and hid them in the thesaurus, operating under the assumption that buying pot would be impossible in small-town North Dakota (which was, in fact, the case). The plan was that Julia could smoke one joint after the first day of class, one on Thanksgiving (which she would have to spend alone), and one after the last day of school in May. The fourth was a spare that could be consumed when (and if) she needed to offset any major unforeseen emergency that might occur over the course of the school year.

Julia sat on her sleeping bag and smoked three of them, all in a row. It was 2:45 p.m.

AUGUST 28, 1983

(Horace)

His life revolved around coffee.

It was central to his existence.

He was that kind of person.

It wasn't even so much the taste, although he did consider coffee to be delicious; he mostly loved the process of drinking it. Every day at 3:00 p.m. (except on Sundays), he drove three miles into town, sat on the third stool in Harley's Café, and drank three cups of coffee, each cup with three tablespoons of sugar. This was not because Horace Jones had OCD or a superstitious obsession with the number three; it was just a coincidence. If you were to ask Horace which stool he sat in (or how many spoonfuls of sugar he placed in his coffee), he would have no idea. These were merely things he did. They were not things he considered.

All of the men in Harley's played poker dice to see who would pay for each round of coffee; the winner paid for everybody, which (curiously) was the goal. There were usually six players, so an entire round of coffee cost $1.50, plus tip. Horace won 16.6 percent of the time. He considered himself extremely unlucky. But winning or losing at poker dice was only a secondary issue, since the conversation at Harley's was always worth the trip into town; stimulating conversation was something Horace could look forward to every single afternoon. These are the topics that were primarily discussed:

1) How current meteorological conditions compared to whatever were supposed to be the average meteorological condi-

tions (i.e., temperatures that were higher or lower than usual, rainfall amounts that seemed out of the ordinary, et cetera).

2) The success (or lack thereof) of the local high school athletic teams, and particularly how contemporary teams would have fared against Owl teams from the late 1960s and early '70s (the conclusion being "not very well").
3) Walter Mondale's potential run for the presidency, an undeniably hopeless venture that only served to illustrate how the state of Minnesota had been destroyed by the same kind of naïve Democrats who crashed all those helicopters in the Iranian desert.
4) The North Dakota State University football team, particularly the number of local North Dakota high school players the school was recruiting in comparison to the number of black, out-of-state, potentially criminal athletes who were already on the traveling roster.
5) The implausibility of specific plotlines on the television show *Dallas*.
6) Acquaintances who had recently died (or were in the process of dying, usually from cancer). This topic was increasing in regularity.
7) Area events they all recalled from the 1950s, generally described as having happened in the relatively recent past.
8) How the market price of hard red spring wheat ($3.51 per bushel) was barely a dollar more than its price during the Dirty Thirties. This made no goddamn sense to anyone.
9) Gordon Kahl.
10) Other people's problems.

"So . . . more problems with the Dog Lover." This was Edgar Camaro speaking. Edgar was the youngest of the coffee drinkers; he was sixty-three. "That idiot kid is going to end up sleeping with Jesus. Did you hear what he said the other night?"

"His statement about the rain?" asked Horace.

"Yes," replied Edgar. "The rain. Just imagine the goddamn scenario: The Dog Lover is tending bar on Saturday night—this is early in the night, maybe seven o'clock—and the idiot is already tight."

"Somebody needs to inform that kid that a good bartender never drinks before midnight," interjected Bud Haugen, a man who had briefly owned a bar during the Korean conflict. "Christ. You'd think everybody would know that."

"Well, sure," said Edgar. "You'd *think* someone would have given that idiot some sense, but I guess he only listens to that hound of his. Heh. But here we go: It starts to drizzle Saturday night, and a few of the guys in the bar—this is like Edmund and Kuch and Woo-Chuck and that whole crew of outlaws—they get up and start looking out the windows, because Lord knows we need the rain. And that idiot—that idiot Dog Lover—he *turns down the jukebox* and says, 'Haven't you farmers ever seen rain before?' Can you believe that? In the middle of the worst drought in forty years, he tells a bunch of *paying customers* that they're stupid for looking at the rain."

"I'm surprised Woo-Chuck didn't snap his spine," said eighty-eight-year-old Ollie Pinkerton, his lazy eye drifting around the room like a child looking for the bathroom. "I mean, don't get me wrong—Woo-Chuck is a nice kid and a hard worker. But let's shoot straight: The man is a criminal." This was true. "Woo-Chuck" was an abbreviation of "Woodchuck." Bob (The Woodchuck) Hodgeman had served in Vietnam, which was something he never talked about. But everyone assumed he must have done (or at least *seen*) some crazy shit over there, because he drank in this awkward, exceedingly antisocial manner, and he drank all the time, and sometimes he punched his own friends for no reason and couldn't explain why. People called him Woodchuck (or, more often, Woo-Chuck) because he used to stash Quaaludes in the upholstery of his Monte Carlo. This seemed like something a woodchuck would do. On balance, he was a good person.

"Supposedly, that almost happened," Edgar continued. "They say Woo-Chuck walked up to the Dog Lover with a really queer look on his face. Remember that night last Christmas, when Woo-Chuck got loaded and threw a pitchfork at his son-in-law? I guess he had those same crazy eyes. But that idiot Dog Lover—probably because he was already seventeen sheets to the wind—he had no fear whatsoever. He just stood there like a concrete shithouse. Words were exchanged. And then the Dog Lover threw everybody out of the bar. Everybody. He emptied the whole place, and it wasn't even seven thirty. Locked all the doors. And then he just sat there, alone, swilling his own booze, listening to the Twins game on the radio. Have you ever heard of anything more asinine? If he's not careful, that bar is gonna end up worse than the Oasis Wheel. Some people just can't stand prosperity."

The Dog Lover's real name was Chet. He had lived a dubious life: Chet's father was (supposedly) one of the most successful bar owners in the Twin Cities; he (supposedly) co-owned five sports bars with Minnesota Vikings quarterback Tommy Kramer. Chet, however, was an irresponsible train wreck: DWIs, dope smoking, girl crazy, gun crazy, car crazy—all the usual interests of the prototypical meathead miscreant. Chet flunked out of St. Cloud State University, was readmitted a year later, and was bounced a second time for selling (fake) pot on campus. His father didn't know what to do with him, and he certainly didn't want Chet hanging around Minneapolis with no job and no prospects; if that happened, Chet was destined to get involved with cocaine or gambling or arson. Chet was a twenty-five-year-old dirtbag. Everybody knew this. As such, his father played the only card he could manufacture: He bought his son a life in a place where it was hard to find trouble. He bought his son a bar in a town where nothing happened, moved him into a four-plex apartment complex, and told him to stay away from Minneapolis until he "learned how the world worked."

That was almost a year ago. Over the subsequent eleven

months, Chet had managed to alienate almost every citizen in town, seemingly on purpose. The first thing he did was change the name of the bar from Teddy's (after the name of the previous owner) to Yoda's (a reference completely lost on the overwhelming majority of his clientele). He had a dangerous propensity for hiring Owl High School students as waitresses, getting them drunk on the job, and openly chiding them for dressing too conservatively; this practice was finally stopped after he fed sixteen-year-old Ann Marie Pegseth so many clandestine wine coolers that she removed her blouse and worked an entire shift in her bra. Two days later, Ann Marie's father threatened to destroy Chet's Z28 Camaro with dynamite. Chet was a prick and a provocateur, constantly outdrinking his patrons and ridiculing the blandness of their conversation. He told Phil Anderson that his wife needed to eat more salad. He told Cindy Brewer that her voice reminded him of "a cuntier version of Joan Rivers." One of his running shticks was insisting that he recognized Randy Pemberton's girlfriend from *Hustler* magazine's "Beaver Hunt" section. He charged way too much for booze (sometimes $2.50 a beer, even for Schmidt). But the one quality that truly drove the citizens of Owl bonkers—and particularly the old men who had coffee at Harley's Café every day at 3:00 p.m.—was Chet's intimacy with his dog. Chet had a black Labrador retriever, and he kept it *inside his apartment.* He turned a hunting animal into a house pet. This was less reasonable than talking to a brick wall. He would bring his dog *inside the bar,* and the dog often sat *in the front seat of his Camaro,* a vehicle *which supposedly cost sixteen thousand dollars.*

Just thinking about that dog made Horace furious. What kind of man treats his dog like a wife? You'd have to be mentally retarded. There were inside animals and there were outside animals, and any dog the size of a Labrador was absolutely, irrevocably, indisputably an outside animal. Oh, you might let a dog inside the pantry during a blizzard or a tornado, but kitchens are for humans. It was almost cruel: Dogs need to run.

Dogs need to herd sheep and chase jackrabbits and retain the few grains of nobility that canines are born with. Only a fool couldn't tell the difference between a man and a beast, and this made Chet a fool; it made him the Dog Lover, which was a deeper insult than that bartender could possibly realize.

Horace wondered how long it had been since he'd set foot inside a tavern. Ten years? Probably ten years. He didn't like them anymore. The bars had changed: These days, all the young men drank beer. When he was in his thirties, men drank OFC whiskey. Nobody knew what the letters "OFC" technically stood for, but they all assumed it meant Only For Cowboys. Norwegians and Polacks were beer drinkers, but no legitimate white man would go into a bar and slurp sixteen fluid ounces of wheat foam. Beer drinkers were embarrassing. Sometimes Horace felt embarrassed for the totality of culture, and for the role he had played in its creation. "That's why all these modern men are soft," he thought to himself as he looked into the brown-black remnants of his sugar-saturated coffee. "They're all beer-gorged and lazy. They have no grit. They're scared of whiskey. They're scared of the world."

It was time for everyone to roll the dice. Horace rolled a pair of fives. It was not enough to win. His luck was never going to change.

AUGUST 29, 1983

(Mitch)

John S. Laidlaw was a football coach, a pheasant hunter, a two-pack-a-day smoker, a notorious cheapskate, a deeply closeted atheist, and an outspoken libertarian. But he was also an English teacher, and—were it not for his preoccupation with convincing female students to have intercourse with him inside his powder-blue Caprice Classic—he might have been among the best educators in the entire state of North Dakota. He was certainly the finest teacher in Owl, even when you factored in the emotional cruelty and the statutory raping.

"Good morning. *Good morning!* I hope everyone who's supposed to be in this room is in this room." Laidlaw spoke to his class while standing behind nothing; he rarely sat at his desk and never used a podium. He spoke with enthusiasm, but he made no hand gestures; his eyes bulged like a Komodo dragon's. John Laidlaw was not handsome, but he was Steve Martin sexy. "At this juncture, I would normally welcome all of you to junior English. However, I'm abundantly aware that none of you would be here if this class wasn't required by the state, so I'm not going to talk to you like cocktail guests. There will be no pretending in this classroom. I am not a showman. I am not a jester or a salesman. This is the situation. The situation is this: For the next nine months, you are my indentured servants."

Much of the class (and certainly all of the girls) laughed at this remark, which is what they were expected to do. Mitch, however, did not chuckle. Mitch fantasized about tying Mr. Laidlaw to a bed and cutting long incisions into his torso with a razor blade before filling the wounds with Morton salt. He closed his eyes and imagined this torture while Laidlaw spoke.

"Now, as many of you may know, junior English is normally when we study 'American Literature,' which means we read literature from American literary figures. These are people like Ernest Hemingway and F. Scott Fitzgerald. These are people like Richard Wright, who was black. These are poets like Robert Frost, who wrote about activities such as chopping wood and walking through a forest after a snowstorm, as these things are often symbolic of disenchantment. Herman Melville was an American author, and he wrote *Moby-Dick,* which is the greatest book of all time. Has anyone here read *Moby-Dick*?"

There were twenty-two juniors in the room. Twenty-one of them had never even seen the cover of *Moby-Dick,* so they remained silent out of necessity. The twenty-second junior, Rebecca Grooba, had read *Moby-Dick* in sixth grade. She remained silent by choice, just as she had (and just as she would) for the duration of every class she ever took (or would take) during her thirteen years inside the rectangular classrooms of Owl public school. During that thirteen-year span, Rebecca Grooba would never score less than 94 on any scholastic examination, except for one 67 on an extra-credit trigonometry test that no one else was able to attempt. Rebecca Grooba taught herself how to read was she was four. She won the state spelling bee in 1976, 1977, and 1979. (She had mono in the spring of '78.) She understood how isotopes operated before she knew what isotopes were. She could count cards and memorize Social Security numbers. As an eighth grader, she read *Finnegans Wake* over Christmas vacation and scrawled the digits "1132" on her Earth Science notebook. No one asked why she did this. Rebecca Grooba was a genius; everyone in Owl knew it, but hardly anyone cared. She was so shy that she wasn't even unpopular. Over time, her wordless brilliance became routine, and then it became boring. People quit noticing.

In 1988, Rebecca Grooba would become a registered nurse.

"So no one here has read *Moby-Dick*?" Laidlaw continued after a pause. "Not one person. Not even you, Rebecca?" Rebecca did not respond. "Jeepers cripes. Not one person in this room has perused the 752 brilliant pages of *Moby-Dick*. That's stunning. That's really, really stunning. Also, this is sarcasm. Do we all know what sarcasm is? Sarcasm is when you tell someone the truth by lying on purpose. Does anyone in this room even know what *Moby-Dick* is about?"

"It's about a guy who kills a whale," said Eli Zebra. "It's about a guy who kills a sperm whale with a harpoon." Zebra answered a lot of questions during class, especially if they were not important. Contrary to what might seem obvious, Eli Zebra's name was not pronounced like that of the familiar black-and-white African horse; his last name was pronounced with a soft *e,* so that it rhymed with *Debra* or *ephedra.* Whenever people got his name wrong (and everyone got it wrong), Eli would say, "It's pronounced exactly how it looks," which only made them more confused. Eli Zebra was one of the few adolescent males in Owl who did not have a nickname, mostly because it's impossible to come up with a better nickname than Zebra, particularly when it's not pronounced *zebra.* He was exotic by default.

"That's true, Zebra," Laidlaw said, unimpressed. "I suppose the killing of a whale is technically what *Moby-Dick* is about, although that's kind of like saying *Where the Red Fern Grows* is about the best way to feed a dog to a wolverine. If whale hunting was truly the point of that book, nobody would care about the point. Do you understand what I am saying, Eli? *Moby-Dick* is about a lot of things. It's about vengeance. It's about making rope. And the reason I bring these things up is because these are all things you would—normally—learn about this semester. This is because—normally—we always read *Moby-Dick* as part of junior English. But not this year. You people won't read *Moby-Dick* until next year, when I teach you senior English, even though senior English is supposed to be 'British Literature' and Herman Melville was an American. Does anyone know why we're doing this? Does anyone know why we're not going to read *Moby-Dick* this year?"

Here again, no one responded. However, this was not due to apathy. It was due to the fact that this was unknowable, even for Rebecca Grooba.

"The reason we are not reading *Moby-Dick*," Laidlaw continued, "is because I want us to read the novel we would normally read *next* year, as this particular novel is British. And we're going to read this book for a very specific reason. Does anyone here know anything about the writer George Orwell? Anything at all?"

Again, Zebra responded without raising his hand. (Now that he was sixteen years old, raising his hand struck him as immature.)

"He was a homosexual alcoholic," Zebra said.

"No," Laidlaw countered. "No, he was not. You're thinking of Truman Capote, who was American. And—quite frankly, Zebra—those are pretty strange things for you to know about Truman Capote, even though both of those facts are true. But I can guarantee you that George Orwell was not gay. Let's be clear on this: *George Orwell was not gay.* More importantly, George Orwell hated Communism. Granted, that detail can be confusing to some readers, because Orwell *didn't* hate socialism. Now, I'm not sure if any of you even know what those two terms mean, and, even if you do, you're probably wondering what the difference is. Here's the simple answer: Right now, in Russia, they have Communism. But socialism doesn't exist and probably never will. Do you see what I mean? It's complicated. The difference is subtle, yet vast."

Mitch wondered what it would be like to have a girlfriend. What would they do together? What would they talk about? What did John Laidlaw talk about with Tina McAndrew? It was always so hard to come up with things to say. When you want to kiss someone, do you ask for their permission, or do you just go for it? Mitch had kissed only one girl in his entire life: It was thirteen months ago. She was a black-haired eighth grader who had moved to Owl only two weeks before. They were both drinking root beer schnapps. It was at a party at the apple grove, and drunkards were throwing apples at parked cars. This fourteen-year-old female stranger was much more romantically experienced than Mitch, and that made everything terrifying. He could recall the conversation directly preceding the physical exchange, but the words had seemed wholly unrelated to the kissing; she asked him about a rock group he was completely unfamiliar with while he asked if she'd ever heard about some implausible movie called *Fast Times at Ridgemont High.* The black-haired girl ultimately made out with three different boys at this same party, and—late in the evening—she casually pulled down her pants and peed in front of everyone. Her motives were ambiguous. Mitch was relieved when she moved away two months later.

"Orwell's greatest achievement was *Animal Farm,*" droned Laidlaw, gaining both momentum and intensity. "That book was about how unpopular ideas can often be silenced without the use of force. That's one of the core dangers of Communism—and of all government, really. The story also involves brilliant, diplomatic farm animals, which is why it's such a classic. However, we are going to be reading Orwell's second-best book, which is called *Nineteen Eighty-Four.* Can anyone here guess why we are going to read *Nineteen Eighty-Four?*"

"Because it's 1983," said Zebra.

"No," said Laidlaw. "But at least you're within striking distance, Zebra. We are not going to read *Nineteen Eighty-Four* because it's 1983. We are going to read *Nineteen Eighty-Four* because it's *going to be* 1984. This is something that's going to happen, and it's going to happen to all of us. Four months from now, when we finally reach New Year's Day, you are all going to see a lot of news stories about *Nineteen Eighty-Four* on the TV and in the newspaper, and everybody in the world is going to be talking about the significance of this book. And the situation is this: I want you all to understand what everyone is talking about. I want you to understand the references. When some bozo on TV says, 'Hey, here we are in 1984, and it's nothing like that book by George Orwell,' you will be able to say, 'Really? Are you sure about that? Maybe you're wrong about that. How much freedom do we really have? Where are my taxes really going?' This is something the whole country is going to be talking about when we attack January. That kind of dialogue is going to be everywhere. So—as always—I'm having the senior class read *Nineteen Eighty-Four*, but I'm also having you juniors read *Nineteen Eighty-Four*. And I'm also having the sophomores read it, and I'm having the freshmen read it. I've also told Mrs. Strickland that she should have her seventh- and eighth-grade English students read this book, and she has agreed to do so. So we're all in this together. Everyone in this school is going to read *Nineteen Eighty-Four*. We will all have this same specific experience, and it's going to be wonderful."

Mitch sketched a three-dimensional cube on his notebook and dreamt about the near future. In three months it would be basketball season; maybe this year he could wear a T-shirt underneath his jersey, not unlike Patrick Ewing.

"The central issue in *Nineteen Eighty-Four* is personal privacy," said Laidlaw. He saw this as the main issue in many novels. "It's about governmental intrusion, which is a complex problem. For instance, I'm sure you're all very familiar with the Gordon Kahl incident that happened six months ago, just up the road from here. Gordon Kahl had a long-standing dispute with the federal government, and he didn't want to pay his income tax. He didn't want *anyone* to pay their taxes. Now, that impulse is completely understandable. But when federal marshals from Fargo tried to arrest him for nonpayment, he shot two of them with a rifle. Gordon Kahl was an excellent shot. Can we defend Kahl's actions? Of course not. We certainly cannot support Gordon Kahl, or at least not his willingness to murder people. The citizens of Medina, North Dakota, will never recover from that tragedy. Their community will never be the same. But such a situation raises many questions: What role should the government play in our lives? What *is* freedom, really? And at what point is freedom more important than respect for the rule of law?

"As you read *Nineteen Eighty-Four,* you will learn about a man named Winston Smith. This is a man watched by the government and hounded by a group called the Thought Police. He is under surveillance twenty-four hours a day. This, obviously, would be horrifying. I'm sure none of you would enjoy being watched twenty-four hours a day. Or maybe I'm wrong. Maybe some of you would love being watched twenty-four hours a day."

Laidlaw smiled and swiveled his skull around the room like an oscillating fan. His arms remained motionless. A few of the girls giggled. They knew what was coming.

"How about you, Vanna?" Laidlaw finally said, fixing his robotic dragon eyes on the ever-slumping Mitch. "Vanna? *Vanna?* Are you not getting enough rest, Vanna? How would you feel if we were all watching you twenty-four hours a day? What would we see behind closed doors? Would it shock us? Would we be shocked?"

There is no viable answer for this kind of query.

"You would not be shocked," Mitch said. "I'm not . . . shocking."

"Actually, I think I might be shocked," Laidlaw said. "I think I would be shocked if I saw you awake, since I can only assume you sleep fifteen hours a night."

The other kids laughed, but not in a mean way. They laughed because someone in a position of authority had told a predictable joke, and it would have made things weirder if everyone had sat there in silence and tried to figure out why Mr. Laidlaw was obsessed with the possibility that Mitch Hrlicka was narcoleptic. It was a joke Laidlaw had been making for three consecutive school years; silence would have made the joke seem meaner than it was, so they laughed for the sake of normalcy.

Minutes passed, or maybe decades. The bell rang. Each of the twenty-two juniors picked up a paperback copy of *Nineteen Eighty-Four* off the top of Laidlaw's desk and power-walked toward their lockers; in three minutes, the seventeen smartest juniors would go to chemistry while the five dumbest would attend the alternative option ("Vocational Technologies"). Zebra walked with Mitch.

"Dude," said Zebra. Because of Sean Penn, saying *dude* had recently become fashionable. "Dude, that dude hates you. Why the fuck does he hate you? I don't understand why that dude fucking hates you so much."

"He doesn't hate me," Mitch replied. "He just knows I don't care what he says." As he said these words, Mitch imagined how wonderful it would feel to jam a screwdriver into Laidlaw's eye socket. He imagined pushing Laidlaw down a flight of metal stairs, possibly toward a bear. He wondered if there would ever be a situation in his life where it would be acceptable to punch John Laidlaw in the face, and he wondered if his fist could shatter another man's jaw.

"Yeah, well, fuck that dude," said Zebra. "And actually, I must say that this book sounds potentially not terrible. It sounds a little like *Escape from New York.* Which reminds me: I got the greatest fucking tape last weekend. Have you ever heard of ZZ Top?"

Mitch had never heard of anybody. Mitch hated rock music, and he could not understand why everyone he knew talked about it constantly. Whenever he tried to listen to FM radio, it always sounded completely ridiculous: All the lyrics were nonsensical and all the guitars were identical.

"These ZZ Top guys have insane Texas beards and a killer fucking car, and it's all super heavy," said Zebra. "They sing about TV dinners. The guitars are heavy as shit. They're heavier than everything. It's like a really heavy Cars album."

"I never understand why you say that," Mitch said. "What do you mean when you say *heavy*? Heavier than what? Sound is just air. Are you saying this band sounds like heavy air?"

"Yes," said Zebra. "It's like listening to a lot of gravity."

"That's incredibly stupid," said Mitch.

The two teens walked into chemistry. John Laidlaw sat behind the desk in his room, completely alone. He was free for an hour. The classroom door remained open, and he could feel the cigarettes in his shirt pocket, taunting him. He was thinking about Truman Capote, and about how his life was in shambles, and about the last time he fucked Tina McAndrew, which had been tremendous.

SEPTEMBER 2, 1983

(Julia)

Much to her surprise, teaching in Owl was easier than Julia had ever imagined.

Julia had spent one semester student teaching in downtown Chicago. It had been part of a collegiate co-op program. It was awful. Half the kids treated her like shit and the other half ignored her completely. It was worse than being a high school student. When she tried to explain the concept of manifest destiny to a fifteen-year-old named Keith, he told her that her breasts were shaped like bananas; this was profoundly embarrassing, particularly since that analysis was accurate. What made things even worse was that she had to spend her sixteen weeks in Chicago subletting a two-bedroom apartment with three other student teachers, two of whom were teetotaling Mormons. The third roommate rarely showered and claimed to be dating an amateur ninja named Tod.

After her experience in Illinois, Julia did not want to pursue a career in academia; she had majored in education only because she had no meaningful interest in any career whatsoever. When Julia registered for classes as a college sophomore, she was required to pick a major: She almost selected business, but that seemed too vague. She briefly considered public relations, but that type of life sounded pathetic, even though she wasn't exactly sure what such a job entailed. Julia ultimately selected education simply because it seemed like a reasonable career for someone in her position to pick. She elected to specialize in history because a) she enjoyed looking at maps, and b) there was no fucking way she was going to relearn the quadratic fucking equation. Those two motives designed the trajectory for the rest of her reality; by the time she received her 1980 class schedule, it was too late to become anyone besides the person she already was. And that had seemed acceptable until she got to Chicago; the following four months made her despise teenagers. She truly, deeply hated them. They reminded her of rats. Upon her return to the University of Wisconsin, she considered applying to graduate school with the myopic intention of finding someone to marry. But her father convinced her otherwise. "There are unlimited teaching jobs in the Midwest," he said. "Find one. Don't worry about what it all means. Just move to some place like North Dakota and teach for two years, and don't spend any money. After that, you'll be able to get a job anywhere in the country, because you will have experience. That's what employers want: experience. That's *all* they want." Julia viewed her father as wise; as such, she decided to take a job she did not want in a place she had never heard of. It seemed like the logical move.

And now she was in that unknown place, and she was doing the logical job she did not want. And it appeared that her father was right: The teenagers in Owl were very, very different from the rats in Chicago. They were maddeningly polite and overwhelmingly blond. They always called her Ms. Rabia, although some of them used the prefix "Mrs." no matter how often she corrected them. More significantly, they just sat there. The students rarely said anything, even when directly asked. Some of them were ambitious and some of them were lazy, but it was difficult to deduce the difference. Almost everyone dressed the same, regardless of gender: A T-shirt promoting an innocuous insignia (often the Led Zeppelin "Swan Song" icon or a Minnesota Vikings logo), acid-washed jeans (Levi's for males, Guess? for females), and white leather Nike Cortez tennis shoes (red swooshes, blue trim). The poorest kids wore Wranglers and low-cut canvas Nikes, which were always blue. There was no system in place for disciplinary detention, and none was needed. It appeared that wearing a windbreaker jacket indoors was perceived as some sign of rebellion, but Julia had no idea why that was. People parted their hair down the middle and feathered it back; everyone used the same brand of mousse. It appeared that none of the students were left-handed. Only one was visually jarring: One of the male seniors was six foot seven, supernaturally muscular, and organically lean. He had muttonchops and a disquieting, distant expression; it was a thousand-yard stare. Julia didn't have this student in any of her classes, but she saw him skulking around the halls every morning, talking to no one. People called him Grendel. His given name was Chris Sellers. He was six inches taller than everyone in the entire building, except for the janitor. (The janitor was six foot four.) He was not popular or unpopular.

Her fellow teachers were friendly, but they did not seem interested in becoming legitimate friends. They mostly talked about the sex lives of the students and sighed indiscriminately. They all seemed exactly forty years old. Barry Rickarski taught science and was either a) gay or b) affable to the point of weirdness. Brenda Giffels taught business classes and dressed almost exclusively in lavender. (Her hair was huge.) John Laidlaw taught English and charismatically smoked cigarettes in the teachers' lounge five or six times a day. Owen Peterson taught the sixth graders and described himself as a kite enthusiast. Julia felt little connection to any of these people; they were all characters in a book she had only pretended to read. The lone exception was Naomi O'Reilly, who was insane.

Naomi taught second grade and had an unusual academic philosophy: She believed small children were always lying. Always. She did not believe that eight-year-olds were *exactly* the same as adults, but she strongly suspected they often used their smallness as a crutch and had been socialized to exaggerate childlike behavior in order to avoid responsibility. Her teaching style involved a lot of accusatory screaming. Whenever Julia walked past Naomi's room, she would hear things like "Come on, Cory! We all know you understand the difference between a clown and a cowboy! You are not fooling anyone in this room!" Naomi was six feet tall. Her haircut resembled an auburn porcupine. At the age of nineteen, she had been a sex kitten; at the age of fifty-nine, she would be sixty pounds overweight. But in the fall of 1983, Naomi was just a normal-sized thirty-nine-year-old lunatic. Naomi met Julia on the last day of Julia's first week, in the women's lavatory, ten minutes after the final bell. Julia washed her paws while Naomi dried her talons.

"Hello," said Julia. "I don't think we've been formally introduced. I'm Julia Rabia, and I just started . . ."

"You live in those apartments," said Naomi. "You live in those apartments with Chet What's-His-Name. Chet Yoda, or whatever. What's it like there? Nice or shitty?"

"What are the apartments like?" Julia asked herself aloud. "I guess they're okay. Who is Chet Yoda?"

"Well, his name really isn't Chet Yoda," replied Naomi. *"Obviously."*

"Who are we talking about?"

"The doofus who runs Yoda's. The sorta cute kid who runs the bar. The mean motherfucker with the dog. The Dog Lover?"

"I have no idea who you're talking about. Is he a cool guy or something?"

"No, he's an asshole. But he's a bartender, so, like, how bad can he be, right? Where are you supposed to be from?"

"Milwaukee."

"So you must drink then, right?"

"Well . . . yeah, I drink," said Julia. "I drink. I like to drink."

"I love getting drunk," said Naomi. "I. Love. Getting. Drunk. We are going to get *intoxicated* together. Do you want to go out and have a few?"

"That would be great."

"What are you doing tonight?"

"I'm still sort of unpacking."

"Fuck that shit. You are getting drunk. With me."

"Where?"

"Well, since you evidently haven't been there yet, meet me at Yoda's at eight o'clock," said Naomi. "There are four bars on Main Street. Yoda's is the one on the north side with the sign that says YODA, in all capital letters. It's not like you're going to get confused: Either you'll walk into Yoda's, or you will walk into the goddamn post office. Does this sound okay?"

"Oh, sure," said Julia. "What is this place like? Is it cool?"

Naomi laughed and shook the water off her hands. She looked like Godzilla, surfacing in the Sea of Japan.

"Is it *cool*?" she responded. "It's a bar."

"True, true," said Julia. "Well, this is great. I'm excited. I'm excited to go to the bar and get drunk."

"Excited? I'm fucking stoked," said Naomi. "I'm jazzed. I knew this was going to be a good year. I'm so jazzed that you're in Owl, Julie."

"Julia," said Julia. "It's Julia."

"Jules!" said Naomi. "Either way, it's gonna end up being Jules. And we are going to rock it up tonight, Jules. We are. Going to. Rock it up. Tonight. You can meet my boyfriend. Well, he's actually not my *boyfriend*—I'm married and I don't cheat on my husband, but I still have a boyfriend. You know what I mean? You know what I mean. *You know what I mean.* So if you have an extra liver, you might want to throw it into your glove box. I might need to chew on it."

Naomi O'Reilly walked out of the bathroom without saying goodbye. Julia was somewhat terrified by her new best friend. But this was still the best thing that had happened since she left Wisconsin.

Julia went home and took a shower, mostly to kill time. She considered hanging her movie posters from *Raiders of the Lost Ark* and *Manhattan,* but they suddenly seemed childish; they needed to be framed. She ate Kraft Macaroni & Cheese and watched the local news out of Bismarck, followed by *Entertainment Tonight.* She decided to wear a skirt and a less comfortable bra. When she arrived at Yoda's it was 8:02 p.m. Naomi was not there; there were ten people in the bar, but Julia was the only woman. It looked like the kind of bar that would be in a made-for-TV movie: One dartboard, one undersized pool table, one jukebox, and one TV hanging from the ceiling (its volume competed with the jukebox, which was playing Billy Joel's "Tell Her About It"). There was one guy behind the bar drying a glass with a towel. Everything was made of fake wood. It was the most bar-like bar she had ever entered.

Being alone, Julia sat by the taps. Seven people looked at her, including the bartender. He did not ask her what she wanted to drink, but she could tell this was what he wanted to know. His eyebrows were raised.

"Rolling Rock," said Julia.

"What?" said the bartender.

"I will have a Rolling Rock," Julia said.

"You're in the wrong place," said the bartender. This was Chet the Dog Lover, but Julia did not yet know it. "We don't serve mineral water here."

"Rolling Rock is beer," she said. "But don't worry, it's cool. It's cool. Everything's cool. What kind of beer *do* you have here?"

"We have Budweiser, we have Bud Light, we have Miller, we have Miller Lite, we have Hamm's, we have Schmidt, we have Old Milwaukee, and we have . . . I guess that's what we have."

"Can I get a gin and tonic?" asked Julia.

"Well, this is a bar," he said. "One can generally order mixed drinks in bars. At least one can at the bars I frequent." He free-poured the gin, added a few ounces of tonic, and slid it in front of her. "Two fifty," he said. She gave him three dollars. He gave her two quarters in return, which she pushed back in his direction as a tip. He didn't take it. Tips made the Dog Lover angry; they were degrading.

Julia sipped her drink through its straw and reflexively gagged. It was 93 percent gin. She took a second sip—this time mentally prepared for the burn—and it went down easier. Before her third sip, someone was standing next to her. He was five foot six and weighed 230 pounds, but his cheeks were boyish and his eyes were squidlike. His cap promoted DEKALB seed corn.

"Hello," said the stranger. "You're Julia, correct? You teach history, correct? And you live in those new apartments. Correct?"

"Wow," said Julia. "I am. Wow. All of that is true. That's amazing."

"Oh, we've all heard about you," said the round little fellow. "It's great to see you out on the town. And you know, I was thinking: I keep hearing about this movie, *E.T.* I'm sure you've heard of it, too. According to the newspaper, it's breaking every movie record that's breakable. And you know what? It's currently playing in Jamestown. So I was thinking we could maybe go check it out tomorrow, assuming you haven't seen it and you're into science fiction. I find science fiction fascinating."

Julia blinked four times.

"Did you just ask me out on a date?" she said.

"Oh, no. No," smiled the little round man. "Unless that's what you want to call it. It's just a movie. Don't you enjoy movies?"

"I just met you, like, eight seconds ago," Julia said. "In fact, I didn't even meet you. You didn't even say your name. I just *saw* you eight seconds ago. Do you have any idea how crazy that seems?"

"Does it seem crazy?"

"Yes," she said. "It seems very crazy. It seems completely crazy. But, I mean . . . don't be discouraged. You might be a great person, for all I know. It's just that there is no way I could *possibly* know whether that's true or false, at least not at this point. You know what I mean? And if this is the case—if you *are* a great person—maybe we could discuss this movie again, sometime in the future. After we've been friends for a while. Okay? Then we could maybe, possibly see a movie. Or not see a movie. Or whatever. Do you see where I'm coming from on this?"

"Oh, no problem. No problem," said the stranger, pleasantly unaffected by Julia's rejection. "Good enough. And nice meeting you." He walked back across the bar and sat down in front of his freshly opened Hamm's, which he finished in four consecutive pulls. Julia took two more sips of her gin and tonic. It tasted like a Christmas tree soaked in gasoline. By the time the fifth mouthful was obliterating the walls of her stomach, another man was talking to her.

"Let me apologize for Bull Calf," said stranger number two. He was also a farmer, but he didn't look like it. He looked like an Italian frat boy. "Bull Calf has no idea how to talk to women. On behalf of this entire bar, I'd like to sincerely apologize for Bull Calf's actions. I know how hard it must be to be the new girl in town."

"Oh, don't worry about it," said Julia. "He seemed like a nice enough guy, from what I could gather. I suppose I should be flattered. Why do you call him Bull Calf?"

"Because he's like a little Bull Calf," said the man. "Isn't it obvious?"

"Maybe. I have no idea."

"Well, let me tell you: It's obvious," said the man. "My name is Kent. Kent Jones." He extended his hand, which Julia shook. "And you're right: Bull Calf *is* a good guy. Sensitive. In fact, I would wager five dollars that he's the person who played this homosexual Billy Joel song on the jukebox. Bull Calf is confused about how the universe operates. But seriously, tell me—how do you like Owl? I had heard you were coming out to the bar tonight with Naomi, so I was immediately interested in hearing an outsider's perspective on our thriving metropolis."

"How did you know I was meeting Naomi O'Reilly here?" Julia asked. "How does everyone know everything? We made these plans, like, less than five hours ago."

"I don't know who told me," he said. "Woo-Chuck, maybe? I think it was Woo-Chuck."

"Who?"

"Never mind," said Kent. "It doesn't matter. But like I said: *Owl.* The city of Owl. What do you think of it?"

"It's nice," said Julia.

"Great! Excellent," said Kent. "I know it must seem boring to someone from Milwaukee, but this is a nice town. I like living here. But I grew up here, so—even if it sucked—I probably wouldn't know the difference. Unfortunately, the movie theater is closing."

"I heard that," said Julia.

"It's really too bad. The owner was simply a bad businessman. I really don't think it had anything to do with the movies themselves. They say it's been a great year for the film industry, all things considered. In fact, I happened to overhear you talking to Bull Calf about *E.T.* They say that movie is supposed to be really good. Really moving, the critics say. There was a huge story about its unprecedented box office success in the Fargo newspaper last weekend. Personally I have not seen the film, but it intrigues me. I think it's interesting that this is a movie about aliens that are *not* attacking us. The alien is apparently a force for peace. We attack the alien, which is a twist."

"Yeah, I know," said Julia. "I read about it when it came out last year. People love it."

"They certainly do," said Kent. He looked at the bartender and gestured to his beer. "So, what do you think?"

"About what?" said Julia.

"Would you like to see *E.T.* on Sunday night?"

Julia blinked seven times.

"You have got to be kidding me," she said.

"Why?" said Kent. "Did you already see it in Milwaukee? I guess it did come out a while ago."

"You just asked me on a date," said Julia. She was trying very hard not to laugh, although this laughter would have been from discomfort rather than amusement. "You came over here and told me your friend was nuts for asking me on a date after only knowing me for eight seconds. But then you talk to me for maybe *eighty* seconds, and then you do the exact same thing."

"Well, I just got the impression you were interested in the movie," Kent replied. "You kept saying how much other people liked it, so I figured you were up for seeing it. I'm sorry. I guess it was my mistake. I guess you don't like movies." Kent got up and walked to the bathroom. The bartender put another gin and tonic in front of Julia. "This one is from B.K.," he said.

"Who?" she asked.

It was 8:06. The juke was now playing Elton John's "Goodbye Yellow Brick Road," another Bull Calf favorite. At long last, Naomi arrived. She was already buzzing, having enjoyed three wine coolers with supper.

"Jules!" Naomi squawked, grabbing Julia's shoulders from behind. "You made it here. I was afraid I was going to have to break into the post office and look for your decomposing corpse."

"Naomi, this place is bonkers," she said in a half whisper. "You would not believe what just happened. That guy over there? The person they call Big Calf, or whatever? The minute I sat down, he immediately asked me to go to *E.T.* with him. Like, on a date. And we hadn't even talked. And then thirty seconds after I said no, some other guy asked me the same question. This all happened in the span of, like, three minutes. What kind of bar *is* this? Am I losing my mind?"

"Jules," said Naomi. "The only new, single women who move to Owl are teachers. That's it. *You're it.* And I don't know what your life was like before, but get ready, because you're Raquel Welch now. And if you pay for even *one* drink over the next twelve months, I will kick the living shit out of you. Just stay sexy and we're all gonna win." As Naomi said this, a third gin and tonic showed up in front of Julia.

"This is from Disco Ball," said the bartender.

"Who are these people?" asked Julia.

"It doesn't matter," said Naomi. "Just drink it. Drink it, or give it to me."

Yoda's closed at 1:00 a.m., which was ten minutes before the two women finally left. Julia awoke the next day at 11:30 a.m., alone in her apartment, fully clothed and sleeping on her face. Her hand was wrapped around a plastic cup that was half full of gin, which had been given to her by the bartender to sip while she drove home. Somebody had told her a bunch of crazy shit about John Laidlaw, but she couldn't remember any of the details.

Julia didn't think she was going to *E.T.* that weekend, but she also wasn't positive that she wasn't.

SEPTEMBER 8, 1983

(Horace)

Horace shook the bones and rolled a pair of threes, a pair of fives, and a lonely deuce. Gary Mauch followed him with three of a kind, so Horace lost again. Horace had not won a round of poker dice since the middle of Monday. He glared at the table through eyeglasses that were too large for his face, silently wondering if he would ever win again.

"Did anyone drive over to Enderlin last Friday?" Gary asked. Gary had posed this same question on Monday, and Horace had posed it again on Wednesday; they were about to have the same conversation that had already occurred on two previous afternoons. Everyone was comfortable with this. Horace was aware that many (in fact, most) of the conversations in Harley's were recycled, but that repetition was useful: It was the only way to figure out who was sincere and who was capricious. Edgar Camaro could have the same conversation five times in five days, but his words and opinions might be different every time; as such, Horace did not trust or respect him. Edgar's views were transitory. He just liked to talk.

"I didn't make it down there," said Marvin, just as he had said on Monday and Wednesday. "I didn't feel like driving forty-four miles to watch that pervert get his butt beat." The Owl High nine-man football team had played Enderlin on Friday and lost 16–12. All six men in the café were unsurprised by this outcome. The Owl Lobos had won roughly 70 percent of their football games over the past twenty years, but the men who shook dice over coffee always expected them to lose. This pessimism was exacerbated by their unified hatred of John Laidlaw, whom they all wanted to see fired. This was not as personal as it might seem; there had never been a high school football coach in the history of Owl they had not wanted fired.

"If it wasn't for that Sellers kid, we'd have lost by three touchdowns," said Ollie Pinkerton, although he hadn't seen the game either. "He's like a man among boys out there. What did he have, three sacks? Four sacks? Five sacks? It's like running a Clydesdale next to a herd of Shetland dykes. The kid must be damn near seven foot tall. But you know what? It don't matter if he's *ten* foot tall. It's never going to matter if they never find themselves an *o*-fense."

"Do you know Laidlaw tried three different quarterbacks in that game?" Gary Mauch asked rhetorically. "He started Chad Becker, then he played Orrin Groff's kid, then he put Becker back in the game, and then he had Hrlicka play for a possession—which was an unmitigated disaster. And then he finished with Groff, although I have no idea why. The boy only completed two passes the entire game. Those kids must be so confused that they don't know the price of tea in Korea. Make a decision, Laidlaw! Find your man and stay with him."

"He was probably too busy looking at the cheerleaders," said Edgar Camaro. "He was probably selecting his next victim."

"No lie," continued Gary, slurping the coffee he alone had paid for. "Can you believe it? An Owl team with no quarterback. Would you have ever imagined such a scenario in a hundred years? I mean, what's next? Cats sleeping with dogs? Wolves flirting with horses?"

This was one of the many great falsehoods about Owl: It was universally accepted that Owl High School had consistently produced legions of top-shelf quarterbacks, and that the Lobo football tradition was built on a legacy of outstanding field generals, and that there was just something about growing up in Owl that made smart young men especially adept at chucking a leather oval with uncommon velocity. This was not true. There had been only three great quarterbacks in the history of Owl

High, and they were all from the same family, and one of them wasn't even great. In 1971, a pugnacious five-foot-nine workaholic named Jake Druid led the Lobos to a completely unexpected state championship. It was the greatest afternoon in the history of the community; all the bars in town gave away free drinks for the entire night. When Jake Druid graduated the following spring, his taller, more confident brother Bobby inherited the QB reins, and he turned out to be even better: He led the Owls to another state championship in 1972 and a runner-up finish in '73. Bobby Druid still holds every meaningful passing record in Owl High history, once throwing for four touchdowns during an ice storm while fighting a 101-degree fever. He eventually married the 1977 North Dakota State University homecoming queen, but things didn't work out. When their youngest brother Vance entered high school the autumn after Bobby left, it was assumed he would be the starting quarterback for at least three seasons. Which he was, although to generally underwhelming results. The Lobos never even won a conference title during that three-year span; Vance never seemed to need football. However, in the final game of his final season, Vance Druid made the greatest, most miraculous play in school (and possibly state) history. And due to an unfathomable collection of coincidences, footage of that play was broadcast on the nationally syndicated TV program *The George Michael Sports Machine* and (eventually) on the CBS pregame show *The NFL Today*. Brent Musburger and Irv Cross both agreed that it was the most thrilling, unorthodox play either of them had ever witnessed in their respective broadcast careers. Citizens of Owl still talked about this singular play all the time; somehow, remembering the Sunday morning it aired on national TV was almost better than the two state championships. It made Vance Druid great, even if he wasn't. But here is the forgotten reality: These three brothers were the totality of the Owl quarterbacking tradition; every other quarterback (before and after) had just been a normal kid with a normal arm and a nonexistent legacy. It was only the three Druids who had been remotely transcendent. But because all three brothers still lived and worked in Owl, and because they continued to be perceived as local royalty, and because everybody would always remember a specific fifteen-second segment on *The NFL Today,* a myth fossilized into truth. This is why old men in downtown cafés were always shocked whenever a kid who happened to play quarterback for Owl High was mediocre, even though they almost always were (and almost always had been).

"We just have to concentrate on our two-point conversions," added Bud Haugen, the only man in the restaurant who had never played football as a teen. "If we make one of our two-point conversions and stop Enderlin on one of theirs, it's a 14–14 game."

"Well, that's classic Laidlaw," said Horace. "If there's a right way and a wrong way, he'll take the wrong way every time. Every damn time."

They all despised John Laidlaw, but none more than Horace. He could not understand how a sex criminal could be allowed to work in an institution funded by public tax dollars. What kind of forty-year-old married man would pursue a romantic relationship with a seventeen-year-old girl? Was he a drug addict? Horace could understand why Tina McAndrew's parents were trying to keep this quiet; their daughter's life had already been destroyed and there was no reason to humiliate her further. Moving her to Bismarck was common sense. But why did everyone else in town allow this to happen? Why hadn't Walter Valentine fired Laidlaw three years ago, after he impregnated Darcy Busch? Why was the man even hired, particularly since there were so many rumors about an incident that had occurred when he still worked in Williston? Why didn't every father in Owl drive to his house at midnight, drag him out of his bed, kick out his teeth, and throw him into the river?

"I think they should turn Sellers into a fullback," said Haugen. "I've never seen a kid that big move that fast. Can you imagine trying to tackle that eight-foot ogre? Even if they knocked him down at the line of scrimmage, the sumbitch would gain three yards by falling forward."

"They say he can barely think," said Ollie. "They say he can barely remember the snap count. They wanted to turn him into a tight end, but he couldn't remember any of the pass patterns. He's a cliché. He's got rocks in his head."

Horace felt terrible for Tina McAndrew, a woman he'd never met. He wondered, What will become of her? She can't even live in her own hometown. What did she think she was doing, making time with a nefarious letch? She will regret that decision forever. She'll never be a normal person; she'll always have a checkered past and a dark secret, not to mention a son or daughter she'll never know, raised by parents she'll never encounter. It was a genuine tragedy. When did the world become so sex crazed? It must have been after the Beatles arrived.

"Kids don't learn things anymore," remarked Marvin Windows, the quietest of the six coffee drinkers. Marvin had nearly died thirteen times over the past seventy-five years. He had been trampled by cattle twice, which was (arguably) the local record. "They go to school all the time, but they don't listen to anyone and they don't read unless you stick a gun to their chest. All they care about is boom-boom music and computer games. And the teachers don't care. The teachers are just waiting for summer vacation. They're worse than the kids. I'm told the new history prof was in the bar Friday night, drinking like an Indian, flirting with every fella in the place, cursing left and right. She was with that gigantic Irish floozy who teaches the little ones. This new history teacher is a kid herself! She can't be more than twenty-four, twenty-five years old."

"Twenty-five? Twenty-four?" asked Edgar Camaro, mildly intrigued. "It won't be long before somebody gets his hooks into that filly."

She'll never be alone, thought Horace. She'll be engaged before June, this drunken new history teacher. She probably wants to get married, because she doesn't want to be alone. Everybody assumes it's so terrible to be alone. It's not. Horace had been alone for half his life, and it was the best thing that had ever happened to him. He knew he could never say that aloud, and (of course) he missed his wife, and (of course) he had loved her, and (of course) the day she died was the worst day he had ever known. But he had grown to love the emptiness of his house even more. He loved that it was just a collection of rooms, and that there were never any questions to answer, and that he could design his own rules for being alive. It was wonderful to be alone: If he wanted to fry up some sizzler sausages at 4:00 a.m., that's exactly what he did. And while it was (of course) sad and (of course) unfair that his wife had passed at the age of forty-four, it wasn't like they had never had a chance to be together; they were married for twenty-five years. What else were they going to talk about? They had run out of things to say after the first decade. He probably enjoyed remembering their conversations more than he had ever enjoyed having them. If people only realized that you don't need someone else to invent your happiness, situations like Tina McAndrew wouldn't happen. Horace was certain of this.

SEPTEMBER 9, 1983

(Mitch)

There were six of them in the vehicle. Mitch, Zebra, and Weezie (whose real name was Waylon Jefferson) sat in the backseat. Ainge (whose real name was Daniel) was driving, as this was, in fact, his father's Oldsmobile. Drug Man (who had never seen or taken drugs) was riding shotgun. Curtis-Fritz (whose name was Alexander Trog) sat between Ainge and Drug Man in the middle of the front seat, riding bitch. Oldsmobiles are humpback whales made of metal. All six riders were wearing farm hats, Levi's 501s, and their powder-blue and fluorescent-maize game jerseys. Mitch was number 7. In two hours and ten minutes, they would be inside the Owl school locker room, strapping on shoulder pads, dressing for the first home game of the season; at the moment, they were driving up and down the same six streets, drinking Rondo Citrus and chewing Skoal. There were multiple conversations happening at the same time; it was like an Altman film, although nobody inside the car had ever seen an Altman film (and four of them never would, mostly by choice).

"Tina was *in love* with Laidlaw," said Curtis-Fritz. He wore number 22, which meant he never, ever played. For the past forty years, no Owl player wearing number 22 had ever been any good; being assigned the number 22 was a humiliating death sentence. Everyone instinctively understood this, except for Curtis-Fritz—he actively requested 22 on the first day of practice. He was that kind of kid. "I mean, she was in fucking *love* with him. I sat by her in study hall, and she would write his name in bubble letters on her notebooks. She wasn't secretive about it. I would ask her, 'Why are you writing the name "John" on all your stuff?' and she would just say, 'Oh, I'm kind of seeing someone named John.' As if I would somehow not deduce who this person was. She was not ashamed of anything. She was so hot."

"He would buy her shit," said Weezie. Weezie wore number 34, which meant he was the starting tailback and the most sexually experienced player on the roster. "He bought her a Black Hills gold bracelet and a Trapper Keeper. I know this for a fact."

"Change it over to Y-94," said Zebra. "All they play on Q-98 is 'Heat of the Moment.' I hate that song." Zebra was number 88, which meant he was supposed to serve as the team's second-best receiver.

"Did Rockwell ever tell you about the time he and Disco Ball witnessed one of their erotic liaisons?" asked Drug Man. Rockwell was a local mechanic named Jason Stonerock. Rockwell was ancient; Rockwell was twenty-six years old. Disco Ball was even older and had a very bulbous skull, which is why he was Disco Ball. "Supposedly, Rockwell and Disco got drunk in the middle of the afternoon and decided to follow Laidlaw's car after track practice. Whenever Rockwell gets drunk, he likes to pretend he's in the FBI. Now, this was around the time when Tina was the team's student manager, remember? And Laidlaw always drove her home after practice, right? And—apparently—he was giving her a ride home, but he was actually giving her a *ride home,* because they drove out to the apple grove and parked out there for, like, three hours."

"We are not listening to gay Y-94 music in my car," Ainge said over his shoulder to Zebra. Ainge wore number 44, which symbolized nothing. "I do not want to hear any gay *Flashdance* music in this vehicle. Women can't weld."

"Vanna, are you gonna play tonight?" asked Weezie.

"I doubt it," said Mitch. In last week's game against Enderlin, Mitch went in at quarterback in the third quarter. The score was 16–6. On his first play he fumbled the snap. On his second play he fumbled the snap again, but was able to pick it up and desperately pitch it to Weezie, who was tackled for a six-yard loss. On the third play he dropped back to pass, and it was unadulterated chaos: The pocket was immediately collapsing, people were yelling, everything was happening at the same time, and it felt like he was trying to defuse a pipe bomb while learning to speak Cantonese. He ended up blindly heaving the ball toward an undisclosed location where he thought a receiver might be, which was actually fifteen yards from anyone on either team. On the play after that, the Owls punted. Mitch did not reenter the game. "I doubt it," he said again.

"You know what would be cool?" Zebra asked rhetorically. "It would be cool if we could somehow plant cameras all over the school, or maybe even inside random houses. Then we could use the photographs to sexually blackmail people."

"I heard," said Curtis-Fritz, "that when Laidlaw's wife left town for three days to take care of her dying mother, Tina McAndrew stayed at his house for the entire time. She would get up in the morning and make him pancakes."

"That did not happen," said Mitch. "There is no way that could have happened. He's got three kids. Don't you think the kids would notice that there's a different woman in the house, having sex with their dad and feeding them pancakes?"

"I don't know," said Curtis-Fritz. "Maybe she stayed in the basement."

"I think you should get to play more," Weezie said to Mitch. "I don't care what Laidlaw thinks. You're way smarter than Becker or Groff, even if you don't always throw so good. And if you *do* play tonight, and if we run Flood Right 64, throw it to me in the flat. I'm always open on that play. Always. Every time. But they never throw it to me."

The opening riff from "Band on the Run" came over the stereo.

"You see what I fucking mean?" said Zebra. "Q-98 is terrible. Wings? Who are these queers? I don't like old songs."

It was at this specific juncture that Ainge's Oldsmobile passed a 1974 Plymouth Barracuda. The 'Cuda was clean and the 'Cuda was yellow. Its driver looked straight ahead, oblivious to the six people staring into his vehicle's interior.

This was the point where five conversations became one conversation.

"Don't even start with that shit," Drug Man said to Curtis-Fritz. "We are not having this argument again. I'm only warning you once."

"We don't have to have it," said Curtis-Fritz. "We don't need to have an argument, because you know I'm right."

"No, it's not because you're right. It's because you're a fucking cum receptacle."

The man in the Plymouth Barracuda was Cubby Candy. He was a senior. He did not play football. He was not involved in any extracurricular activities, unless you counted dove hunting and water-tower vandalism. He was the most disturbed individual anyone who knew him had ever met.

"Curtis, we all know Candy is nuts," said Drug Man. "He's a maniac. If he doesn't go to prison when he turns eighteen, he's going to be dead before he's twenty-one. No one is disputing these facts. But have you ever *looked* at Grendel? Have you ever watched him lift weights? Do you know what he can bench-press? Three hundred and forty pounds. He can lift three hundred and forty pounds, just with his arms. *Three hundred and forty.* That is probably two hundred more pounds than whatever Candy weighs!"

"Doesn't matter," said Curtis-Fritz. "It is not the size of the dog in the fight, it is the size of the fight in the dog. My grandfather says that all the time."

Drug Man said, "Your grandfather is talking out of his ass. He hasn't watched enough dog fights."

Cubby Candy was five foot seven and 133 pounds. He had a very suspect mustache and a horrifying scar from a botched appendectomy. He drank Lord Calvert in his car before school and used to get beaten by his alcoholic father four times a week. Everybody knew this. He had also been sexually abused by his grandfather at the age of eight, and his mother spent most afternoons crying in front of the television, babbling about how she wanted to kill herself. Nobody knew this except Cubby. More critically, the prefrontal cortex of his brain was 14 percent smaller than that of a normal human, and that particular section of the mind is responsible for developing a person's sense of moral conscience; this means Cubby should have been medically diagnosed with a borderline personality disorder generally classified as sociopathy. Absolutely nobody knew this, and nobody ever would.

Cubby Candy saw no connection between his actions and the rest of society. He would do things that were so incomprehensible that they often couldn't be defined as bad, even though that was the only viable option. Once, when he was a sophomore, he was sitting quietly in biology, waiting for Mr. Rickarski to correct a quiz; Candy suddenly stood up, picked up his desk, and threw it through a plate-glass window. He claimed it was because the sun was in his eyes. Candy's threshold for pain was beyond comprehension. Once, when he was trying to show Tina McAndrew that he had a crush on her, he burned his left biceps with the cigarette lighter from his Barracuda. When Tina freaked out, he said, "No no no, you don't understand." He burned himself again. When she freaked out even more, he did it a third time. He gave himself eleven circular scars in the span of fifteen minutes, and he never seemed to care. He felt nothing and cared about nothing, except possibly his car. Which is why it's (probably) no surprise that Cubby Candy was the greatest teenage street fighter in all of south-central North Dakota.

"You've never even hung out with Candy," said Curtis-Fritz. "I have. I used to go to street dances with him in the summer, because he always had booze. I've seen him obliterate fuckers. He'd fight two, three, four guys at once. He loves it. He turns into this subhuman animal. He doesn't care what happens. If he ever got Grendel on the ground, he would kick him to death. I'm serious. He would kick Grendel until *he was dead.*"

"But that would never happen," said Drug Man. "That's what I keep telling you. I'm sure Candy would start screaming and do his whole werewolf routine, and he'd foam at the mouth and lose his shit. And then Grendel would punch him—*once*—in the face. And then Cubby Candy would be a headless werewolf. It would be like when Larry Holmes pounded Tex Cobb."

This specific discussion—this hypothetical fistfight between Chris "Grendel" Sellers and Cubby Candy—was the single most polarizing debate in the universe of Owl High School. For people like Drug Man and Curtis-Fritz and Mitch and Zebra and every other male between the ages of fourteen and nineteen, this was *Roe v. Wade*. Sure, Cubby was insane. Sure, his career fighting record was something like 79–0–1 (the lone tie coming when he attacked a cop in eighth grade). But what would happen if he fought Grendel, the greatest titan any of them had ever known? Who would win? It was a question that defied clarity. Granted, Grendel had never been in a fight in his adult life, and—granted—Grendel and Candy had no dispute with each other (they probably had not even spoken in five years). But the notion of such an epic conflict was eternally intoxicating. It seemed to represent everything. It was the one subject everyone could always talk about.

"I still think the central issue is reach," said Ainge. "Grendel is six foot seven, but he has the wingspan of a guy who's seven foot six. I think he'd hit Candy five times before Candy could get close enough to shoot the leg."

"What are you saying?" said Curtis-Fritz. "Reach? What difference would that possibly make? Candy would just hit him over the head with a bottle. He's done that to tons of guys."

"Here's the thing," Zebra said. "Grendel's stupid. He can't read. He can't count. For all we know, he probably thinks wood comes from cows. If you told him that cow bones were made of wood, he probably wouldn't question it. But Candy is smart, kind of. I know he gets shitty grades, but he's *kind of* smart. Like, we were talking about Ozzy records one night, and he had some very interesting ideas about the lyrics off *Diary of a Madman*. So if there was ever a point where strategy became involved, Candy would have a major edge."

"There isn't going to be any goddamn strategy," said Drug Man. "It's a fight. They would be fighting. They would not be discussing Ozzy Osbourne. Grendel would be tearing Candy's arms off and crushing his bones into powder. Grendel would be eating Candy's stupid yellow car."

"No," said Curtis-Fritz. "No way that happens. No way. Besides, no one could ever punch Candy any harder than his dad did all the time."

"Mitch, will you intercede here?"

This was Mitch's deepest source of personal pride: For reasons that had never been clearly defined, he was universally viewed as the intellectual authority on who would win an imaginary fight between Grendel and Candy. It might have been because Mitch had spent more time thinking about this theoretical conflict than anyone else, or it might have been because he just seemed like the kind of person who *would* spend an inordinate amount of time thinking about an event that had never happened. But regardless of how this assumption came to be, Mitch loved that it was believed it to be true. He loved that this was an issue everyone had an opinion about, but—somehow—his opinion counted more. Whenever people discussed the Grendel vs. Candy Hypothetical, he never had to interject himself into the conversation; he always knew someone else would eventually ask him what he thought.

"As I have often noted in the past," began Mitch, "context is everything. If you locked Grendel and Candy in a room and said, 'Okay, start fighting,' I'm sure Candy *would* win. Locking him in a room would be more than enough motivation to make him go wolfshit, because he wants to die. If you locked up

Candy in his kitchen and said, 'Okay, start fighting,' he would beat the shit out of the oven. That's just who he is. He's like Gordon Kahl. But we have to assume this fight would be happening for a reason. Something would have to be at stake, and it would have to be something that Grendel was extremely *emotional* about, because he doesn't have the capacity to get pissed off intellectually. So if this fight did happen, it would have to be because Grendel went insane. And if Grendel was insane, I don't see how anyone could stop him. Candy could hit him with a bottle. Candy could hit him in the chest with a sledgehammer. It wouldn't matter. Grendel would always win."

"I disagree," said Curtis-Fritz.

"This conversation is over," said Drug Man. "Vanna has spoken."

Ainge made a U-turn in front of the abandoned lumberyard, and the Oldsmobile retraced the Main Street pavement for the twenty-first time that afternoon. Steve Miller's "Swingtown" came on the radio.

"Vanna, I am serious about this," said Weezie. "Flood Right 64. I'm always open in the flat. Always. Tell the other quarterbacks I told you this. They will trust you."

SEPTEMBER 26, 1983

(Julia)

It was extraordinary to be this new kind of person.

It was exhausting. It was a little embarrassing. And sometimes it was the opposite of embarrassing, even though no such word exists. Julia had never met a person who was remotely similar to the person she had suddenly become; had she seen such a character in a film, it would have made the movie implausible.

Oh, she had certainly known attractive girls in her life. Her freshman-year roommate at Wisconsin: That girl should have been illegal. She looked like a Spanish runway model on anabolic steroids. One of the Mormon teachers from her co-op in Chicago: That woman was joyless, but her skeleton was faultless. In truth, beautiful women were not as rare as poets from the Romantic period seemed to indicate. They were everywhere. They were almost as common as ugly girls. In fact, for the first twenty-three years of her life, Julia had never been considered the prettiest or the least attractive member among any random collection of her female friends; for some reason, she always ranked third. Julia had also known lots of popular girls in life (some who had deserved the attention and some who had not). Charisma is an undeniable thing; some people are just naturally dynamic, regardless of what they say or how they behave. You want to be around these people, even if you don't know why. Similarly, she had occasionally encountered women who were more desirable than logic would suggest; she assumed this amorphous quality was what people meant when they used the word *sensual.* Her sister had that quality. Obsessive, bookish guys were always falling in love with her older sister, even though she was oddly shaped and smelled like a hippie. Her sister never had to make men want her, and that was an attribute Julia had always envied.

But not anymore.

Not here. All of those preexisting, archaic perceptions of beauty and charm were no longer relevant to Julia's day-to-day life. She had been wrong about everything. As it turned out, and much to her surprise, Julia Rabia was the most attractive, most charismatic, most enchanting woman in North America.

Every day was the same: Wake up hungover. Go to work. Sleepwalk for eight hours: Tell kids that Balboa discovered the Pacific Ocean; pretend to care that Angie Dickinson was born in Kulm; grade a few multiple-choice tests about slavery. Return home to an empty apartment. Nap. Eat Chunky soup. Take shower. Put on Guess? jeans. Put on a sweatshirt. Leave the door unlocked at 8:30 and drive the Honda seven blocks. Park diagonally on the street. Enter the bar. And then—from the moment she sat down until the moment she drunkenly climbed back into her car—be aggressively (but politely) pursued by virtually every unmarried man in town.

It was beyond her comprehension, but she got used to it.

Most nights began in a corner booth with Naomi and Ted (usually at Yoda's, Mick's Tavern, or the Owl VFW). Ted was Naomi's boyfriend, although they were both married to other people and had no physical relationship; they just seemed to enjoy calling each other "my boyfriend" and "my girlfriend." It was hard for Julia to understand the nature of this relationship, or how they were able to sustain their respective marriages. She never asked. Ted was eight years younger than Naomi and referred to himself as an underemployed farmer; he had a beard, drank Schmidt, and continually grinned. That was the sum of his persona. His primary role in Julia's life was to provide biographical information on the suitors who were simultaneously pursuing her. This was more complicated than it might sound, simply because everyone had two names. If you met ten people, you had to remember twenty. As of the evening of September 26, these were the ones Julia could consistently recall:

- Derrick Decker. He was "Bull Calf." They called him Bull Calf because he once pulled his groin during a junior high football game and, while lying in agony on the trainer's table in the coach's office, he moaned like a baby bull.
- Leonard McCloud. He was sometimes called "Koombah," because as a sixth grader his haircut reminded people of an older, long-graduated student named Keith Koomersbach.
- Greg Blixer. He was called "Disco Ball." His skull was a globe of bone.
- Brian Pintar. He was known as "the Drelf," which was an abbreviation for "the Drunken Elf." Brian Pintar was five foot four and a part-time alcoholic.
- Kurt Flaw. He was called "Ass Jam," because someone once noticed that he ran the 220-yard dash with an awkward, upright posture, almost as if a wooden stick had been jammed into his rectum. This was not intended as criticism.
- Kelly Flaw. This was Kurt's younger brother. He was "Baby Ass Jam."
- Tyler Smykowski. He was called "Buck Buck," because he spent the summer of 1976 listening to Bill Cosby comedy albums in his basement and repeating the skits verbatim.
- Phil Buzkol. This person actually had three nicknames, but he was customarily called "McGarrett." This was because he once tried to pay for a single can of Coca-Cola with a $50 bill he'd received as a confirmation gift, an unusually large denomination of currency that made the cashier think of *Hawaii Five-0*, a TV program whose main character was named Steve McGarrett. He was also called "Busload" (because that vaguely sounded like "Buzkol"), and he was occasionally referred to as "Vanderslut," because there was a

rumor he had received fellatio from a promiscuous girl named Vickie Vanderson in 1975 (this, incidentally, was not true).

- Steve Brown. He was officially nicknamed "Little Stevie Horse 'n' Phone," but most people referred to him as "Horse 'n' Phone" (or even just "Horse," but only by his closest friends). The origin of all this was unknown; it was the name his father had always called him, and now the father was deceased.
- Chuck Voight. He was called "B.K.," an abbreviation for "Brother Killer." This was because he once threatened to stab his older brother with an ice pick during an ill-fated attempt at installing an air conditioner.

These nicknames fascinated Julia; their inexplicable specificity was confounding. During her formative years in Milwaukee, nicknames had always been obvious and derivative: A left-handed person might be called "Lefty," or a big-boned girl would be labeled "Moose." Milwaukee slang was also less adhesive; if you put peroxide in your hair, you might get called "Blondie" for one summer (or maybe even for half a school year), but that kind of moniker was never permanent. This was not the case in Owl. In Owl, nicknames were spawned by random, unmetaphoric events that offered no meaningful reflection on the individual. Yet these nicknames would last decades. A man like Bull Calf might be called "Bull Calf" until he reached retirement (or at least until he married and became a father). Julia noticed that a few of Ted's peers referred to him as "Kleptosaur." One night she asked him why; it was because he got caught shoplifting a plastic dinosaur as a third grader. Ted did not find this name problematic. "It could be worse," he said. "I could have been stealing rubbers."

Julia's nights were not all identical, but they were more similar than different. She would sit next to Naomi, who sat across from Ted. The three of them would start the evening discussing the teachers Naomi did not like (this was almost all of them), the students Naomi felt should be thrown out of school (this was an ever-changing roster, although it always included Cubby Candy), and the fact that all of them were making less than fifteen thousand dollars a year, which was less than they deserved but more than they needed. As the night wore on, a revolving door of nicknamed men would take turns occupying the booth's remaining seat, each one trying to make casual, dynamic conversation with a semi-intoxicated twenty-three-year-old Our State instructor. Often, this meant a discussion about grain prices. Every male contestant would buy the entire table a round of drinks (Ted occasionally declined, only because he feared men would lose respect for him if he never paid for his own booze). If the initial table talk went smoothly, the contestant would buy them all a second round of cocktails; if those beverages made the bachelor confident, he would ask Julia to play a game of pool. She agreed to this offer 51 percent of the time. And if the billiard game was playful, and if the man convinced Julia to let him buy her one more drink, and if he was likewise drunk (or at least unsober), the curiously nicknamed man would inevitably ask Julia to see a movie in Jamestown. And Julia always said no.

She had to.

That was one of the first things Naomi explained to her.

In Owl, people did not date; if you went on one date, you were *dating*. If you went on two dates, it was an exclusive relationship. If you went on three dates, it was a serious relationship and there was potential for marriage. You could hang out with members of the opposite sex whenever you wanted, and you could get drunk with them in public, and you could even find yourself having clandestine sex with one of them, possibly on multiple occasions. But you couldn't make *plans*. Going on a proper, recognized date was different; when someone asked you on a date, they were actively asking if you'd be interested in a committed relationship. When all those curiously nicknamed men asked Julia to see movies, they were really asking if she might consider sharing her life. Because—if a shared life was the life you wanted, and you wanted to share such a life without leaving Owl—there were no other options. If Julia didn't like you, no one could ever say, "Well, there's a lot of other fish in the sea." There was one fish, and it lived in a lake with no tributaries, and all the competing villagers read *Field & Stream* with extreme prejudice. The arrival of an unattached female teacher was a romantic race against time. And no matter how much she enjoyed her insular celebrity (and regardless of how nicely these desperate, lonely men seemed to treat her), Julia knew that was perverse. She thought about it all the time.

In fact, she was actively thinking those specific thoughts when she re-noticed a person she'd noticed several times before.

Julia, Naomi, and Ted were sitting inside Mick's. It was Tuesday. It was almost midnight. They were all different levels of drunk. Naomi was smoking Ted's cigarettes. Julia had played four games of pool. And there was a man sitting at the bar and everyone was talking to him, but he was barely talking to anyone. It was impossible to tell if he was completely intoxicated or mostly sober. He was wearing a blue denim jacket, a white denim shirt, and blue denim jeans; it was as if he were wearing the world's most comfortable tuxedo. His teeth were unusually large and uncommonly white. He looked sad, or possibly angry, or theoretically bored.

"Ted," said Julia. "Who is that?" She gingerly pointed at the man in denim. "I've seen him here before."

"Vance Druid," said Ted.

"What do people call him?" she asked.

"Vance Druid," said Ted.

"Really. Why doesn't he get a nickname?"

"I'm not sure," said Ted. "I guess he just doesn't need one. He's famous."

"Famous? For what? For wearing denim?"

"Well, not *famous*," said Ted. "He's just . . . you know, he's a different kind of person."

Oddly (and inevitably), that was precisely the quality Julia had noticed about this denim-clad man on the previous occasions she had watched him drink Old Milwaukee: Everyone treated him differently, and for no comprehensible reason. They did seem to behave as if he was a celebrity. He only paid for his drinks when he felt like it. He didn't look at people during conversations, almost like he was a mafia boss. Whenever some random drunkard told a joke that made Vance laugh, the joker would be visibly pleased with himself; somehow, making this man laugh was viewed as a cultural victory. Vance Druid possessed an abstract surplus of interpersonal leverage. Everyone liked him, even when he didn't like them back.

During the entire month of September, Vance Druid had never tried to buy Julia a drink. He never chatted her up or challenged her to billiards or asked if she wanted to see *E.T.* or *War Games* or *Cujo.* And this (of course) made him seem like the only attractive man in the entire town. And that (of course) is a romantic cliché, which (of course) only serves to illustrate Julia's damaged self-perception. It was all (of course) too predictable to believe. Which is how life always is. In baseball and sex, clichés are usually true: Pitching beats hitting, and people always want to be loved by anyone who doesn't seem to care. So when Vance walked out of the men's room at 11:58 and stopped to look at a jukebox he never played, Julia decided she would initiate conversation with this unfriendly man, much to the quiet chagrin of every bozo in the bar. She could do this. She was the most attractive, most charismatic, most enchanting woman in North America. She could do whatever she wanted.

"Hello there," she said. "I don't think we've met. I'm Julia."

"We've met," Vance said, still looking at the letters and numbers behind the Plexiglas. "I've met you."

"We have? When?"

"Some other night. It was a while ago. I don't remember. You were drunk."

"I don't think we've met," she said.

"Well, then maybe we haven't."

Vance was not putting any money into the machine. He was just looking at it. Seven uncomfortable seconds disappeared.

"It's nice to meet you," Vance said suddenly.

Four seconds passed.

"It's nice to meet you, too," Julia said. "You're Vance, right? Your name is Vance."

"Sure," he said. "Why not?"

Eleven seconds passed. He still had not looked at her. It was like talking to a prison guard.

"What songs are you going to play?" asked Julia.

"This jukebox is terrible."

"What kind of music do you like?"

"The Rolling Stones," said Vance.

"Yeah, they're cool. Who else?"

"That's it," he said.

Five more seconds passed.

"The only band you like is the Rolling Stones?"

"Pretty much."

"That's impossible," said Julia. "No one only likes one band. You must at least like the Beatles."

"Not really," said Vance. "Their songs are boring."

"Wow. That's really interesting," said Julia. "I've never met someone who didn't like the Beatles. What about Foreigner? Or Boston? Or Styx? Or Journey?"

"I can't tell any of those bands apart."

"Yeah, yeah. I know, I know. You're probably one of those Led Zeppelin people. Guys like Zeppelin."

"No, they were gay."

"What?" said Julia. "You thought Led Zeppelin was gay? Weren't they, like, sex fiends?"

"Their singer always seemed gay to me," said Vance. "I haven't listened to that shit since ninth grade."

"How about Fleetwood Mac?" she asked.

"I don't like female singers."

"The Eagles?"

"Nobody listens to the Eagles."

"Quiet Riot?"

"That trash is for dope addicts and twelve-year-olds."

"Van Halen?"

"Mother of God," said Vance. "That clown is even gayer than the queer from Zeppelin. Plus, their guitar player is boring. Why would I want to listen to a guitar that sounds like a police siren?"

"I'm running out of possibilities," she said. "How about . . . oh! I know: ELO? I love ELO. You better not say anything bad about ELO!"

"They're like a combination of the dullest parts of the Beatles with the gayest parts of Led Zeppelin."

"This is crazy," Julia said. "I don't think I believe what you are saying. I don't think any person could hold such opinions. Do you at least *appreciate* music that's made by people who aren't in the Rolling Stones? Do you *appreciate* Bruce Springsteen?"

"He seems like an asshole."

"Oh, he does not."

"He tries too hard," said Vance. "He's needy. He needs people to like him. It's undignified."

"Pat Benatar?"

"There again, girl singer."

"Cheap Trick?"

"You know, I actually saw Cheap Trick during college," he said. "They came to West Fargo and played the fairgrounds. Some dipshit asked me to go with him. The band played for fucking ever and dressed like circus freaks. It was ridiculous."

"The Police?"

"Never heard of 'em."

"I suppose I shouldn't waste my time with the Sex Pistols," Julia said.

"That's not music."

"Are you one of those people who says, 'Disco sucks'? Are you actually going to say the words 'Disco sucks' if we keep talking about this?"

"I can't speak to that," he said.

"You must hate Steely Dan."

"Steely Dan," Vance repeated as he looked deeply at the words *Bat Out of Hell.* He seemed to take her question very seriously; this further confused Julia, as she had been operating under the assumption that he'd been answering her questions thoughtlessly and without justification. "You know, they're not terrible," he eventually said. "I like 'Deacon Blues.' That's a song. But still: boring. I'd never waste money on their records."

"So you're serious about this," Julia finally said. "You only like the Rolling Stones. Inside your house, the only music you play is by the Rolling Stones."

"Yes. Why not? They have plenty of albums," he said.

"Do you have a favorite?"

"Probably *Black and Blue* or *Goats Head Soup.*"

"I thought guys like you were supposed to love *Exile on Main Street,*" she responded. "The records you like are generally considered to be their worst ones."

"I don't think that's true," he said. "Well, nice meeting you again."

Vance walked back to his bar stool and finished his sixteen-ounce Beast, and then he drank two more. Julia went back to her booth, deflated by the awkward, baffling conversation with a man who did not seem to care about anything she said (or about anyone, except possibly Keith Richards). Had she not been inebriated, it would have been both embarrassing and discouraging.

But they would talk again tomorrow. And things would go better.

OCTOBER 12, 1983

(Horace)

"It's not even in the newspaper." This was Bud Haugen talking. "Not on the front page, not on the editorial page. Nowhere. It's like it didn't even happen."

Today's afternoon coffee was stronger than usual, depositing black acid bitterness into the blood of its disciples. It was an entertaining anomaly. The old men embraced their caffeinated anger. It felt good.

"You know, I saw the school bus running this morning," added Gary Mauch. "The kids don't even get the day off anymore. Only the postman."

"I don't care about the children," said Bud. "It's the newspaper that gets me. Think of all the crap they run in that rag. Think of all the idiocy that constitutes somebody's version of public information. They will put *anything* in there. Did you see last week's Sunday paper? The region section? They ran a picture of a dog wearing a neckerchief. It was the front of the region section. That was news. Yet what do they do on the anniversary of the most important event of the past thousand years? Nothing. I guess they'd think differently if America had been discovered by a dog wearing a neckerchief."

"The problem," said Marvin, "is that reporters have no sense of history."

"That's not the problem," said Bud. "The problem is that you can't celebrate Columbus anymore because it perturbs the Indians. That's the entire issue. And now that they run the casinos, they control all the money. It's politics."

"Bud makes a halfway valid point," said Marvin. "The way

young people talk these days, you'd think Christopher Columbus was the Caucasoid Pol Pot."

"Doesn't matter," said Marvin. "Doesn't matter what kind of person Columbus was. Doesn't matter how many Indians he killed or didn't kill, or if he was or wasn't an asshole. From what I've read, Columbus probably was an asshole. He probably deserved to get hung. But here's the thing: He *didn't* get hung. The man climbed on a wooden watercraft and collided with North America by accident. It doesn't matter what happened afterwards or what his motives were. He found it. It happened. He's what history is. It was his destiny to be that particular man, and it was his destiny to do those specific things. But nobody at that newspaper cares about anything that happened before they were born, which is why they don't give space to things like Columbus Day. Which is why I stopped reading the newspaper in '74. After they busted Nixon, it all became bullshit and advertising."

It was difficult to argue with Marvin. It was difficult to argue with anyone who'd ever a) fallen off a thirty-five-foot corn crib, b) broken four vertebrae in the process, yet c) elected to return to work the very next day. (He shoveled grain while wearing a full-body plaster cast underneath his overalls, sweating like a mule.) Marvin Windows was unkillable, which meant he was unassailable. In 1971, a raccoon bit him in the neck and he had to undergo a series of fourteen rabies shots in the abdomen. Everyone in town remembered this incident except for Marvin; within the catacombs of his mind, the raccoon had bitten his brother. He had no recollection of seeing any doctor. This sort of thing happened a lot. Marvin could not remember how many times he had been thrown through the windshield of a moving vehicle, but it was at least three. He was the godhead, and he had no rival. Who could win a debate against a man who did not recall how many times he should have died? It was like trying to beat Rasputin at chess. As such, Horace did not voice his disagreement with Marvin's thesis; he just swallowed his unusually strong coffee. But he *did* disagree with what Marvin was claiming, particularly with all that business about Columbus having a destiny.

For most of his youth, Horace had believed in destiny. He believed it was his destiny to fight in a war. But this was not some romantic, self-destructive fantasy; he did not believe it was his destiny to fight and die. He believed it was his destiny to fight and *live.* He believed it was his destiny to kill faceless foreigners for complex reasons that were beyond his control, and to deeply question the meaning of those murders, and to kill despite those questions, and to eventually understand the meaning of his own life through the battlefield executions of total strangers. He had believed this since he was a boy. Wars changed men, and often for the better. Unfortunately, Horace had been born in December of 1910, a terrible year for anyone who hoped to experience militaristic calamity. He was still a child during World War I; to Horace, WWI was just a radio show. He was thirty-one at the start of World War II, but too responsible to leave the country—his three younger brothers all enlisted the day after Pearl Harbor, so someone had to stay home and take care of the cows. He was forty-two during the Korean Conflict; that was too old to help Ted Williams kill any Asian of consequence. Vietnam had been for the kids. Four wars, and he missed them all. And (of course) Horace knew he was supposed to feel fortunate about this. He had fallen through the few slender chasms that buffered cataclysmic events. He knew that all wars were brutal (especially the Civil War) and that he might have been tortured or emasculated (especially by the Japanese), and perhaps he would have gained nothing from the experience beyond what he more easily learned from reading books (most notably *All Quiet on the Western Front*) and ignoring the lies of television (most notably *M*A*S*H,* a program whose pro-Communist themes consistently enraged him). He was not naïve about the realities described by people like Stevie Wonder and Michael Herr, despite the fact that he had no idea who those people were. Horace was a reasonable man. Everyone believed this. But there was simply no way he could accept that his destiny was to *not* fight in a war. There was no way the defining experience of his life could be the four experiences that he missed.

This is why Horace stopped believing in destiny, sometime during 1955.

His wife had not believed in destiny either, but she had different, less creative reasons: She felt the concept of predestination was lazy. She thought destiny was a mental construction for people who did not want to take responsibility for their own actions; she thought destiny made life too simple. Horace felt destiny made life harder. In a predetermined world, people were like slaves unaware of their enslavement. If not for free will, every human action would be work; every human achievement would be devoid of meaning, or at least devoid of credit. And that would be acceptable—except that you'd still have to do all the shit that came along with it. I mean, let's assume Marvin was correct. Let's assume it *was* Christopher Columbus's "destiny" to discover the New World, and let's pretend he was consciously aware of that fact. What possible difference would that have made in his day-to-day life? He still had to build the boats. He still had to beg Queen Isabella for funding, and he still had to significantly underestimate the circumference of the earth. He still had to wait for someone else to invent the compass. He still had to wake up in the morning. As far as Horace could decipher, destiny was a concept that forced you to live a certain kind of life *on purpose,* even though you were already living that life *by accident.* And that seemed immoral, not to mention stupid. Why would existence be designed as a redundant system? Destiny made God seem like an unconfident engineer.

"I don't know what you're so hot and bothered about," said Edgar Camaro, directing his words away from the unassailable Marvin and toward the eternally assailable Bud. "What, exactly, do you expect the newspaper to write about Christopher Columbus in 1983?"

"They should recognize the man," said Bud.

"Why?" asked Edgar.

"The man deserves recognition."

"That's not an answer to the question. You're just repeating what you already said. That's not an argument."

"Why should I have to explain why Columbus is important? You're acting like a two-dollar jackass."

"I just think it's idiotic that we don't get mail today, simply because Columbus was a bad explorer. You do realize he discovered America by accident, right? He thought the Indians were pygmies."

"We all know that," said Bud. "That isn't the point. Have you not listened to anything we've been saying for the past twenty minutes? Do you have shit in your ears?"

"You know, they say Columbus was a rapist," said Edgar. "I don't know if that's fact or fiction, but it's certainly not impossible. And I'd hate to think we didn't get our mail this morning in tribute to an Italian rapist."

"Now that's just downright stupidity!"

"Jesus wheels," said Gary, almost laughing. "Ed Camaro, you are a piece of work. Anytime there's something to be against, you're ready to be against it."

"Edgar was born thirty years premature," said Marvin. "He would have made the ideal hippie. He could have moved out to California and lived among the orange-juice drinkers."

It was at this juncture that Burna waddled out of the kitchen to refill everyone's cup. Burna was Harley's daughter-in-law and the café's lone employee between lunch and dinner; she was thirty-eight and pregnant, and she usually thought about Elvis Presley when she made love to Harley's son. She always smiled and rarely eavesdropped, which made her a better-than-average waitress. "What are you rascals arguing about?" she asked the group. "I could hear Bud caterwauling from the kitchen."

For a moment there was silence.

"I think Edgar would like to order a glass of orange juice," said Marvin.

They all laughed at this for a very, very long time. Gary had to remove his eyeglasses in order to wipe away his tears with a napkin. Five years from now, Edgar would recount the memory of this joke at Marvin's funeral, and they'd all remember the details perfectly. It was so Marvin.

"Burna, this is coffee," said Horace. "*This* is *coffee.* You've really outdone yourself, Burna."

OCTOBER 17, 1983

(Mitch)

"Explain his world to me," said Laidlaw. He was an upright Gila monster wearing a polo shirt. It was Monday morning, 8:45 a.m. "Explain what the world of Winston Smith is like. We know he's in London, and we know the year is 1984. But what is it like to live in that place, at that time, within this story? Who can tell me?"

As he spoke these forty-six words, twenty-two autonomous teenagers stared into his transfixing reptilian face, thinking the following twenty-two respective thoughts:

1) How awesome it would feel to be sleeping.
2) Unaffordable denim skirts. Fuck.
3) What it would feel like to be asleep.
4) Sleeping.
5) The lack of cool guys living in Owl, at least when compared to how the guys in Oakes were described by a cousin during a recent telephone conversation.
6) An empty room, filled only with white light and silence. (This was Rebecca Grooba.)
7) The iconography of Teresa Cumberland, chiefly the paradox of why no one else seems to realize that she is a total back-stabbing bitch who talks shit about everybody in school and then acts as if she is somehow the victim whenever anyone calls her on it.
8) The potential upside of being comatose.
9) Theoretical ways to make a Pontiac Grand Prix more boss, such as painting a panther on the hood or moving the entire

steering column and floor pedals to the passenger side, which would likely be impossible without a cherry picker and extremely expensive tools.

10) The meaning (and linguistic derivation) of the phrase "Gunter glieben glauchen globen," as heard during the preface to Def Leppard's "Rock of Ages."
11) Being asleep, possibly inside a ski lodge.
12) Robot cows.
13) That one eighth grader with the insane tits, and the degree to which it would be life-changing to tickle her when she was naked. Was her name Judy? That seemed about right.
14) Sleeping.
15) My boyfriend has amazing hair.
16) I wish Grandma would just hurry up and die.
17) Nobody knows I have a warm can of Pepsi in my locker.
18) The carpeting in Jordan Brewer's semi-unfinished basement that smells like popcorn and would provide an excellent surface for sleeping.
19) The moral ramifications of stealing beer from a church rectory, which—while probably sinful—would just be so fucking easy. I mean, it's almost like they *want* you to steal it.
20) Being gay.
21) The prospect of a person being able to successfully ride on the back of a grizzly bear, assuming the bear was properly muzzled. (This was Zebra.)
22) Firing a crossbow into the neck of John Laidlaw while he received fellatio from Tina McAndrew. (This was Mitch.)

"You're all 106 pages into this story," Laidlaw continued, "or at least you're *supposed to be* 106 pages into this story. I'm sure many of you feel like nothing is happening. Do not be alarmed. All great books are like this. All great books seem boring until you're finished reading them. But for the time being, let's focus on the atmosphere that Orwell is creating. What is the world of *Nineteen Eighty-Four* like?"

Laidlaw pointed at Jackie Andercrash, a thin, big-toothed girl best known for her mild scoliosis. "Bad," she answered.

"You paint a vivid picture," said Laidlaw. "But you need to elaborate. What is so bad about Orwell's universe?"

"The government watches everyone all the time," Jackie said. "I don't know what the problem is, exactly. I guess that it's just a bad society. They tell people things like 'Freedom is slavery,' which seems—you know—pretty obviously wrong."

"What Orwell has done," Laidlaw said, "is create something called a *dystopia.* To understand what that means, you first have to know the meaning of the word *utopia.* A utopia is a perfect civilization, which generally means there isn't a government to interfere with the lives of its citizens. This, of course, is an impossible dream. There is, however, an extremely long book called *Atlas Shrugged* that's about what would happen if all of the most brilliant individuals in the world separated themselves from the flotsam and jetsam of society and built a utopia. Rebecca, you should read this book. You'd probably relate to it, especially if you're interested in trains. But here is my larger point: In *Nineteen Eighty-Four,* we have the opposite of a utopia. In Orwell's *dystopic* society, the concept of the individual has been completely eliminated."

Laidlaw walked to the blackboard and wrote the words *utopia* and *dystopia* in large cursive letters, circling the latter for emphasis. Half of the class copied those two words in their notebooks, anticipating a true-or-false question that seemed utterly inevitable. Mitch did not take notes. He knew what a utopia was. There was actually an Intellivision game called Utopia, and the whole objective was to build a flawless society on a desert island; you had to raise food and build hospitals and protect your mindless villagers from hurricanes. If there were any abstract "utopia vs. dystopia" quandaries on this test, he would crush them like spiders. He was, however, less confident about questions regarding the book itself, as he did not comprehend anything about it. He had looked at all 106 pages that had been assigned, and his pupils had scanned across every sentence, and he understood all the individual words and all of the meaningful phrases. Yet—somehow—Mitch had ingested nothing. He could not recall the qualities of any of the characters (although their names now sounded vaguely familiar), nor could he outline any element of the book's plot (beyond feeling an abstract sense of darkness and formality). Had he forgotten to bring the book home over the weekend, he would still be in the same position he was right now. This sort of thing happened all the time. The things he did on purpose were usually no different from the mistakes he made by accident.

Mitch stared forward, blinking himself awake. Laidlaw was now nattering about someone who was working in a record-keeping department and something about the availability (or lack thereof) of sugar and potatoes. Is this, he wondered, the kind of conversation Laidlaw made with Tina McAndrew? Is this why she fell in love with a mean-spirited, chain-smoking lizard? Yes, Tina was an airhead. That was true. But still. How do you make other people believe that you are interesting? Is this the key? By talking about a story that isn't even real?

"How about you, Vanna?" said Laidlaw.

"What?"

"What do you think about this?"

"I didn't hear the question," said Mitch. "The radiator is too loud."

"The radiator is not working, Vanna," said Laidlaw. "However, I'm not surprised that you are hearing things. That is, after all, a sign of psychosis. As such, I will pose my question again, this time above the din of the imaginary radiator. WHO. ARE. THE THOUGHT POLICE?"

It was too bad the movie theater went bankrupt, thought Mitch. If the theater was still in business, he could buy a ticket for the 7:30 showing of a Saturday-night horror movie and slip out the rear exit during one of the scenes that were set at night, because the theater would be pitch-black and no one would notice his departure. He could then leave his car in the parking lot and cross town by foot, arriving at Laidlaw's house at 7:55. John Laidlaw was Lutheran, but his wife was Catholic, and she always went to Mass on Saturday night. This would mean Laidlaw would be alone, probably watching *Love Boat* or *Fantasy Island.* Mitch could enter the house through the garage, creep into the living room through the kitchen, pounce up from behind the La-Z-Boy, throw a potato sack over Laidlaw's skull, and bash him over the head with a brick. He'd hit him twice, or maybe three times. All the blood would stay on the inside of the bag. Then, while Laidlaw was unconscious, he would drag him down the stairs and tie him (crucifixion style) to the Nautilus machine in the basement; Mitch knew the family owned a Nautilus machine because Laidlaw talked about it all the time. He would rouse him by throwing ice water in his face, and then—right at the moment when John Laidlaw became aware of his surroundings and conscious of his captor—Mitch would crush his shoulder blades with a crowbar. "Do you like that?" Mitch would ask rhetorically. After that, he'd burn Laidlaw's pupils with cigarettes. He would use the same cigarettes that Laidlaw always smoked. "This is what *I* call sarcasm," Mitch would say over the muffled screaming. At 8:15, he would put on a pair of leather gloves and beat his reptilian coach to death, supplying some extra-violent attention to his ultra-vulnerable kidneys. Mitch would then exit the home at 8:28 p.m., roughly twelve minutes before Mrs. Laidlaw and her children would return from church to discover the corpse. She would probably be relieved. And because he would still have the ticket stub from the movie theater (and because the stub would list the time and date of the show), Mitch would have a seamless alibi. Even if he somehow became a suspect (which was unlikely), he'd be untouchable. The murder would likely be blamed on a paid hit man from Fargo or Winnipeg, undoubtedly hired by the father of some pregnant teenager; Laidlaw's lifelong history of sexual misconduct had undoubtedly created countless enemies, so it wouldn't be illogical to assume that someone finally decided to make him pay for the things he had done. Moreover, no one would ever believe an unassuming sixteen-year-old quarterback would (or even *could*) inflict that level of concentrated, clinical, unadulterated damage against a local authority figure. The crime would be so brutal that a boy such as himself would be above suspicion.

Damn.

Why did they have to close that movie theater?

"The Thought Police are cops who can read your mind," replied Mitch, guessing through the power of context. "They can stop crimes before they happen, because they know what you're going to do before you do it."

"Close," said Laidlaw. "You're not completely right, Vanna, but you're close."

OCTOBER 22, 1983

(Julia)

Rugby, North Dakota, has a population of three thousand people, most of whom are blond and none of whom play rugby. It is the geographic center of North America, and the community features a rock obelisk that proudly marks that location. This obelisk has been relocated several times since 1971, possibly because a) many geologists suspect the true vortex of North America to be about fifteen miles outside of town, but primarily because b) it is technically impossible to pinpoint the precise center of any landmass that doesn't have discernible sides. There is no middle to America. It does not matter where they stick the Rugby obelisk; Rugby is not the geographic center of anything. But everyone believes that it is, including all the people who admit that it isn't. As such, Rugby celebrates this (almost true) fact by staging an annual three-day street festival, always punctuated by a handful of hyper-intoxicated locals who consume fried bull testicles in public.

If you are from North Dakota, these are things you learn in eighth grade. It's part of a class called Our State.

Julia taught Our State while falling in love with the concept of Vance Druid.

"The longitude of Rugby is forty-eight degrees north," she said to a room of edgy, *Thriller*-purchasing eighth graders. "The latitude of Rugby is ninety-nine degrees west. You will need to know this." Julia had no idea why anyone would ever need to know such things, but multiple-choice tests required her to create questions that had irrefutable answers. She read Rugby's geographic coordinates off a translucent plastic sheet that rested on an overhead projector, but she did not hear her own words as she spoke them aloud. By now Julia could lecture about Teddy Roosevelt or answer questions about Lake Sakakawea without hearing or remembering anything she said. Teaching history to eighth graders is like being a tour guide for people who hate their vacation. She still didn't know much about North Dakota, so she unconsciously fabricated many of the tangential details (including its second-most-lucrative industry, which she claimed to be cobalt). No one cared, including Julia; inside her skull, words and sentences sounded like side three of *Metal Machine Music,* an album she had never heard of. She had little sense of time and no interest in society. Today, all she thought about was Vance Druid and how much fun it was to be in love with him.

Julia's fake love for Vance was exhilarating and idiotic; it was the kind of love you can only feel toward someone you don't actually know. Julia was wholly aware of her electrifying stupidity; she fully realized that she'd only spoken with Vance on four occasions and that none of the conversations had lasted more than ten minutes. The first had been twenty-six days ago, when they both stood by the jukebox while he criticized rock groups that did not include Charlie Watts. The second time had been the following evening at the same bar; they talked about which characters they liked on the sitcom *Alice* and the failure of technology. "Whatever happened to lasers?" Vance wondered. "Why don't cops have laser pistols? Wasn't that supposed to have happened by now?" He seemed legitimately annoyed by this. Their third encounter probably didn't qualify as an actual chat, as this had been a group discussion about *Alice* that Vance mostly ignored; all he said was that the show went downhill after Flo left, and then he resumed drinking. But their *fourth* encounter—the one that had just happened the night before, and which had focused on nothing in particular—had somehow triggered that neurological mechanism all humans possess: He had struck the cerebral switch that makes someone *actively decide* they are going to be in love with a specific individual, simply because that is the person they are going to be in love with.

There is no feeling that can match the emotive intensity of an attraction devoid of explanation.

Julia knew this was ridiculous. She felt like a ridiculous person. She did not care. It was so much fun to imagine theoretical conversations the two of them might have, and to mentally replay their previous conversations in the hope of finding subtext. Julia found the latter activity especially time-consuming: Vance generally spoke in short, cryptic sentences. It was akin to code breaking. "That's like salt through a widow," he once remarked after Julia swallowed a complimentary shot of tequila. What, exactly, did that phrase mean? Was this some kind of all-purpose rural platitude, or was it specifically about her? Were widows addicted to sodium? Was he suggesting that she had a drinking problem? "You've got a lot of ideas," he once remarked before getting up to piss, and he said it in a way that did not sound complimentary or sarcastic—it was oddly neutral. There was just something tragically endearing about this person; he reminded her of a character Paul Newman would have played during the 1960s, back when he exclusively portrayed charismatic alcoholics. No one seemed to care that he was a broken person, including himself. Vance was the most obviously depressed individual Julia had ever met, but no one else in town seemed to notice; they all treated him like he was the host of *The Joker's Wild.* He would sit on a bar stool and pound thirteen cans of Schmidt and utter (maybe) one hundred words over a span of four hours. He did this 250 nights a year. Nobody found this troubling. People would look at his behavior and say double-true things like, "That guy is a pretty laid-back guy." They envied his life, or at least the life they assumed he had. He was a sad Ben Franklin. He was Mr. Owl.

Julia fantasized about saving his life. She imagined him saying, "I didn't even have a life until you moved here." She imagined him taking a shower in her apartment and sitting on her couch in boxer shorts, politely looking at the pictures in her photo albums; he would ask who certain people were and how and when she knew them. He would be mildly jealous of her male friends from college. He would ask if she ever hooked up with any of them. She'd tell him about her problems, and he would say, "I understand where you're coming from on this." He would constantly want to make out, but never in public. People would ask Julia questions like, "What is Vance *really* like?" and she would say, "Different than he seems." She would understand his secret darkness, and it would make their sex life unbelievable. "We need to buy a bigger bed," he would suggest sardonically, and they would lie on the mattress and laugh and laugh. Vance Druid had said or done nothing to prompt such fantasies. Still, these were the things Julia thought about while she taught Our State. She felt like she was on cocaine, a substance she'd never tried but had read about in magazines; she assumed this is how cocaine made people feel.

It was Friday. She could not wait to see him. Julia decided to wear a black turtleneck sweater with a bra that made her boobs look extra spherical and a pencil skirt that made her look like she was going to a bar in a town that wasn't Owl. The color of her lipstick was labeled Fireball Orange; it tasted like black licorice. Her hair achieved its maximum volume, which required eight dollars of Aqua Net. Julia waited in her apartment an extra forty-five minutes before going out. She did not want to appear as if she was waiting for anyone in public. When she showed up in Yoda's at 8:55, Vance was not there. Julia had a quick gin and tonic and headed over to Mick's Tavern. He wasn't there either. She drank a Tom Collins and drove to the VFW; the only people in the lounge were Disco Ball and Little Stevie Horse 'n' Phone, both of whom insisted on buying her G & Ts in rapid succession. She drank only one before heading to the White Indian, where she did not find Vance but did enjoy an extremely potent Greyhound. It was gone in seven minutes. She was on a roll. She peeped inside the Oasis Wheel but left immediately. There were a lot of vehicles parked outside Doc Jake's Saloon, but Vance was not inside (still, she had a rum and Coke). At quarter to 11:00 she checked back at Mick's Tavern; somebody whistled when she walked in. Julia felt like an idiot. She ordered a shot of Jägermeister and pretended not to be looking for Vance, who was not there. She eventually fell out of the bar's back door, a move that was not particularly dignified. When she finally staggered back to Yoda's, Naomi and Ted were sitting in their usual booth, throwing peanuts at each other.

"Holy shit," said Naomi. "Jules, you look like a thirty-thousand-dollar hooker. You look *fantastic.* We are going to get a million free drinks tonight. That skirt is like a Burmese penis trap."

"Where's Vance?" asked Julia.

"Um . . . what?"

"Vance," she repeated. "Why isn't Vance here? Or anywhere else?"

"Did he say he was going to be here?"

"He is always here! Or at least he's always somewhere," said Julia. "Fuck that guy."

"Why are you looking for Vance?" asked Ted.

"Who said I was looking for him?" said Julia. "Besides, fuck that guy." She was saying these things much louder than necessary.

"I don't understand this," said Naomi. "Is there something going on between you and Vance Druid? Why have I not been informed of this?"

"Nothing is going on. Fuck that guy. I just had to tell him something."

"What did you have to tell him?" asked Ted.

"I don't remember," said Julia. "Who wants a drink?" She walked toward the wall of bottles. Chet the Dog Lover was smiling from behind the bar, totally pissing her off. The Dog Lover only smiled at people when he wanted to piss them off.

"Give me three fucking rum and Cokes," said Julia. "And

quit looking at me. I know I'm drunk. I know I'm fucking drunk. Since when do you care who's drunk?"

"Since when do *you* buy your own drinks?" replied the Dog Lover.

"Give me a break, man. I mean, come on. Fuck. You know what I mean? Jesus Christ."

"Classy," said the Dog Lover as he mechanically injected streams of Coca-Cola into glass cauldrons of Lord Calvert and ice. "You know what? Fuck it. You can have all three of these drinks for five bucks, just because I'm such a swell guy. And—for the record—I think you look great tonight. I don't care what the inbred morons around here think. They don't know shit about fashion. In my opinion, strippers always look hot."

Julia wanted to move to Rugby.

OCTOBER 26, 1983

(Horace)

"I think Jeannette is trying to poison me," Edgar Camaro said. This was a surprising thing for anyone to say, even if that anyone was Edgar. The old men rarely spoke about their spouses over coffee; this was mostly out of respect for Horace's dead wife and Marvin's two dead wives. Today would be an exception. "Last night she made her knephla soup, and I swear it tasted like Treflon. Even the dumplings! I'm certain I could taste Treflon. She must think I'm a ragweed." Treflon is an herbicide used to kill weeds like foxtail and kochia; it is (theoretically) as safe as table salt, and you often see farmers eating their lunchtime sandwiches with hands that are stained yellow from the chemical's application.

"A little Treflon won't hurt you," said Marvin. "It'll just make your piss glow in the dark. Saves money on the electric."

Farmers die from cancer.

"If that soup is poison, you should bring the whole pot over to my house," Gary Mauch remarked. "I will eat the whole goddamn kettle in one sitting. In fact, tell Jeannette to throw some strychnine in with the milk. If your wife is really trying to kill you, I'm envious. I'd rather sleep with Jesus than spend another night hearing war stories from the Crusades."

Everyone chuckled. Everyone knew what Gary was referring to. Gary's wife, Vernetta, was currently embroiled in an intense religious standoff, and it was the only thing she had talked about for the past two weeks. He had no choice but to listen. Three months ago, the bishop in Fargo assigned a new Catholic priest to the Owl parish; his name was Father Steele. This sort of transformation happens to every small-town Catholic church every half decade—the diocese never wants any priest or congregation to become too comfortable. In this instance, the change had been especially welcome: The previous padre had been Father Brickashaw, one of the most intimidating rural clergymen of the late-twentieth century. For six years, Father Brickashaw ruled the Catholics of Owl like Attila the Hun, except this warlord a) didn't care about Mongolia and b) despised Vatican II. He once punched an altar boy in the chest for ringing a bell incorrectly (which, to be fair, did improve the overall quality of pre-Mass bell ringings by an unbelievable degree). His homilies were rhetorical interrogations of society as a whole, and his vocal style employed the soft-loud-soft pattern that would eventually be perfected by rock bands such as the Pixies. His most famous sermon focused on a college football game he happened to watch before the Saturday-evening Mass; Nebraska had defeated Oklahoma, prompting Cornhusker running back Mike Rozier to hold up his right index finger at the game's conclusion. "I see this very often in the world of sport," Father Brickashaw began timidly. "I see a young man who feels good. I see a young man who feels special, and he wants to tell this to the world. He has won this big football game, you see, and this makes him 'number one.' The world tells him this. He wants to find a television camera and hold up his finger and proclaim that he is number one. We all want to do this. We all want to show other people how proud we are about all the wonderful things we have done. We all want to be number one. But there is one problem with this desire: YOU ARE NOT NUMBER ONE! YOU ARE NOT NUMBER ONE! ONLY GOD IS NUMBER ONE! YOU ARE NOT NUMBER ONE. YOU ARE NOT NUMBER ONE. THERE CAN ONLY BE ONE NUMBER ONE, AND IT IS NOT A MAN CARRYING A LEATHER BALL. IT IS NOT A BUSINESSMAN, IT IS NOT JOHN WAYNE, IT IS NOT THE PRESIDENT OF THE UNITED STATES. IT IS JESUS CHRIST. IT IS JESUS CHRIST, WHO WAS NAILED TO A TREE TO SAVE YOU FROM SIN. HE CHOSE TO DIE

FOR THE SAKE OF THE ENTIRE WORLD. *HE* IS THE ONE. BUT *YOU*? YOU ARE NOT NUMBER ONE! YOU ARE NOT NUMBER ONE! YOU ARE NOT NUMBER ONE!"

He paused to wipe the sweat from his balding skull. The earth did not rotate.

"You are not number one," Brickashaw finally continued, audible only because of his microphone. "And yet that is how you continue to live."

Not surprisingly, there was a degree of unspoken relief among Owl parishioners when Father Steele suddenly arrived that summer, mostly because he did not seem interested in reminding everyone they were (probably) going to hell. On the contrary, Father Steele was a young, fat, affable, nebulously feminine individual who—in stark contrast to his predecessor—did not assume all women were the intellectual equivalent of cows. He delivered short, nonconfrontational homilies about the sanctity of fidelity and the symbolic value of herding sheep. He especially enjoyed organizing the housewives of the congregation into religiously themed activities they could pursue throughout the week. One of these endeavors was an ad hoc quilting collective, which worked out brilliantly. The other was a weekly Bible-study group, and that ignited the Crusades.

Traditionally, Roman Catholics are not big Bible scholars. Catholics focus on the Gospels; the rest of the Bible is what Protestants arbitrarily memorize for no obvious reason. But Father Steele wanted to change this. He told the ladies of Owl that there was merit in reading and discussing less familiar passages of the Bible (even the Jewish parts), because this would allow them to place their everyday life into a religious context. His perspectives seemed fresh. As such, five of these middle-aged women agreed to meet with Father Steele every Wednesday morning in the basement of the church rectory to debate the Word of God. That was September. By October, Vernetta Mauch hated Melba Hereford the way Nixon hated JFK.

The feelings were mutual.

Melba Hereford had always been a polarizing figure, which is something that cannot be said about most fifty-four-year-old housewives with an interest in ceramics. She was born on a farmstead two miles north of town and had remained there her entire life; it was a personal detail she loved to tell anyone, regardless of how much (or how little) they cared. "I *am* Owl," she was wont to say unironically. Melba was a workaholic, a born leader, and a better-than-average house painter. Her father was Irish and her mother Italian; even when exhausted, she was mildly attractive. She didn't take naps and rarely gossiped. She was involved with every civic organization in town, even breaking the gender barrier of the (previously) all-male volunteer fire department. Had her residence been inside the city limits, she almost certainly would have run for mayor. And all of this was somewhat bizarre, because Melba Hereford felt life in Owl was mildly absurd and totally unfulfilling. She hated what the simplicity of her rural existence implied to East Coast strangers she would never meet, and she felt her life had been a minor waste. This was her darkest insecurity, and she never told it to anyone. Instead, she just worked harder. In 1946, Melba ran for Miss North Dakota, inexplicably assuming she was virtually guaranteed to win the title (along with the one-hundred-dollar academic scholarship that came with it). She placed fourth. When her rival was crowned, all the other girls swarmed around the weeping winner, passively delivering congratulatory hugs. Not Melba. Melba walked straight over to the program's host, pointed two fingers in his face, and stoically said, "You don't know what you're talking about." This sentiment didn't make much sense, particularly since the host had not been involved with the voting. But this is what she told him, and she never stopped saying it. It became her mantra. "You don't know what you're talking about." She would say this to anyone, and she always believed it. She told people they didn't know what they were talking about during school board meetings, and she told people they didn't know what they were talking about at funerals. She said it during wine-fueled political arguments, and she said it during casual conversations about the best way to hang a birdhouse. She said it to people she agreed with, sometimes while actively agreeing with their fundamental point. She once said it during sex. (Melba Hereford's husband lived an existence of perpetual despair.) "You don't know what you're talking about." Whenever she said this, she was correct 50 percent of the time. And that, obviously, is what made Melba Hereford so polarizing: No one else in Owl was remotely like her. No one was as disagreeable, no one was as self-assured, and no one was so deeply committed to a life that was imperfect. She was a nag, but she always hauled the water.

Melba was the reason why Gary Mauch wanted to consume poison soup.

Vernetta Mauch didn't want a Bible-study group. She wanted therapy. She needed it. For the previous seventeen years, she had lived her five-foot-two existence in a four-bedroom house with three empty bedrooms, sharing her declining years with a man who only liked to talk three hours a day, and only with other men, and only in a café she wasn't inside of. Vernetta wanted other people to understand her life; she felt her life was tremendously interesting, and she wanted other people to know this. Prior to the creation of this Wednesday-morning Bible-study group, having such dialogue was impossible. (It seemed rude and egocentric to talk about oneself in normal conversation.) But now—suddenly—that process was easy. In a way, it was almost the point of the entire exercise! Moreover, it seemed obvious (at least to Vernetta) that God *wanted* her to talk about these things. He must have. Because why else would he have made the entire Bible about her life?

There was not a single anecdote from either testament that Vernetta could not connect to specific dramatic events in her own personal history, or even to semidramatic events from the previous Friday. The story of Samson and Delilah was exactly like what happened to her brother-in-law, a promising collegiate wrestler who had a terrible relationship with a Korean girl (this was a fourteen-minute anecdote). The story of Cain and Abel was *exactly* like a situation that happened to Vernetta and her baby sister ten Christmases ago, except they both behaved more like Abel and there really wasn't a Cain figure, unless you count the UPS man (this was a twenty-six-minute story, told in two parts). Vernetta closely related to the plight of Job, mostly due to an ill-fated attempt at growing strawberries. There was no theological train that Vernetta could not derail. By the third week, Melba Hereford could no longer contain her annoyance.

"You don't know what you're talking about," Melba interjected when Vernetta tried to use Christ's damning of a fig tree as a means to criticize her husband's insistence on buying a new lawn tractor. "Buying a lawn mower has nothing to do with the Son of God. You're ruining the Bible for everyone."

"I'm talking about my life," said Vernetta. "My goodness, Melba. How can you say I don't know what I'm talking about when I'm talking about *my own life*?"

"Because if you actually knew what you were talking about, you wouldn't be talking about it here," Melba said. She then turned to Father Steele and pointed two fingers in the general direction of his chubby, cherry face. "I want to make a new rule: From now on, no one can talk about their own life during Bible study."

Father Steele did not know how to respond to this demand. However, he did know that he was very afraid of Melba Hereford, and he was very glad his overwhelming sexual confusion had led him away from a life where he might have married such a person. "That would be rather unorthodox," the priest said softly. "I mean, the idea behind having these discussions is to understand how the Word of God can be part of our everyday world. I'm really not sure if this is a good idea, Melba. I'm not sure if placing a ban on all expressions of human discovery would be an effective way to pursue divinity."

"You don't know what you're talking about," Melba said.

"When we agreed to form this committee three weeks ago, you described it as 'Bible study.' To me, that means we should be studying *the Bible.* I am very interested in *the Bible.* I am not interested in listening to jibber jabber."

"My life is not jibber jabber!"

"I think we should vote on it," said Melba, already tearing an 8½ x 11–inch piece of paper into five pieces. "We will use a secret ballot, so as not to hurt anyone's tender feelings. Mark down an X if you want a ban on people talking about themselves, and mark an O if you want to continue perverting God's autobiography."

The voting process was predictably efficient. Father Steele collected the ballots and counted them carefully, unwillingly supporting the election by allowing its very existence. The swing vote was June Cash, the pragmatic wife of a dairy farmer; June didn't like Melba, but not as much as she disliked self-indulgence. The final tally was 3–2. As a result, Owl now had the only Bible-study group in America where it was forbidden to tell any story less than two thousand years old. This is why Vernetta Mauch hated Melba Hereford: Through sheer force of personality, Melba invalidated her entire life. And this public invalidation had been—pretty much without exception—the only thing Vernetta had talked about since the votes were counted. Over the last two weeks, there had never been a conversation in the Mauch household that did not devolve into a one-sided, singularly repetitive declaration of the fatwa against Melba Hereford.

This made Gary want to eat Treflon.

"I can't take it," he said. "I just cannot take it. It's like I'm living with the goddamn Ayatollah. From the start of supper until the end of Carson, all she does is rant about how Melba Hereford is a witch who needs to be thrown into the river. I keep telling Vernetta to just quit the goddamn Bible group if it causes her so much suffering, but she refuses. She thinks that's what Melba wants. As if Melba cares about anyone who isn't named Melba! The crazy old biddy. That goes for both of them. I don't know which biddy is loonier. I'd really like to know if my wife is crazier than Melba."

"If it's a horse apiece," said Marvin, "who gives a damn?"

"No shit," said Gary.

Horace smiled and blew his nose. Marvin Windows knew what he was talking about.

"So what are our thoughts on Grenada?" asked Horace. "Do you have an opinion on our situation, Marvin?"

"Do I have an opinion on what?"

"On Grenada," said Horace. "We invaded the island of Grenada yesterday."

"Where the Sam Hill is Grenada?"

"East of Central America," said Horace. "They only have twelve hundred men in their entire military. The war is already over. Reagan just made the announcement. We won."

"Why did we invade Grenada?" asked Marvin.

"We had to rescue some American medical students," said Horace.

"There was a Marxist coup," said Gary. "The Marxists are against medical students."

"Huh," said Marvin. "Well, I don't have any opinion on the matter. I didn't see the newspaper."

OCTOBER 29, 1983

(Mitch)

People often recall their childhood school bus smelling like vomit, but this is a misremembered cliché. In reality, the smell people recall is vomit cleanser. This misremembrance is the second-most interesting fact about school buses. The first-most interesting fact is that school buses vibrate. Anytime a yellow busload of children exceeds forty miles per hour, the seats and windows vibrate in place like an air hockey table; it always feels like the vehicle is on the cusp of molecular disintegration. Mitch imagined this happening as he looked out his window at the darkening horizon and the prewinter sky. Bodies would fly everywhere, peppering the highway with blood and bone and fragments of clothing. It would be violent, but he would survive.

His bus was rolling toward Wishek, a Germanic community where the Owl Lobos were about to close out the '83 football campaign against the WHS Badgers. This was a big deal for two reasons. The first was that playing well in Wishek was always important, because Wishek High was populated by an inordinate number of attractive, disarmingly voluptuous girls; this had been the case for decades and was known throughout the region. The mothers of Wishek had hot-blooded bloodlines. The second reason was purely mathematic: The Lobos currently had a record of 4–4, so tonight's game would dictate the symbolic value of the entire season, along with the civic worth of every person on the roster. If the Owls won, they would finish the year as a winning team; everyone in town would be mildly satisfied and deeply relieved. A record of five wins and four losses was acceptable to all. However, if they lost, they would become the first Owl team in two decades to end the year below .500. Going 4–5 would be a disaster; in theory, Mr. Laidlaw could even lose his job. This struck Mitch as strangely arbitrary, but it probably made sense: Everything needed a cutoff. Tonight he would be fighting to save the job of a man he despised.

The season had gone precisely as Mitch had anticipated, which meant the season had been completely undramatic. The Owls had won the three games in which they were plainly the better team, they had lost the three games in which they were generally outclassed, and they had split the two contests that were genuine toss-ups. The squad never found a legitimate quarterback. Mitch had played sparingly, but consistently; Laidlaw often inserted him into ballgames whenever the team was floundering, almost as a way to publicly express his dismay with the other players. Mitch's lone highlight had been against the Napoleon Imperials in early October: After not playing a down throughout the first three quarters, he entered the game with the Lobos trailing 14–0. Laidlaw kept calling Flood Right 64; as promised, Weezie was open in the flat every time. Mitch threw ten desperate passes and completed six of them, including the only touchdown of his entire career. (The toss had even spiraled, partially.) Owl still lost the game, but everyone told Mitch he had played wonderfully and slapped his helmet with enthusiasm. "I bet you'll start next week," Weezie told him after the game. "You are the quarterback of the future." For most of the weekend, Mitch believed that. He spent Saturday afternoon throwing a football through a Firestone tire his father had hung from a tree. He spent Sunday afternoon watching Tommy Kramer take downfield gambles while looking foxy and hungover. Mitch could not sleep, and he did not want to. Things in his life were (possibly) about to change (completely). And they did, but not in the way he had hoped. When Mitch arrived at practice the following Monday, he immediately noticed something: Laidlaw liked him *less*. "Completing a few passes doesn't make you Johnny Unitas," he barked at Mitch during calisthenics, apropos of absolutely nothing. "I've seen a million kids heave a touch-down pass after the cows were already in the corn. That's not what I need to see, Vanna. I need to see *leadership,* Vanna. *Be a leader.* For once in your life, be a leader. Do you even understand what that means?" Mitch did not. In fact, he had no clue what that was supposed to mean in any context that wasn't theoretical. By Wednesday it was clear that Mitch was not the quarterback of the future, or even the present. The Lobos faced Cando High School on Friday, and Mitch didn't play at all. He spent most of the next three days pretending not to care about this, except when he was alone in his bedroom. Bedrooms are good places for crying.

Tonight Mitch sat at the back of the bus, adjacent to Zebra's ghetto blaster. They could not play the stereo before the game, but—if they won—they could play it on the ride home. (And if this happened, Mitch would sit near the front of the bus, away from all those stupidly deafening songs about legs and TV dinners and sharply dressed men.) Grendel sat across the aisle from him, staring blankly ahead; even without his shoulder pads, he seemed like a piece of machinery, wrapped in horseflesh and gorilla leather. Grendel was the undisputed star of the Lobos; his nineteen sacks had already shattered the school record and he would probably get three more tonight. There had been numerous newspaper articles written about his dominance, and it was rumored that he was being recruited by the University of Nebraska, a college he could not locate on a map. In the game against Cando, he had broken an opposing running back's femur; the bone sounded like a deer rifle when it snapped.

"Grendel," said Mitch. He received only silence in response. "Hey, Grendel," he said again. "Grendel. Grendel? *Chris.* Hey, Chris."

Grendel eventually turned his head. His eyes were piercing and vacant at the same time, which shouldn't be possible.

"What," said Grendel.

"Can I ask you a question?" said Mitch. He felt a little like

Zebra when he asked this. He found himself trying to talk like Zebra, which almost worked.

"Yes."

"What do you think of Cubby Candy?"

"Cubby Candy," repeated Grendel.

"Yeah," said Mitch. "What do you think of Cubby Candy?"

"He's crazy."

"Sure," said Mitch, "but do you *like* him?"

"I've never thought about it," said Grendel.

"Do you think you could beat him in a fight?"

"Yes."

"Really," said Mitch. "That's interesting. That's really, really interesting. And I totally agree with you. Absolutely. But you know what's weird? What's weird is that a lot of people think he could beat *you* in a fight, simply because of that aforementioned craziness. Which, I think, makes for an intriguing hypothetical."

"Nobody thinks that," said Grendel. "Who thinks that?"

"Well, it's not like anyone *specifically* thinks he could kick your ass," said Mitch, not showing his sudden nervousness. "It's not like this is something people *talk about,* or anything like that. It's just that Candy gets in a lot of fights, and he *is* a decent fighter, and the only fight he's ever lost was with that cop, and that doesn't *really* count, because the cop cuffed him and hit him with a *billy club,* which I think we'd all agree was a total cheap shot. So I guess certain people just wonder if maybe Candy could fight *anyone* and possibly win, even if the person he was fighting happened to be *you.* Because—like you said—he *is* crazy. And, you know, *unpredictable.*"

"I'd wreck him," said Grendel. "I would destroy."

"But what if he did something outrageous?" Mitch asked. "Like, what if he tried to bite your neck? Or what if he attacked you with a ball-peen hammer or a saber saw or a folding chair?"

"I would fucking wreck him worse for trying," said Grendel. "I'd rip out his heart and jam it into his fucking mouth. I wouldn't let some bastard hit me with a folding chair. You can't let people get away with shit like that."

"True, true," said Mitch. "You're right about this, Chris. You're completely right. I was just curious about your opinion on this subject."

"You say a lot of bozo shit, Vanna." Grendel hated the fact that kids like Mitch could use so many different words whenever they spoke. Like, he knew what the word *hypothetical* meant when someone else used it in a sentence, but there was just no way he could talk like that during normal conversation. Every time he tried to use a complicated word, people looked at him like he was speaking Spanish. Fuck them all. He resumed staring at the front of the bus and feeling unstoppable.

"Sorry, man," said Mitch. "I apologize for breaking your concentration. I was basically just talking to myself."

Owl beat Wishek by forty points. Grendel knocked their 130-pound quarterback into an eighteen-hour coma, but at least the dude lived.

NOVEMBER 1, 1983

(Julia)

At first, Julia thought the horrible sounds she heard outside her window were the result of not being drunk, which made her fear that she was an alcoholic. Could she no longer sleep sober? Julia had stayed inside on Halloween night, unsure if she would spend the entire evening greeting trick-or-treaters; as it turned out, she was visited by only five kids, leaving her with two extraneous bags of mini Butterfingers. She watched *Newhart* and *After MASH* and missed being in college, remembering how Halloween was always a universal party night: She and all her girlfriends would dress like slutty nurses or slutty witches or slutty KISS members, as this was the lone night when slutty attire was expected. It was something to look forward to, and it was something to remember later. However, this Halloween had been a lonely, depressing night; she briefly considered smoking her last joint, but did not. Instead she simply went to bed, hoping she would dream about 1982.

Her slumber was broken by the sounds of animal torture.

Sometime after midnight, Julia heard a living creature scream and hiss and cry; it sounded like someone was forcing his own hand into a food processor. She could hear drunken men laughing on the lawn below her bedroom. Was one of these men Chet the Dog Lover? Possibly, but she could not tell for certain. Was this a dream? No. Something outside her window was dying, choking on its own windpipe. People were opening beer cans; every so often, the creature would expel a high-pitched screech of grotesque terror, and a handful of guys would go, "*Ohhhhhhh!,*" almost as if they'd just witnessed a particularly stunning golf shot. She wanted to look outside and see what was happening, but she was afraid (even though she did not know why). The noises finally ended around 1:00 a.m.; the men disappeared inside, and she fell back asleep. She dreamt of ambulances being attacked by apes.

Julia awoke at 7:15 the following morning, surprised by how good she felt. Not drinking was really refreshing. During her shower, she slowly remembered the previous night's howling. After dressing and applying mascara, she walked out behind the apartment and found the corpse of a mutilated cat, beaten with a hammer and ripped to shreds. Its intestines had been pulled from its guts with a stick, and the neck of a beer bottle was jammed into its rectum. The cat's eyes were wide open and its jaws were locked; its tongue had been ripped out with a pliers.

Julia immediately recognized the taste of lukewarm vomit on her tongue.

She did not know what to do next.

Had she seen this cat before? She thought that maybe she had. It used to be fat and orange. There was a house across the street, and the fat orange cat sometimes sat on its porch. Julia walked to the door and rang the doorbell. A middle-aged woman answered the door; she was wearing a terry-cloth robe.

"Good morning," said Julia. "I live in one of the apartments across the street. I hate to be the bearer of bad news, but last night I heard some really awful sounds."

"Good Lord," said the robed old woman. "What kind of sounds? A burglar?"

"No, no," said Julia. "Not a burglar. However, I have to ask you an unhappy question: Do you have a cat?"

"Yes," said the woman. "We have a cat."

"Is your cat okay?"

The old woman knew what happened to cats on Halloween.

"Kenny," she said over her shoulder, still looking at Julia. "Do you know where Rocky is?"

Kenny came to the door. He was eleven years old. He had a crew cut.

"Have you seen my cat?" Kenny asked.

Julia started to cry. "Maybe," she said.

"Where is he?" asked Kenny. "Is he all right?"

Kenny already knew that he was not.

Julia and the boy walked over to the corpse. They stood above its body. Kenny poked at it with a stick, very gently. Julia swallowed another thimble of her own vomit.

"Was he a friendly cat?" Julia asked.

"Rocky was a good cat," said Kenny. "He was my sister's cat, and then he was my cat when my sister went to college."

The cat was so dead. It was extra dead. It looked like it had been electrocuted, but that was impossible.

"Do you think other kids did this?" Kenny asked.

"I don't think it was kids," said Julia. "I don't know who did it, but I don't think it was kids. I think it was grown-ups. I think it was some drunken grown-up idiots."

Kenny kept staring at the body. He wondered if he had time to bury it before school.

"I will find out who did this," said Julia. "I will ask around. I will do some sleuthing. They won't get away with this. Whoever did this to Rocky will get caught. We will catch them, and they'll have to pay a fine and maybe go to jail and absolutely buy you another cat. We will involve the police. The police will be involved."

"They would just deny it," said Kenny. "They would probably just say you did it, because you found him. And it really doesn't matter if we catch them, anyway."

"Yes, it does," said Julia. "It matters. Your cat was important. Don't ever think this wasn't important. Rocky was a good cat."

"Oh, that's not what I mean," Kenny replied. "I just mean that it doesn't matter if *we* catch them, because all the people who did this will eventually die, because everybody dies. And then they'll burn in hell forever."

Kenny walked back to his garage to get a shovel. Julia went back to her apartment to reapply her mascara and re-hate the world. They were both late for school.

NOVEMBER 8, 1983

(Horace)

"They shot his dog," said Edgar Camaro. This was not the first time this point had been made. "They walked into his yard and shot his dog in the throat. For *barking*. They shot his dog for being a dog. What does that tell you about their motivations? Does that sound like the work of credible law-enforcement personnel?"

"They said they had no choice," Gary replied.

"No choice? It was a dog! Were they afraid he was gonna give them rabies? I don't support what the man did, but there was no justification for shooting his dog. None. They just decided they wanted to shoot something, and that dog was the only thing available."

This was all true. On February 15, 1983, FBI agents assassinated Gordon Kahl's black Labrador.

"The dog. The dog! The man murdered two U.S. marshals, and all you want to talk about is the hound." Bud said these words with the frustration one can only feel from having an argument for the tenth time. "Who do you think you are, the damn Dog Lover? You talk like a fish. You talk like a dope smoker!"

"Gordon Kahl killed men who were trying to kill him and his family," said Edgar. "I don't support what the man did, but he was the one who didn't have a choice. What were his options? He had no options."

"He could have paid his taxes," said Horace. "All he had to do was pay his taxes."

"It was too late for that," reiterated Edgar. "By the time those federal marshals arrived, it was too late. They had no intention of asking him for a check. Someone was going to die. They were going to make an example out of him. What would you do if the government tried to shoot your own son? What was he supposed to do? I don't support what the man did, but what he did was not so wrong."

Born in Heaton, North Dakota, in 1920, Gordon Kahl spent his childhood hunting gophers and playing piano. He spent a few years farming and a few years working in a lumberyard; he tried to join the U.S. Army Air Corps in the autumn of '41, but they wouldn't take him. They said he had a bad nose. (He'd broken it as a boy and still didn't breathe right.) When Japanese kamikazes destroyed Pearl Harbor that same December, the military changed its mind about his nose. He became a turret gunner on a B-25 bomber and shot down ten planes while receiving two purple hearts. The M*A*S*H surgeons in North Africa were never able to get all the shrapnel out of his body; he lived most of his life with metal inside his face. Gordon married a woman named Joan Seil in 1945, whom he had met when she was only fourteen. They moved to North Carolina. He gave her a double-barreled shotgun as a wedding gift.

Gordon Kahl was a skeptical person. How was the attack on Pearl Harbor allowed to happen, he often wondered, sometimes during conversations that were not about war, Hawaii, or Japan. He read a book written by auto magnate Henry Ford called *The International Jew: The World's Foremost Problem.* Had Zionist bankers convinced FDR to goad the Japs into launching their attack? Had there been a clandestine 1918 meeting among Russian Jews focusing on world domination? Perhaps. Were the Jews truly trying to take control of the banking system, the media, and the farm economy? It often seemed like it. His friends in Carolina told Gordon he was crazy, but he did not believe them. They seemed crazier than he was. He elected to move back to North Dakota.

Gordon and Joan had six children. During the 1950s, they lived a semi-itinerant lifestyle: They farmed wheat in the summer and traveled to California in the winter. It seemed as if absolutely everyone in California already owned a car, and Gordon was naturally adroit at fixing anything that had the potential to break. He was a quiet, patient person. One West Coast winter, someone introduced him to a theology called the Christian Identity movement. It was a doomsday religion that split the world into two groups: The Good and The Evil. That distinction made sense to Gordon. The Christian Identity movement believed there was a coming nuclear war between the U.S. and the Soviet Union, and that the Aryan Race was superior to all others. Previous to joining the Movement, Gordon and Joan had converted to Mormonism for spiritual guidance, but they quit when Gordon concluded that Mormon ceremonies were replications of the rituals practiced by the Bavarian Illuminati and the Masons. Gordon Kahl was nobody's puppet.

By 1960, Kahl was positive that the government was corrupt; the creation of the Federal Reserve was the last straw. He considered joining the John Birch Society, but they weren't radical enough. In the summer of '64, he decided that the sixteenth amendment was illegal because it hadn't been formally ratified by three-fourths of the states. Moreover, the IRS collected taxes on behalf of the Federal Reserve, an organization controlled by eight international bankers of Jewish descent who wanted to overthrow the Christian government; as such, paying one's taxes was directly financing the destruction of Christianity. In fact, that's why John F. Kennedy had been murdered in Dallas the previous winter: He knew about this conspiracy and refused to participate.

Gordon was extremely confident about these things.

"Never again will I give aid and comfort to the enemies of Christ," Kahl wrote in 1967. He proceeded to mail these words to the IRS, who responded by demanding that he appear before a federal tax court. He ignored that request (and all similar requests that followed). Around this same time, he quit hauling his family to California; instead, he spent his winters working in the oil fields of Texas. In 1973, he joined an organization called the Posse Comitatus. The Posse Comitatus believed that governments did not exist above the county level; being the kind of man who refused to accept even a driver's license from the state, such messages fit Gordon's worldview. Kahl soon became the Posse's coordinator for all of Texas. It was at this point that Gordon Kahl truly became an enemy of the United States; in 1976, he went on television and told everyone in America to stop paying their taxes, just as he had done for the past nine years. "When you become a Christian," he said into the camera, "you put yourself on the opposite side of government."

Kahl's thirty-minute television appearance earned him eight months in Leavenworth prison. Questions remain over what truly generated this penalty: Did Kahl go to jail for not paying his taxes, or did he go to jail for bragging about it on TV? Either way, he certainly didn't help his cause on the trial's opening day when he told the judge, "I didn't fail to file my taxes. I *refused* to file my taxes."

Prison did not reform him.

Everybody said Gordon Kahl was (or at least *had the potential to be*) a likeable old man. He did not drink alcohol, smoke tobacco, or use foul language. This was mildly unusual for a racist anti-Semite who wanted to destroy the government. All he wanted (or so he would argue) was merely to be left alone; he wanted to be able to farm without government intrusion and to live without "oppression," which he defined as having to write the IRS a ten-thousand-dollar check. On Sunday, February 13, 1983, a group of federal marshals from Fargo tried to arrest Gordon Kahl for his ten-thousand-dollar disobedience. They were going to send him back to jail. But Gordon Kahl was not going back to jail; the day he walked out of Leavenworth, he vowed that he would sooner die than return to prison. And—in keeping with his interpretation of the King James Bible and the Articles of Confederation—this vow was not a metaphor.

Medina, North Dakota, is a community of 520 people that's 125 miles west of Fargo, 71 miles east of Bismarck, and 11 catawampus miles from downtown Owl. It was here that five-foot-seven, 160-pound Gordon (along with his equally vigilant twenty-three-year-old son, Yorie) came to live, and it was here that they had a shoot-out with the law. It happened on a road just north of the Medina city limits, fifteen minutes before 6:00 p.m.; it was six hours and fifteen minutes from Valentine's Day. The federal authorities blocked the road and pulled their guns on Gordon, Yorie, Joan, and two of Kahl's companions as the quintet drove away from a chapter meeting of the North Dakota Constitutional Party, a group of perhaps two dozen local citizens who had just voted in favor of secession from the Union. Gordon was not surprised by the confrontation. He had long been certain that someone in Medina was a Mossad informant. "What do you guys want?" Kahl asked, crouching behind the open passenger door of a '73 AMC Hornet, a gun leveled at his enemies. "All we want is you," a marshal yelled in response. "Put the guns down, we'll talk about it." Almost everyone at the scene had at least one weapon (and most had more). For a few insane minutes, both parties stared at each other with weapons drawn, twenty-five feet apart, their breath visible in the winter air. It was 5:55 p.m.

Eventually people stopped talking.

And then people started shooting.

As is so often the case in situations like these, no one knows who shot first. However, Gordon Kahl's rifle definitely shot last; he blew the head off a U.S. marshal named Robert Cheshire from point-blank range (skull fragments landed twenty feet away). The shoot-out lasted only thirty seconds, but the sixty-three-year-old Kahl had murdered two marshals and forced all the others to flee on foot. Yorie had absorbed a near-fatal bullet in the abdomen (he was hemorrhaging and moaning for his mother), but he lived (and eventually went to prison for life). His father, now a loner, managed to slip out of North Dakota under the cover of night, traversing the desolate rural roads that cops never really understand. He was probably across the South Dakota state line by the time the FBI raided his empty home on Tuesday the fifteenth. The operatives were greeted by the Kahls' dog, which they subsequently shot. "When human life is on the line, you don't worry about a dog," said FBI agent John Shimota.

The Gordon Kahl incident was the most violent regional news event since the 1975 Leonard Peltier shootings on the Pine Ridge Indian Reservation. It was all anyone in North Dakota could talk about; everything else on the local news seemed like meaningless filler (which it was, but now more than usual). The fact that Kahl was able to elude arrest for weeks after the murders made the story even more compelling: How could this elderly, diminutive man outwit an FBI manhunt? How was he able to outshoot U.S. marshals? Was he some sort of agricultural supervillain? People tried to forget that he was a hatemonger; fourth graders played "Gordon Kahl" during recess and reenacted the Medina standoff. When people would debate the shooting, they never said that Kahl was a hero; it was essential to preface any statement about the shooting with the phrase "Well, I don't support what he did." But 1983 was a good time to hate the government, especially if you were from North Dakota. Many, many farmers had been duped during the prosperity of the 1970s; every small farmer had been told that there was a worldwide food shortage and that they would all get rich by feeding the planet. Skyrocketing inflation artificially magnified the price of land, so everyone was suddenly a theoretical millionaire. There just wasn't any cash. Through a credit system they could not understand, farmers were persuaded into purchasing new equipment they could not afford. Every year, they got better at crop production; every year, the yields for wheat and corn and beans surpassed bumper crops from years past. And then, seemingly from the moment Jimmy Carter issued a grain embargo against Russia, everything collapsed. It was rudimentary supply and demand: Grain prices fell through the floor. It did not matter how successful farmers were at growing food; suddenly, no one wanted to pay for it. Around 1981, everyone started to go bankrupt and no one seemed to understand why. They had been tricked by modernity. Gordon Kahl thought this was the work of ZOG, just as Henry Ford had indicated; almost everyone else assumed it was a combination of bad luck and worse government. Every weekend there was another foreclosure, which meant another wrecked family and (occasionally) another suicide by a middle-aged farmaholic who no longer had anything to do with his life. The government was stealing the way people lived. And now that same government was willing to exchange gunfire with a sixty-three-year-old man . . . *for ten thousand dollars.* People did not support what Gordon Kahl was, but they (kind of) supported what he did. And they wanted him to win. Which is probably why so many people convinced themselves that Gordon Kahl was still alive, even when he wasn't.

"That ornery sumbitch is still out there," said Marvin Windows. This had always been his position. "He'll shoot somebody else before he's done. He'll probably shoot ten more of those stupid bastards, assuming they're still crazy enough to try and take him down."

"You're the crazy one," said Bud. It took guts to say this.

"We'll see," said Marvin. "We'll see."

The FBI allegedly killed Gordon Kahl in Arkansas on June 3. They burned him up. According to the government, there is nothing *alleged* about this claim, and most sane people (and certainly most dentists) agree. But it did seem curious that there was another shoot-out at the Arkansas residence where Kahl was finally caught, and that another law-enforcement agent (this time a sheriff) was killed, and that the home where Kahl was hiding was burned to the ground during the encounter, and that the charred corpse that was believed to be Gordon's was mutilated (both legs and one hand were severed from the torso). None of those bizarre details indicated that Kahl was still at large; however, they also did not make the FBI seem any more sympathetic, which produced the same effect.

"I don't support what the man did," Marvin Windows said, "but I know he's not dead."

"Oh, I'm pretty sure he's deader than a dinosaur," said Edgar.

"You guys talk like San Francisco hippies," said Bud.

Horace pushed his eyeglasses against the bridge of his slender nose and hoped the conversation would change; he was tired of talking about this person, dead or alive. Horace always paid his taxes and didn't mind Jews, and he certainly didn't think Gordon Kahl had the right to kill anyone, particularly since he had already been granted the opportunity to kill strangers within the context of a war. The Feds probably didn't need to burn him alive or chop off his hand, but somebody had to take him down. Kahl wasn't like that innocent Labrador those marshals shot in the neck. Kahl was like a dog that bites children: Who cares what his motives are? Why was this still an issue? Kahl didn't represent anyone but himself.

And if he *was* still alive? If Marvin *was* correct?

Well, thought Horace, if he's alive, he's alive. But he didn't say this aloud.

NOVEMBER 21, 1983

(Mitch)

"Why do we get out of bed?" Mitch wondered. "Is there any feeling better than being *in* bed? What could possibly feel better than this? What is going to happen in the course of my day that will be an improvement over lying on something very soft, underneath something very warm, wearing only underwear, doing absolutely nothing, all by myself?" Every day, Mitch awoke to this line of reasoning: Every day, the first move he made outside his sheets immediately destroyed the only flawless part of his existence. He could still remember the spring of 1978, when he (along with over half of his fifth-grade classmates) contracted mononucleosis. It was the best month of his life.

Peering out from beneath his electric blanket, Mitch looked toward his lone bedroom window. He slept in the basement. Outside, it was still semidark. Soon it would be pitch-black when he awoke and pitch-black when he returned from basketball practice. By mid-December, dusk would come before 4:00 p.m. and dawn wouldn't break until after 9:00 in the morning. "How did pioneers spend their winters before the advent of electricity?" he wondered. "Did they just eat supper and go to bed? Did they essentially hibernate? What else was there to do?" Perhaps they sat around and talked about their lives. But what would they have talked about? Before electricity, nothing really happened. Every conversation would have been identical, unless somebody got cholera or was mauled by a badger.

Unlike virtually every nonadult he knew, Mitch did not decorate his bedroom. He could not relate to people who did, which meant he could not relate to anyone. Zebra, for example: Zebra covered the walls of his bedroom with cut-out pictures of an (evidently) British band who were (evidently) called the Dead Leopards, alongside some buffoon named Billy Squier. They all wore tight, colorful pants. What did Zebra see in these people? He worshipped all the freaks he would hate in real life. Zebra was constantly buying magazines about musicians from the grocery store, always trying to decipher what their ponderous songs were about and whether these people were addicted to heroin. Whenever Zebra talked about the Dead Leopards, he referred to all the band members by their first names, almost as if they were casual acquaintances. It was embarrassing. Zebra was cool, but sometimes he was like a ten-year-old kid who still believed in Santa Claus. Lots of his classmates were like this. The guy who really blew Mitch's mind was Curtis-Fritz: That kid decorated his bedroom with *Star Wars* toys and Bo Derek posters. He had X-wing fighters hanging from the ceiling on fishing wire, and he had all his little Wookiees and stormtroopers posed on his bookshelves with their laser guns drawn—but then he added this glossy 36 x 24 photograph of Bo Derek running along the beach, undoubtedly hoping to mitigate the possibility of his parents suspecting that a seventeen-year-old who owns ten plastic tauntauns might be atypical. Society is so confused, Mitch thought. Everyone wanted to become the person they were already pretending to be.

What Mitch wanted most was what he already had: a room. *A room.* He wanted a rectangular room with a bed in the middle, a dresser, a nightstand with a lamp, a desk, and (in theory) a phone and a thirteen-inch TV (neither of which he currently possessed, but Christmas was only a month away). Mitch wanted to live in a motel room. He wanted to sleep in a room that expressed nothing, because rooms were supposed to be meaningless. He did not want to give anyone the opportunity to glean anything about his personality via his sleeping quarters. Last summer, his mother gave him a poster of Viking quarterback Tommy Kramer. (It had been a free gift with the purchase of four radial tires.)

Mitch liked Kramer, but he never hung the poster. He didn't know the man. Did Tommy Kramer have a poster of Mitch in his living room? Of course he didn't. They had no relationship. Mitch preferred staring at his off-white wall. He had a nice rapport with the wall.

It was odd: While discussing the early pages of *Nineteen Eighty-Four,* Mr. Laidlaw had noted that its protagonist lived in an apartment called a flat. It was essentially a colorless, spartan space that expressed nothing about its inhabitant. This was supposed to be metaphoric and depressing (and all the girls in the class took notes when he mentioned its details), but Mitch saw no symbolism whatsoever. It was impossible to construct personality, and it always seemed ludicrous when somebody tried to do so by buying furniture or throwing shit upon the walls. That's what restaurants tried to do. Did they really think they were fooling people? It was one of many things he did not understand about *Nineteen Eighty-Four,* and he was only on page 230. The remainder of his befuddlement was as follows:

1) The book's main character (Winston Smith) works in the Records Department for the government, and his vocation is rewriting documents and newspaper articles in order to make them correspond with the updated social condition. This actually seemed like a good job, not to mention an incredibly easy way to get paid. Mitch would not have complained about this.
2) Though he always assumed this story was set in England, that wasn't explicitly clear. There had also been some kind of major war, but he could not understand a) who fought in it and b) who won.
3) In the world of *Nineteen Eighty-Four,* having sexual intercourse for mere pleasure was illegal. This was probably a good idea, all things considered. Everybody he knew who was having sex without justification seemed to have a defective life; it was all they ever thought about, and it seemed to

dictate every decision they made about everything. Tina McAndrew's life had been ruined by her desire to have sex with Laidlaw, and Laidlaw's sexual obsession was proof that he was a bad person. Many of the laws in *Nineteen Eighty-Four* seemed practical. The world would be better off if everyone had to publicly validate why they were having sex with someone.

4) Laidlaw spent an inordinate amount of time railing against "doublethink," which he seemed to view as some brilliant commentary on the way modern real estate agents sell houses. It was supposed to be satire. But here again, Mitch did not see much detachment from common sense. One of Orwell's examples was that if a war went on forever, it would just become the normal state of existence; as such, "war is peace." Well, wasn't that usually true? America was supposedly in a Cold War with Russia, but nothing ever happened; people weren't even that worried about it. Just last night, NBC had aired a made-for-TV movie called *The Day After.* People had been talking about this for weeks. Father Steele told the entire Catholic congregation not to watch this movie because it would only make them worry about something God would never allow to happen. This made Mitch want to watch it even more, so he did. It was ridiculous. Basically, *The Day After* claimed that you could survive a nuclear holocaust by hiding in your basement, eating candy, and buying a horse. Nuclear war was so improbable that it could not even be properly imagined on television. There was no way the U.S.S.R. was going to bomb Kansas and there was no way America was going to bomb Siberia. And since *everybody* knew this, war *was* peace. Mitch could never tell which parts of this book were supposed to seem absurd.

5) More than anything else, the point that *Nineteen Eighty-Four* kept ramming home was that Big Brother knew everything about everyone, and everyone just accepted this as part of being alive. No shit! How was this remotely different

from reality? Everyone in Owl knew Laidlaw had impregnated Tina McAndrew. Everyone. Everyone knew they were having sex, and some people even knew *where* they were having sex. Everyone knew that Bull Calf Decker was afraid to shower without wearing his eyeglasses. Everyone knew that Vickie Vanderson once received cunnilingus in a Porta Potti. Everyone knew Naomi O'Reilly used to be a bulimic shoplifter. Everyone knew Marvin Windows had genital herpes and didn't care when (or from whom) he got it. Mitch had no idea how he knew these things, but he knew them all; very often, he knew the stories without having ever met the people they were about. Everyone knew everything. So how was *Nineteen Eighty-Four* a dystopia? It seemed ordinary. What was so unusual about everyone knowing all the same things?

Mitch lay on his side and squinted toward his alarm clock, which read 7:43. He heard his mother padding around upstairs, possibly making waffles or Malt-O-Meal. Now the clock read 7:44. His blankets were so warm; it was like being buried beneath a bear. His mattress was a cocoon made of bread. The world did not exist. He was inside a black hole. But then the clock read 7:45 and started saying *bonk-bonk-bonk-bonk-bonk-bonk-bonk,* and then he was not in space. He was in the world, and it existed. He turned off the alarm, emerged from beneath his bear, and lumbered toward the bathroom. Time to piss. There was nothing left to look forward to.

NOVEMBER 22, 1983

(Julia)

Julia arrived at Yoda's forty minutes later than usual; she had been correcting essay tests about the Underground Railroad while scrubbing her bathtub with Ajax. Naomi and Ted were already eradicating their second and third cocktails when she stomped into the building. Julia made her cursory hellos and jackknifed toward the bar. Vance Druid happened to be standing there, waiting for his first beer, playing with his car keys. Having spoken four times before, they nodded their heads in mutual salutation; Julia smiled warmly and Vance smirked, possibly by accident. It was the first encounter they'd ever had in which their combined blood-alcohol level was 0.00. This unexpected clarity was the catalyst for an important three-minute conversation, even though neither of them knew it at the time (or even in the future).

What she said: "So . . . tell me . . . how do you spend your non-drinking hours? Are you a farmer, too? Everyone I meet is a farmer."

What she meant: I don't know anything about you. You look like every other guy in town, you don't talk very much, and you don't seem to do anything except drink. *But I suspect you are different.* Somehow you seem unlike everyone else I've met in this community, even though there's no tangible evidence that would suggest my theory is valid. This is my gamble. So here is an opportunity for you to describe yourself in a manner that will confirm my suspicion and possibly make me love you forever, mostly because I am searching for any reason to increase the likelihood of that possibility.

What he said: "Yeah, I farm with my two brothers. It's their operation, really. I'm basically just a hired hand. It's not bad, though. It's fine. I enjoy it."

What he meant: I was my father's third son. When my father died, the ownership of the farm went to my oldest brother, because that's how it always works. I own nothing in this world.

What she said: "What kind of farm is it? Do you raise any animals?"

What she hoped to imply: I will talk to you about things that don't interest me at all. Just be different from everyone else I've met in this town. It doesn't matter how you're different. I'm flexible.

What he said: "We raise bison."

What he believed: Two years before he died, my goofy fucking father read an article in *Modern Farmer* magazine about alternative food sources, one of which was American bison. He believed this animal was going to revolutionize the livestock industry; it must have been a pretty persuasive article. Bison are larger than beef cattle, they produce leaner cuts of meat, and they're easy to feed. A buffalo will eat absolutely anything. You can feed buffalo hay, grass, silage, cornstalks, or even straw. You could probably feed buffalo coal briquettes and they wouldn't notice the goddamn difference. A buffalo is the only animal stupider than a moose, which is why they were so easy for bored cowboys to execute during the nineteenth century. So because of the low overhead and the alleged fiscal upside, my goofy fucking father decided to sell all our farm equipment and invest in 150 head of two-year-old bison. They were shipped in from Wyoming on the Great Northern railroad and cost three thousand dollars apiece; we had to take out a massive farm loan, but this was the 1970s and that's what farmers did. So—pretty much overnight—we became bison farmers. And this was scary as fuck. It was like suddenly trying to shepherd a bunch of mastodons. Unlike conventional cows, a buffalo will charge at your pickup truck for no apparent reason. If a mama bison thinks you're staring at her calf for too long, she will try to kill you. They have no sense of space or domesticity or captivity, so they'll walk right through a barbed-wire fence without even noticing it's there. You can't herd them or control them or anticipate how they will react to anything, because these are undisciplined beasts who belong on *Wild Kingdom.* It also turned out that buffalo were almost impossible to sell on the open market. Nobody eats bison meat. Nobody wants alternative food. I don't think we were able to sell more than thirteen calves that first year, which was an unmitigated disaster. We were headed for bankruptcy in eighteen months. Everybody in town said my father was insane for trying to raise buffalo, and everybody was right. And it killed him. He was so embarrassed that he had a heart attack. He died in church. My brother Jake (who had always been called Jason until he became a quarterback) inherited the farm, and—because Jake is the kind of guy who likes to be admired for seeming ethical—he decided that these idiotic bison were going to be our father's postlife legacy, and that these bison (somehow) represented our father's unorthodox personality, and that he would devote his life to making this bison farm succeed. He even talked about this during the funeral, which would have been hilarious had the corpse been anyone who wasn't my father. Jake convinced our mom to pay off the loan for the bison with Dad's life insurance, and she immediately agreed with the decision. My mother always admired Jake's simulated ethics. As such, my livelihood continues to revolve around a pasture of dangerous, unmanageable, fiscally insolvent ungulates. Ironically, they are now beloved by the community. *The Bismarck Tribune* has written two feature stories about our bison, and tourists (from as far away as Sioux Falls) will slowly drive their station wagons past our farm to show their children what the Old West theoretically looked like.

What she said: "Bison? No way! Like, buffalo? You have a farm full of buffalo? That's astounding."

What she meant: I knew you were different. I knew it!

What he said: "Well, it's not really as interesting as you might think. Bison aren't that different from stock cows, except they're bigger and meaner and dumber."

What he hoped: Someday one of those bastards will charge through the barbed-wire fence and gore an onlooker to death. He'll hit a car with his skull and plow it off the road. My brother will probably get sued.

What she said: "That must be a crazy way to live, though. I mean, relatively speaking. You're certainly the first buffalo farmer I've ever met. Everybody else just talks about corn."

What she meant: There is something about you that I like, but I cannot deduce what that quality is. You are attractive, I suppose, but that is not the reason behind my attraction. I sense that you do not belong in this town, but that is a minor detail. Perhaps if I give you vague compliments, you will become self-confident and expose your secrets by accident.

What he said: "Well, at least I'm good for something. I'm That Guy With All The Buffalo."

What he knew: I'm an idiot.

What she said: "Is that why you're famous?"

What she understood to be true: I am not afraid to say what is obvious, even if the obvious is uncomfortable to all involved.

What he said: "What in the hell are you talking about?"

What he meant: I know what you are talking about.

What she said: "You're famous around here. Everybody in this bar treats you like you're a celebrity. It's like you own the place. Is this because of the buffalo?"

What she decided: What have I got to lose?

What he said: "No, no. None of these dopes gives a shit about the buffalo. I'm not famous. Nobody treats me like I'm famous. It's just that people treat you a certain way when you're in high school, and that never changes. If people know me, it's probably because of my brothers."

What he knew: I am worshipped by the stupidest people in the world. I can't openly complain about this, but I'm totally aware of it. It's disturbing to be the center of another person's universe, especially if you've never interacted with that person in any meaningful way. Their misplaced adoration makes them seem foolish and immature, so you cannot reciprocate their respect. It instantaneously makes the relationship unbalanced. And this imbalance makes you feel guilty, so you start to unconsciously resent the idolization. Over time, you find yourself hating people for loving you too much, which seems like a terrible thing to do. So you worry about those feelings of hatred all the time, and you wonder if maybe you're a jackass. Because it's not their fault. They're just confused.

What she said: "What did your brothers do that was so great?"

What she meant: What did your brothers do that was so great? I'm legitimately curious about this.

What he said: "They were football players. We all played football, and that's always a big deal around here."

What he remembered: When Jake won the state championship, it was the greatest day of my life. It still is. I was eleven years old. Do you have any idea how philosophically galvanizing it feels to watch your older brother kick everybody's ass in public when you're eleven? Jake's mental toughness was obscene. There's never been a tougher five-foot-eight quarterback in the universe. This was back when Owl ran the wishbone. He was so focused. He was one of those live-on-your-feet-or-die-on-your-knees maniacs who would insist on getting everybody pumped up for games that barely mattered. People loved him. His teammates would have swallowed cyanide capsules if he told them to do so. He was that kind of guy. I could never relate to him. And Bobby . . . well, Bobby was better than Jake. Just naturally, effortlessly unstoppable. Bobby was six foot two, covered with acne, probably dyslexic, and absolutely the best football player I've ever seen. He was an ice-nine death machine. He was on par with Shanley's Roger Maris during the 1940s, and maybe even with Lidgerwood's Arnie Oss from before the Great War. When Bobby was twelve years old, he could throw a tennis ball at a stop sign on the other side of the street and nail the *O* every time. Bobby never seemed excited or surprised by this. He didn't seem to have normal emotions. His passing was so flawless that Owl dumped the wishbone and started throwing the ball twenty-five times a game. For a high school team in North Dakota, this was unheard of; it was like showing up at the Civil War with an AK-47. Bobby set records that will stand forever. A bunch of colleges recruited him (even Michigan and Ohio State, although they didn't offer scholarships). He ended up attending North Dakota State, and he married a girl who regularly won high school beauty pageants. What a whore she was. She destroyed their marriage and she destroyed my brother. I still hate her. Bobby quit the team when he was a senior, dropped out of school, and came back to Owl to help with the buffalo. It's kind of a sad story, I suppose. But—of course—Bobby is still a god in this town, just like Jake. And just like me, although that never should have happened.

What she said: "Oh, yeah, that's right. Somebody told me about this. You were the proverbial high school football star, no?"

What she hoped he would infer: This really isn't important to me. Where I come from, being remembered for things you did in high school usually means you had a baby before you wanted one. Still, the rules are different here. I realize that.

What he said: "No, not me. I was no football star. My brothers were football stars. I was just another good guy."

What he never stopped thinking about: They never should have turned me into a quarterback. I couldn't do the things quarterbacks needed to do. All my life, I've never done anything that was more difficult than trying to complete a downfield pass. People always claim that athletes are morons, and I suppose some of them are. But playing quarterback was *complex*. It was harder than any class I ever took or any job I've ever quit. You have to memorize so much shit. You have to make so many decisions.

When I was in high school, I used to vomit all the time. My stomach was a sack of acid. Do you remember dissecting frogs in biology class? I do. I remember looking at the frog diagram in the textbook, and all the individual frog organs were clearly defined and coded by color. The diagram was lucid. But then we cut open the *real* frog, and it was just a ball of meaningless brown guts. There was no clarity whatsoever. This is how it feels to play quarterback. I would drop back in the pocket and try to find the open man, but the pocket always seemed to be collapsing before it ever existed. You'd hear this cacophony of shoulder pads colliding and linemen grunting and snorting and saying things like *oof*. Everything happens within the same four seconds. My receivers never appeared where I assumed they would appear; whatever you plan in the huddle never really happens the way it was designed. This, I suppose, is what military generals refer to as the fog of war. I was never comfortable in this kind of scenario, and many people (including all of my teammates) seemed to inherently recognize this. But because of my brothers and because of my last name, there was never any question about what position I would play for the Owl Lobos. They turned me into a quarterback in fifth grade, and I always did the best that I could. Which was slightly better than almost okay, most of the time.

What she said: "But didn't you supposedly have some amazing moment? Somebody told me this—I think it was Ted. Ted told me you were involved with some crazy football play, and this play was on TV, and everyone still talks about it. But maybe he meant it happened to one of your brothers."

What she meant: Sometimes I have conversations about you when you are not around, and I remember insignificant details about your life. You should appreciate this. But I only do this *casually*. I am not a freak.

What he said: "No, no, that *was* me. I know the situation Ted was talking about. That was me."

What he meant: Even though the football play you are referring to essentially ruined my life, I secretly love that strangers know about it and talk about it when I'm not around. I hate when people bring it up to me in conversation, but I like to imagine people discussing it during conversations that don't involve me directly. My vanity conflicts me. My problems are clichéd and predictable.

What she said: "What kind of play was it? I used to watch the Packers with my dad. Was it a flea-flicker? I love flea-flickers. If I were a football coach, my team would run a lot of flea-flickers. The flea-flicker would be the key to our offense."

What she was attempting to convey through means that made no sense: By espousing an exaggerated affinity for a specific NFL gadget play, I am displaying an awareness of how football is played (which is central to the conversation we are presently conducting) along with a willingness to watch football on television (in case that quality is important to you when looking for a romantic partner). However, by playfully claiming that I would employ said ludicrous gadget play all the time (were I somehow an NFL offensive coordinator), I am indicating that I'm still a girl in the traditional, conventional sense and no threat to your masculinity. It's win-win.

What he said: "No, it wasn't a flea-flicker, sadly. It was just a crazy play where I scrambled around a lot and then completed a dippy, lucky pass. It was a fluke. Everyone knows it was a fluke."

What he perceived as the deeper truth: It was the last game of my senior year. We were playing the Langdon Cardinals; they were headed for the play-offs and we were not. It was a physical, boring affair: Langdon was the better team, but we blocked a punt in the fourth quarter, putting us in a position to win or tie. With eighteen seconds left, our fullback scored from the one-yard line, making the score Langdon 14, Owl 13. At the time, there was no overtime in high school football, so we decided to go for the win with a two-point conversion. The ref placed the ball on the two-and-a-half-yard line. I assumed this would be the final play of my wholly unremarkable career. I remember thinking that specific thought as I walked toward the line of scrimmage: I thought, "I guess things could have been worse." We called a bootleg pass; I faked the handoff and rolled to my right, but Langdon blitzed the outside linebacker on that side. I was a dead man rolling. In an act of desperation, I reversed my field and ran back to my left, but there was a defensive lineman in the backfield, waiting to clobber me. Seeing no other option, I ran *away* from the goal line, zigging and zagging lengthwise across the field, fleeing from a growing swarm of defenders and surrendering yardage at every turn. I had no plan, so I just kept running away. I could hear the crowd making a peculiar noise; they sounded excited, but also *amused.* The play seemed to go on for several weeks. At long last, I decided to simply square my shoulders toward the goalposts and fling the ball in the general direction of anyone who looked like they might be on my team. I really didn't care what happened. I was ready to surrender. But when I finally squared my shoulders, I noticed something bizarre: The goalposts were *distant.* They were almost on the horizon. Somehow, I had retreated all the way to the fifty-yard line. This is why the crowd had been cheering and laughing at the same time. I scanned the field. It was chaos. Players from both teams were scattered at random, running at full speed but unsure of what to do. It was beyond the fog of war; it was like I had sliced open my biology frog and discovered a human fetus. I was terrified, and—somewhat amazingly, considering that the play was still actively unfolding—*embarrassed* by what I had done. I had turned the last play of my life into a cowardly exhibition of Smear the Queer. I had always assumed my brothers (or at least Jake) had long been disappointed by my mediocre quarterbacking skills; now they would be shamed by my on-field buffoonery. Since there was nothing else for me to do (and since I certainly couldn't throw the ball fifty yards), I started running back toward the original line of scrimmage, assuming I would be tackled in the process. But something unusual happened as I did this: Everyone who tried to hit me missed. I wasn't juking or jiving or spinning away from prospective tacklers; they all just seemed to mistime their tackles and graze me. They were Hong Kong extras and I was Bruce Lee. I kept getting knocked off balance, but I never fell down; this happened five times. The crowd no longer sounded amused; they were now generating the kind of rising anticipatory murmur that always preceded the stunts of Evel Knievel. When I reached the twenty, I hurdled over somebody's body and angled toward the orange pylon in the left corner of the end zone. I remember thinking, "It's kind of remarkable that this is happening." I had one defender to beat at the five-yard line; I lowered my shoulder and turned my head, preparing for the first collision I had ever looked forward to. I was going to try and run this bastard over. But as I tucked my head and locked my jaw, I glimpsed the numerals 8 and 0, way across the field. This, I instantly recognized, was Hank. Hank Zulkey was our tight end (and something of an imbecile, truth be told). He was standing in the corner of the end zone, all the way across the field, waving his arms like a castaway trying to get attention from a search plane. As the crow flies, he was at least thirty-five yards away. I should have ignored him. But for reasons I will never understand, I did not. I spontaneously threw Hank the football. I reflexively chucked it at him sidearm, as if such behavior was an intrinsic part of my nature. As if this had been my plan all along. It was an ill-advised, extraordinarily difficult throw, and Hank had hands made of mahogany. I could not have made a worse decision. But that ill-advised pass turned out to be the tightest spiral I ever released. It was like I fired a crossbow into the stomach of a scarecrow. It was perfect. Hank fell back on his ass, the ref threw his arms toward the sky, and the entire crowd (or at least everyone under the age of thirty) stormed the field; they looked like freed Egyptian slaves. There weren't any grandstands at that time, so the older, lazier fans would always park their cars around the perimeter of the field and watch the game from their front seats. They would honk the horn whenever something exciting happened. I really remember all those horns blasting forever—people just laid on the steering columns. It was terrifying and apocalyptic, but still pretty great. About twenty people immediately dog piled on top of Hank, then thirty others piled on top of me. They all smelled like beer and cigarettes. They tried to tear down the goalposts, but that didn't work. The game's final eighteen seconds were never even played. It was madness. The school eventually had to call the cops. We could hear the sirens from the locker room. I've never been to Northern Ireland, but maybe that's what it's like there all the time.

What she said: "But why was this play on TV?"

What she almost said: The concept of a high school football game being on national television is insane. I'm not going to say that directly, but come on—that's fucking preposterous.

What he said: "I have no idea. It just sort of worked out that way."

What he didn't feel like explaining: Because Langdon High was going to the play-offs that winter, the game was being covered by WDAZ-TV, the Grand Forks affiliate for ABC. They weren't televising the game in its totality; they just wanted a few highlights for the nightly newscast. What this meant is that WDAZ sent one cameraman to Owl with instructions to videotape the first ten or fifteen minutes of that particular contest.

(This is so that they could glean one or two key moments from the affair for the 10 o'clock news.) The cameraman was supposed to show up in Owl for the 7:00 p.m. kickoff, shoot the first two offensive sequences, drive to another high school game in another town (in this case, Cavalier), tape fifteen minutes of *that* game, drive to yet another town (possibly Ellendale), tape the final minutes of the game that was happening there, and then rush back to the WDAZ headquarters in Grand Forks in order to edit all the footage by 10:22 p.m. But on this specific evening, this specific cameraman's Chevy Blazer died in Owl (it was the alternator). Unable to drive anywhere else (and seeing no other way to spend his evening), the cameraman elected to film the entire Owl-Langdon game, including its memorable, impossible conclusion. It proved to be a fortuitous breakdown. On the following Monday, WDAZ replayed that two-point conversion three times in a row. It was, they argued, the play of the century. I have no idea what play it allegedly usurped. They showed it again on Wednesday, supposedly because of viewer response but probably because nothing ever happens on Wednesday evenings. (Wednesday is church night.) That weekend, the footage was picked up by an ABC station in Minneapolis. "You will not believe what you are about to see," the mustachioed sportscaster said as a prelude. "The following fourteen seconds will quite possibly change your life. These fourteen seconds are, in many ways, what high school football is all about." That, of course, was not true; those fourteen seconds represented nothing about high school and very little about football. But people loved it, and things took off from there. It was like a fourteen-second version of *Rocky*. It made average people happy to live in America. It was outrageous and impossible and authentic, and it seemed as if every TV market in America (and especially those in Texas) found an excuse to show it whenever there wasn't any real sports news. This was before normal people had VCRs, so every replay was an event; you had to wait for it, and that made it better. The fact that this play happened in a tiny North Dakota town no one had ever heard of didn't hurt, either: It turned watching TV into rural sociology. Even before Brent Musburger said my name on *The NFL Today*, it had become the most important event in the ninety-eight-year history of Owl. Most of the world does not know that Owl exists—but if they do, it is almost always because a Chevy Blazer broke down on the only night I ever played football like one of my brothers, at least for fourteen seconds.

What she said: "I bet that was exciting."

What she assumed: Everybody wants to be on TV.

What he said: "It was okay. It was different."

What he meant: Everything is fucked now. If I had just let one of those pricks tackle me, I wouldn't even be here. I was good in school. Nobody remembers this, but I was awesome in math. I should be an engineer right now. Wouldn't it be cool to build a bridge? I always wanted to do that. That would have been a satisfying way to live. I was going to go to college in Arizona—ASU had already accepted my application. All I needed were the student loans and some khaki shorts. But something happened after that episode of *The NFL Today*: All of a sudden, I was a good football player. Everybody seemed to come to that conclusion. I made the All-Conference team, even though I was only the third-best quarterback in the conference. I made the All-Region team, even though I was probably the tenth-best quarterback in the region. It was like everyone in North Dakota received a concussion from watching television, and my mediocrity was erased by the collective amnesia. The *Grand Forks Herald* wrote a huge story about the history of Owl quarterbacks, describing me as "the third Druid legend." They even took a photograph of me with my brothers, standing in front of a cardboard diorama of Stonehenge; my mom framed it for the living room. People who had never spoken to me before had no qualms about reinventing my existence. I had never had a girlfriend in my entire life. I had never kissed a girl with my mouth open. Now I was dating the hottest sophomore in school, and she would regularly take off most of her clothes in my car. Older dudes would toss me beers for no reason and buy me hamburgers. I would walk into Harley's Café to buy a Kit Kat, and all the old codgers would put down their coffee mugs and compare me to deceased athletes I'd never even heard of. It's hard for Americans to differentiate between talent and notoriety; TV confuses people. It confused me, too. It made me naïve. That March, I received a phone call from the offensive coordinator at the North Dakota State School of Science. NDSSS is a two-year junior college in Wahpeton. It's really just a high school with ashtrays. You could smoke cigarettes in class—that was the institution's main selling point. This unknown man on the telephone claimed I could "potentially" play quarterback for NDSSS, even though he'd only seen fourteen seconds of my entire career. He insisted I had "intangibles," which seemed like a nice compliment at the time. I believed him. The man convinced me to believe I possessed intangibles, and I enjoyed being convinced of this. I enjoyed the possibility of being a less tangible character. So I went to NDSSS to play football. And this—of course—was a disaster. It was instantly obvious to everyone (including the offensive coordinator who had convinced me to go there) that I could not compete at that level. I could not compete *at all.* I was slower than most and weaker than all. I'm not sure I even completed two passes in any given practice. Most of my teammates hated or ignored me, except for the black guys—they thought I was hilarious. They called me Barney Fife. I eventually became the second-string holder for the field-goal unit. Let me reiterate the reality of that designation: *I was the back-up holder.* This is like being a prostitute's intern. During my two seasons at NDSSS, I played exactly one down of football, and the kick was blocked. I did, however, spend a lot of time getting drunk in my dorm room, never going to class, and eating half-frozen corn dogs twice a day. To be fair, life in Wahpeton wasn't so terrible. I had some good times. But I never earned a degree and I never learned a goddamn thing, and I moved back home because I couldn't think of anything else to do. I felt like a failure. But everyone in Owl still loved me; in fact, they seemed to worship me more than when I had left. And that made me feel worse, because it proved how confused they had been all along.

What she said: "Well, I'm going to get back to the booth with Naomi and Ted. They probably think I fell down a ditch. But you should come over and hang with us. It was nice to have a chat before one of us got drunk. Or both of us."

What she resigned herself to: You know, this was not the conversation I was hoping we'd have. You didn't tell me anything meaningful about yourself, and you didn't ask me a single question. Our sentences seemed forced and innocuous, and now I feel weird and aggressive and uncomfortably sober. It's actually kind of impossible to talk to you when we're both not intoxicated, which is undoubtedly why I just said the exact opposite. Sometimes I say the reverse of what I feel, and I don't know why. But still . . . I *like you,* man. How obvious do I have to be about this? I will give you two hundred chances to be interesting. All you have to do is try.

What he said: "It was. A rare pleasure, I suppose. At least for people like us."

What he meant: This woman makes me nervous, and I suspect she might be making fun of me. But I wonder what it would be like to have sex with her?

What she said: "Check you later, Famous Mr. Bison Man."

What she meant: Sometimes I can be snotty. You love it.

What he said: "Whatever."

What he meant: What can I do to make you like me?

NOVEMBER 23, 1983

(Horace)

Edgar Camaro was Lucifer. Or at least an idiot. Or at least he was when he rolled dice, or at least that's how it seemed to Horace.

Horace had two great secrets in his life. One of them was dark and sinister, as most noteworthy secrets tend to be. The second was less awful but more embarrassing, which is why it became the secret he despised more.

Horace's wife, Alma, died on the morning of June 5, 1972. That was a Monday. The funeral was the following Friday. Because she was only forty-four, the turnout was larger than the church could hold: Overflow guests sweated in the building's social hall, silently mourning the passing of an acquaintance without being able to hear any of the actual service. It was ninety-six degrees. Horace wore a brown suit and had the same conversation with all 477 guests. It was the most complicated thing he'd ever done; he smoked two packs of cigarettes and vomited twice. "Thank you so much for coming. It means a great deal," he said over and over and over again, and—every time—it was true. "Alma always liked you so much," he told all the mourners; this statement was true about 60 percent of the time. Alma was sweet, but discerning. Horace knew just about everyone in attendance, including most of the visitors from out of town. He had met nearly all of them at least once; in fact, Horace encountered only one new, unknown person at the burial of his wife. The man's name was Chester Grimes.

He was, as far as Horace could tell, the nicest man he'd ever met.

"I feel so terrible about your loss," Chester said while he

slowly shook Horace's right hand with both of his own. "What an awful way for someone to pass. She was an amazing woman, and you were the love of her life. *The love of her life.* I know this to be true." Horace thanked Chester for coming to the funeral. He wanted to ask how Chester knew his wife, but he did not need to pose the question. "I suppose I did not know Alma very well," Chester admitted. "Most of my personal memories are from when we were schoolchildren: I would see her at family reunions and at Easter, and we would play childish games around the yard. We made up this silly game called Rah, where you collected piles of grass and leaves and crawled around on your hands and knees like a mountain lion and sometimes you yelled *Rah!* at the other players. It seems foolish now, but I miss those afternoons of Rah. We were distant relatives—I am not sure if we were second cousins or if we were third cousins. Maybe we were only related by marriage. Who remembers such details? I don't think I've seen her more than twice since I moved out to Fargo in '61. But family is family. Right? Family is family. So how could I *not* go to her funeral? *How could I not go?* She was such a wonderful woman."

"Alma always liked you so much," said Horace, and he hoped he wasn't lying.

There was something about this Chester Grimes fellow. Horace didn't know what that quality was, but he knew he liked it. There was something about the way he talked; he seemed unnaturally open and unpretentious. He was conversationally fearless. Moreover, Chester was handsome in a manner that was almost confusing; he looked like someone famous, but it was impossible to say whom. It was equally impossible to estimate his age; Horace didn't know if this man was twenty-nine or forty-nine.

All the other guests liked him, too.

After Alma's casket was covered with dirt, everyone returned to the church social hall to solemnly consume ham and scalloped potatoes. (This is standard funeral fare.) Such a meal is always uncomfortable for the widower, as he is inevitably surrounded by female relatives insisting that he eat more ham. However, Horace got lucky: For reasons that he would not understand until later, he found himself eating with Chester. They had met only ninety minutes before, but Chester sat right across from him. Despite the circumstances, their conversation was outstanding. This Chester Grimes could talk about anything, even at a funeral. "I just have to be honest: Your pastor seems like a nice enough guy, but that eulogy was subpar," he said. "I realize a funeral is ultimately for the living, but let's not forget the dead. Dammit, give the dead their due! Is that too much to ask? I don't feel like the portrait he painted of Alma was very sophisticated. I didn't hear much genuine insight." Horace agreed with this man. He had opinions.

"I deliver booze for a living," Chester told Horace as they walked toward their respective vehicles at day's end. "Can you believe it? That's my job. Every week, I drive a booze wagon to Wahpeton and Grand Forks and Bismarck and every other crazy city in this whole crazy state. I have driven through Owl every Saturday afternoon for ten years. Can you believe that? I drove through downtown Owl once a week for a decade, and I never stopped to see Alma once. What a fool I was."

"You can't blame yourself for that," said Horace. "Nobody can predict the future."

"Actually, we can," said Chester. "The only thing we can't predict are the details. I knew Alma was going to die. I didn't think she'd die this young, or in such a bizarre, horrific manner. But we're all going to die eventually. So what was my plan? Did I think I'd start stopping over to say hello when she hit her sixties? Of course I didn't. I had no plan, because I didn't realize I needed one. And now she's dead. What a fool I was."

"Well, let's not make that same mistake, Chester."

"You're goddamn right we won't," he replied. "I will see you tomorrow, friend."

The next afternoon, Chester's beer truck pulled into

Horace's yard at 6:30 p.m. This happened every single Saturday evening for the next four months. A new friend! It was precisely what Horace needed during his period of stoic sorrow. Every Saturday night, the two men sat in the kitchen and sipped a little scotch, chatting about the news of the world. They rarely talked about Alma or farming or Owl. They had big talks about big things. It was refreshing. Chester dominated these conversations, mostly because he seemed to understand things that no one else in America could possibly know. His insights were electrifying and wildly specific. He knew why America didn't have an effective light-rail system. (It was killed by GM, the Nazi-controlled Daimler-Benz, and the Nazi-influenced Ford Corporation.) He knew that FDR had been aware of the December 7 attack on Pearl Harbor on November 28. He knew the precise location where Marilyn Monroe had sex with Robert Kennedy (a swimming pool at the Biltmore Resort in Phoenix, Arizona). He knew an inordinate amount about deep-sea fishing, despite the fact that North Dakota is a landlocked state. But the subject Chester *really* understood was sports. He could talk about any sport, in any context, for any length of time. Moreover, he knew the kind of arcane details than only an insider would have access to. He knew, for example, which major league baseball players were closeted homosexuals, and he knew which NBA players were addicted to narcotics. He knew exactly how low they cut the grass at the Augusta National Golf Club (1.25 inches on the fairways, 0.4 inches on the putting greens), and he knew the reasons why those lengths were selected (they were specified in Bobby Jones's will). And the main thing he knew—the thing that he somehow managed to slide into every conversation they ever had—was that virtually every professional football game was fixed.

"The NFL is a league run by gamblers," he would say. "So was the AFL—they were even worse. There's probably *never* been an Oakland Raiders game that wasn't fixed. Going to a pro football game isn't that different from going to a Broadway play. It's theater, my friend. It's scripted."

"But how can that be?" Horace always countered. "How can every football player in America be corrupt? It's unthinkable."

"They need the money," said Chester. "For every $400,000 contract they give to Joe Namath, there are 50 guys making $40,000 and 300 more making $14,000. It's the casinos that have the money. It's the gamblers. Every week, the men who run Las Vegas find themselves a quarterback and a cornerback and a couple referees, and they throw ten grand at each of them. What, you think Len Dawson was *framed*? If you're making $14,000 a year by working your ass off, how would you feel about making an extra $10,000 in one day, just for being lazy on a few plays during the third quarter? Why would those slaves care about the integrity of the sport? What is football doing for those fellows, besides giving them a few moments of glory and a lifetime of arthritis?"

"It just seems like such a complicated conspiracy," said Horace. "I don't even know how it would work."

Chester, of course, understood completely. It was all about point spreads. "Let's say Minnesota is playing Dallas," he would explain. "In a legitimate situation, the Cowboys would probably be favored by four points. As such, the bookies would hope that fifty percent of their clients picked Minnesota and the other half would pick Dallas. This is referred to as a balanced ticket." Chester seemed amazingly familiar with the lexicon. "In a legitimate situation, bookies want a balanced ticket, because they still get their piece of the action from the Juice. That's what bookies call their commission: the Juice. If you bet fifty dollars on a game and win, you don't win a hundred—you only get ninety-five. That extra five dollars is the Juice. In other words, the house takes *everything* from losers, but they still skim *a little* off the winners. So if you operate at a high enough volume, the house never loses."

Horace deeply enjoyed this brand of banter.

"But here's the twist," Chester continued. "At some point, bookies decided the Juice wasn't enough. They realized it made more sense to just manipulate the spread and fix the outcome: Instead of making Dallas a four-point favorite, they might make Dallas a nine-point favorite. Every small-time gambler sees a spread that size and immediately thinks he's a genius. He thinks he understands what everyone else can't see. He assumes picking Minnesota is a lock, so all his money goes on the Vikings. And there are dupes making that same bet in every city in America. That's when two guys in Nevada get on a plane, fly to Minneapolis, and deliver a suitcase full of money to Fran Tarkenton or Alan Page or Bud Grant. Whoever needs it the most, you know? Whoever's willing to take it. Tarkenton inexplicably throws three interceptions in the second half, and the Cowboys win by two touchdowns. There's nothing subtle about it. It's that easy. It happens all the time."

"Incredible," said Horace. It did seem incredible. "I can't believe that Fran Tarkenton would ever do something like that. His father was a minister."

"You'd be surprised," said Chester. "It's just business. And the players obviously can't talk about it, because it would kill their careers. Remember what happened to Karras and Hornung in '63? By being such a fascist hard-ass, Pete Rozelle guaranteed that no one would ever admit they're in bed with gamblers. Still, everybody gets what they need. Nobody gets hurt. And the guys who really clean up are the Drones."

Chester took acute pleasure in discussing the Drones. The Drones were the true geniuses, he said. According to Chester, Drones were accidental insiders to the world of high-stakes gambling. They were people who did not play a role in the fixing of games but occasionally knew when a fix was happening; typically, they were employed by bookies in some minor capacity and would simply overhear the right kind of gossip. Once they knew a few key secrets, they were fiscally unstoppable. All they had to do was find a different bookie in a different city, make a huge bet on a guaranteed winner, and await an outcome that was never in question. They were the cheaters who cheated the cheaters, and Chester spoke of them with reverence. And over time, Horace began to suspect what Chester eventually admitted: Chester was, in fact, a Drone.

"It's true," he said one Saturday in September after consuming a thimble more scotch than usual. "The only reason I run the booze wagon is because I need an excuse to drive all over the state every week. I'm a bet collector. I work for a guy in Fargo named Keith Beetle. He's a bookmaker. And bookmakers are hard to find in rural areas, so we have to cover the whole state. We do okay, all things considered."

"Do you ever have to beat people up?" Horace was excited. "Do you ever deal with deadbeats? Do you break legs?"

"Oh, Jesus. Never," said Chester. "Everybody pays what they owe, unless they honestly don't have it. North Dakota gamblers are still North Dakota citizens."

Once this confession was on the kitchen table, it became the only subject Chester and Horace discussed. One might have guessed that Horace would have been dismayed by this unlawful revelation, but the opposite was true; he loved being friends with a criminal. A criminal! That's what Chester was. He committed crimes. But his crimes didn't seem that bad to Horace. Being a Drone seemed smart, and intelligence warranted a reward. The criminal world, suspected Horace, was probably more fair than the one in which he lived. Chester told a story about the time he made fifteen thousand dollars on a 1969 Browns game. "I wasted every cent of my winnings on a twenty-two-year-old whore named Laura Lawless," he said. "Every penny was gone in six weeks' time, and all I had to show for it was a busted box spring and a drawerful of jewelry receipts. But that was still the greatest fifteen thousand dollars I ever made. Nobody could figure out why Jim Brown was so easy to tackle that afternoon. He was devoid of heart. He gained forty-four yards on twenty carries, and nobody could understand what his problem was. But I knew what his problem was. His problem was that he didn't have any problem whatsoever."

This, at its core, was what made Chester Grimes the most dynamic personality Horace had ever encountered: He was inside. For the first time in his life, Horace was aligned with a person who knew consequential secrets. The possibility of every pro football game being rigged was crazy, but maybe it was true; sometimes crazy things are true. There was even a cliché about that. Perhaps Horace had been wrong about everything. Maybe the world was controlled by conspiracies, and maybe that was immoral. Maybe that was depressing. But maybe it just meant the world was *complicated,* and maybe he was just starting to understand the complications. Which was why he found himself fantasizing about the day when Chester would let him become a criminal, too.

That conversation happened on September 30, 1972.

"I have some information," Chester said almost immediately upon his arrival. "Nine days from now, Oakland is playing Houston on *Monday Night Football.* The Raiders will be heavily favored. The spread is going to be set at fifteen points. It won't be that high in the Vegas casinos, but it will be fifteen on the street. That kind of number is unheard of. Everybody and their mother is going to take Houston, especially since they're playing at home. But Oakland will cover the spread. They will win by more than fifteen points. I can assure you of this."

"How do you know?" Horace asked. In truth, he did not really care.

"I overheard my boss on the telephone," said Chester. "He was talking to someone in Reno, and he kept using the term *jailbreak.* That's code. That means they have at least three Oilers on the take, plus a zebra."

"Code!" said Horace. "You speak in codes."

"When my boss went to the can after he got off the blower, I glanced at the legal pad that was sitting on his desk. The wheels are already in motion," Chester said cryptically. "Now, I realize this might not be something you'd want to be involved with. Maybe this makes you uncomfortable. It is, after all, illegal. And what we'd be doing is not only illegal, but also unethical. But if you have money, and if you can reconcile your own conscience, we can make a lot of cash in a short amount of time. We're gambling, but we cannot lose, which means we're not gambling at all. I will drive to Minneapolis the day before the game. I know people there, but they don't know me. They might suspect I know something, but they won't be able to decline my bet, even if it's massive."

For a moment, they silently looked at each other like criminals. It felt important. At the end of the pause, Chester spoke again.

"How much money do you have?"

"I have most of Alma's life insurance." Horace felt no apprehension. "I have $22,000."

"That's perfect," said Chester. "That will get us forty-four grand, minus the Juice, which will put us at—what—$42,000? No, wait . . . more like $41,800. I will give you your original $22,000, plus fifteen grand. I'll keep the last $5,000 for myself, if that's acceptable."

"Oh, absolutely," said Horace. "In fact, you should take a bigger cut. I insist that you take more. You're doing everything. I'm just lucky to be involved with any of this. I'm just lucky to have met you."

"Absolutely not," said Chester. "The opposite is true. You may not be *working* for this money, but it's money you deserve nonetheless. Whether I make $5,000 or $50,000 for myself, it will be gone before Christmas. But God owes you money for taking your wife. And I know you are worried about this, because you're trusting me with a lot of your retirement. But here is the terrifying truth, which I cannot stress enough: This is a crime, Horace. And in order to commit a crime, you need to trust at least one other person. You have to trust them completely. In order to live outside the law, you have to be honest. I heard those words in a song, and the words are true. The words are true."

Horace had never met a man as noble as his criminal-in-law.

Because this transaction required cash, Horace went to Owl National Bank on Monday morning and tried to withdraw twenty-two thousand dollars from his savings account in hundred-dollar bills. It took the bank four days to fulfill this request; he claimed he was considering buying some quarter horses from a Mennonite colony and they did not accept checks. It was an extremely solid lie. When Chester's booze wagon finally arrived on Saturday night, Horace hoped they would get profoundly drunk together, which had never really happened; he even bought some Dewar's, which was expensive. Chester nonetheless declined the offer of a third drink, stating that he still had too many miles to drive that night, not to mention the following day's trip to Minneapolis. Horace delivered the cash in a metal lunchbox. They shook hands, and Chester drove away.

Forty hours later, Oakland defeated Houston 34–0 on *Monday Night Football.*

But something occurred to Horace as he watched this game.

It did not seem fixed.

It seemed like Oakland was a vastly superior team, but not in any sort of nefarious way. They simply had better players. He started to wonder how a football game could be successfully rigged. Wouldn't such a ploy seem obvious to everyone watching? There were always twenty-two men sprinting and colliding on every single play—how could this be scripted? And how could he have been blind to this reality for so long? How could everyone in America not know this was happening?

His stomach started to feel strange. It felt the way stomachs feel when your wife dies, or when you reach your hand back to get your wallet and realize it is no longer there.

At midnight, he found himself wanting to call Chester for reassurance; he could claim it was a celebratory call. But he could not find Chester's phone number. Had Chester ever given him his number? He must have. But if he did, why couldn't he remember this exchange ever happening? Horace's neck was getting warm. He could feel his heart beating, and then he could hear it. Where did he keep his phone numbers? This was bad. He picked up the phone and dialed 0. It rang eleven times. It was 1972. When a woman's voice answered, he asked for the number of Chester Grimes in Fargo. There was no Chester Grimes in Fargo. There were two listings for Grimes, but no Chester. Was it possible he still lived with his parents? How could he not know these things? What in the hell had they talked about on all those Saturday nights?

It was too late in the evening to try the two Grimes numbers at random, so he sat in the kitchen and waited for the clock to say 7:00 a.m. He called both. The answering parties did not recall anyone named Chester living at their respective residences. Horace tried to remember what liquor distributor Chester worked for. He had no idea. Wasn't the company's logo written on the truck's door? He could not recall. All he could remember was that the truck was red, or possibly orange. He called the operator and asked for any residence or business involving the surname "Beetle" in the Fargo-Moorhead area. Nothing. There was nothing.

All week, Horace tried to talk himself into normalcy. "I'm overreacting," he repeated inside his own mind. "Chester will show up on Saturday. He is not listed in the phone book because he is a criminal. A criminal would not list himself in the phone book. I'm overreacting. This is an overreaction. We've never spoken on the phone before, so why would we start now? Everything happened as he predicted. It was a jailbreak. All we will lose is the Juice. I am overreacting. I am overreacting. This is how it feels to overreact, which is what I am doing."

But Horace never saw Chester Grimes again.

That red (or possibly orange) truck did not pull into the yard on Saturday night. Horace waited five hours, the last four hours and fifty-eight minutes devoid of hope. He drank most of the bottle of Dewar's but did not feel drunk. He felt like a child who had been beaten with a wooden spoon without being told why. He wondered, Did this actually happen? Is it possible that Chester Grimes never knew Alma at all? Is he just a person who looks for funerals in the newspaper and trolls them for vulnerable marks? Could such a human exist? Was he brilliantly calculating, or was he simply amoral? Had all of their conversations been fake? Had Grimes consciously manufactured a four-month friendship? Wouldn't that be as much work as holding down a regular job? How did he know that Horace would give him the money? How did he know that Horace wanted to break the law? What did Chester Grimes immediately know about Horace that Horace did not know about himself? It all seemed so impossible.

And yet . . . it was still more plausible than the likelihood of every pro football game being fixed, which is what he had chosen to believe when he gave a con man twenty-two thousand dollars before shaking his hand.

This was Horace's most despised secret.

He thought about this secret all the time. This was usually because Edgar Camaro was an idiot, or at least he was when he rolled dice. Whenever Edgar was rolling especially well, he liked to gingerly taunt his opponents with clichés that were not remotely applicable to what they were actually doing. His personal favorite was "That's just like catching a can of corn," which was a baseball term he only halfway understood. Sometimes he would say things like "You mess with the bull, you get the horns," or "The fox is back in the henhouse." Edgar just liked the way these phrases sounded, regardless of their context (of which there was usually none). Most of the time, no one was even listening. However, Edgar consistently misused one platitude that a) made no sense and b) forced Horace to reexperience his deepest shame: When things were really going well, Edgar would slam the dice cup onto the Formica tabletop, examine its contents, and stupidly decree, "You can't con an honest man."

Edgar Camaro did not understand what that phrase meant. But Horace did, and he knew that it was true, and it reminded him of what he was not.

NOVEMBER 24, 1983

(Mitch)

"Post pattern," he said. "Sprint upfield thirteen steps, plant your outside foot hard, and break toward the center of the field at a forty-five degree angle. The ball will be coming over your left shoulder. It should be a pretty deep route. Watch out for the flagpole."

Mitch was speaking to his twelve-year-old sister.

Kate Hrlicka trotted toward the imaginary sideline and took her position as an imaginary wide receiver. She rested her hands on her hips and placed her left foot slightly in front of her right, mimicking the two-point stance of James Lofton (a Green Bay Packer whose football card she kept inside a music box). Kate was still built like a boy. "Red eighty-four! Red eighty-four!" yelled Mitch. "Down . . . *hut hut!*" Kate sprinted off the nonexistent line and counted the thirteen steps in her head. She planted her outside foot and broke upfield, which means she broke toward the barn. The hood of her sweatshirt flew off her head. Mitch dropped back five steps and heaved the football toward his sister. The throw was high. Kate had to jump and twist, but she caught it.

If women played football, Kate Hrlicka would not have to worry about how she was going to pay for college. If women played football, Kate Hrlicka would be going to Notre Dame for free.

"Nice route," said Mitch. "You're awesome." As he spoke, clouds of white rolled out of his nose and mouth and slowly grew invisible. The air was twenty-eight degrees.

Kate flipped the ball back to her brother. "All I do is run

under the ball," she said. "You're the quarterback. I could never throw anything that far. Not even a golf ball!"

"I'm a terrible quarterback," said Mitch. "And that was probably as far as I have ever thrown a football in my entire life. But *you* are awesome. This time, I want you to run a hook-and-go: Go down ten steps, fake a buttonhook, and then break it back into a fly pattern."

Kate jogged back to her point of origin and returned to her familiar two-point stance. Mitch rebarked the cadence. Kate counted the ten steps and pivoted inward; Mitch pump-faked the ball, freezing the imaginary defenders who were trying to stop his sixth-grade sister from going to the Pro Bowl. Kate made a rapid 360-degree revolution and sprinted down the sideline, which means she sprinted alongside a shelterbelt of evergreens. Mitch threw the ball as far as he could, actively trying to overthrow her. He failed; the ball nestled in her paws and did not move. Jesus, she was so good at this.

"You are awesome," he said again. "I cannot believe how awesome you are. You are a witch."

"It's just fun to run after things," Kate said. "Do you think it's almost dinnertime?"

"Doubtful," said Mitch. "Grandma isn't even here yet. We probably won't eat dinner until two o'clock. Let's try a flag pattern. Do you remember how to run a flag pattern? It's exactly like a post, except you cut to the corner instead of the middle."

"I remember," she said. This time Kate caught the ball one-handed.

"Do you have any idea how good you are at football?" asked Mitch. "I really think you have no idea how good you are at playing football."

"I'm good," Kate said. "I just wish we lived in town. Then we could play against other people."

The Hrlickas' nearest neighbor was two and a half miles away; if you looked to the west, you could distantly see the house. They lived nine miles outside of Owl; at night, you could see the town's feeble lights flickering to the south. It was flat in every direction. The only trees on any horizon were the ones people planted to stop the wind.

"No, it's better to live out here," said Mitch. "Besides, town kids are stupid. All they do is ride their bikes and play Atari. They don't even know how to change a tire."

"Yeah, I know town kids are stupid," said Kate. "But still. It would be fun to run pass plays against other people."

"No, this is better," said Mitch. "Besides, there is no possible way any other girl could possibly cover you one-on-one. It wouldn't even be fun. You would kill them."

Kate spit on the ground and pulled the hood over her auburn hair.

"Run a buttonhook," said Mitch. "Ten yards."

She did as she was told. This time, Mitch fired the ball with unnecessary velocity. For the first time all morning, it slid through Kate's hands, bouncing off her concave twelve-year-old chest.

"My hands are getting cold," said Kate. "We should go inside."

"You're probably right."

They started to walk toward the house. They could see their mother in the window, mashing potatoes.

"That was a hard throw," said Kate. "I think I have a mark where it hit me. It's a good thing I don't have boobs yet."

"Don't swear," said Mitch.

"That's not swearing," said Kate.

"How do you know that?" asked Mitch. They went inside and watched the Detroit Lions until dinner. The Cowboys played after that. They were thankful for things they were not conscious of.

NOVEMBER 25, 1983

(Julia)

"I want to smooch Vance Druid," Julia said. "I'm so serious. I want to walk up to his house, knock on the door, and just smooch away. I want to enforce the Smoochie Rule. I'm serious. Nobody believes me, but I want to smooch him hardcore."

Julia said this from the backseat of Ted's car. Ted was behind the wheel and Naomi was in the passenger seat. They had been drinking for seven hours. Ted was trying to drive off his buzz.

"You don't wanna kiss that guy," Naomi said in response. "That guy . . . you don't need that guy. You can do better than that. He's just a small-town drunk who needs new pants. You deserve a real man. And what the fuck's the Smoochie Rule?"

"The Smoochie Rule is in effect!"

"You're a crazy woman, you crazy woman."

"Don't tell me who isn't crazy," said Julia. "I'll tell you who the crazy woman isn't."

Ted turned onto a gravel road. A fox ran across the path of his Chevy Cavalier, but no one inside the car noticed.

"Kissing is a problem," slurred Ted. "Smooching, kissing, human relations, whatever you want to call it. It's complex."

"What are you talking about?" said Naomi. "You don't know how to kiss people? Is that why you never kiss me? Because you don't know *how* to kiss people? It's not like driving a speedboat. It's easy. A child could do it."

"No, no. Shut your mouth, woman." Ted drove with his knees while lighting a Camel with the car's cigarette lighter. He shook the still-glowing lighter and threw it out the window. It was that kind of night. "That's not what I mean. You don't even know what I'm talking about. You never listen to me."

"Then what are you talking about?"

"Here is what I am talking about," said Ted. "I had a kissing problem when I was in college. Before I quit college. It was complicated. I still think about it."

"What is this regarding?" Naomi demanded. "If you're homosexual, I'm going to shoot myself. And you. And Jules, probably."

"What the fuck did I do?" screeched Julia.

"Just tell the goddamn story," Naomi said to Ted. Her right foot was resting on the dashboard. She suddenly looked like Faye Dunaway in *Mommy Dearest,* which may have been the look she was going for.

"When I was a freshman at Mayville State," said Ted, "my two closest friends were a guy named Tiger Lyons and a girl named Sarah Greenberg. Tiger Lyons was from a farm outside of Hazen, which is about five miles from Beulah. Sarah was from Saskatchewan, and she also happened to be Jewish. An authentic Jew, for real. I didn't even know that until we'd been friends for over a year. She never went to church or anything. I guess Greenberg is—supposedly—a very Jewish name."

"No shit," said Julia. "Christ. Don't you people have Jews here?"

"Not really," said Ted. "She's still the only Jewish person I've ever met. It was very interesting. For example, are you aware that Jewishness is more than just a religion? It's also an *ethnicity,* like being black or white or Japanese. Sometimes there are even atheist Jews."

"What the hell is wrong with you?" said Julia, now laughing. "Who doesn't know those things?"

"I didn't know those things," said Ted. "I guess that notion had never occurred to me. I had always thought Jews were just white people. But here's the thing: Sarah loved to kiss strangers. She did this wherever she went. She would get drunk at a party and suddenly just kiss a man she'd never met before. Right in front of everybody. This happened a bunch of times."

"Was this because she was Jewish?" asked Naomi. "Is this normal behavior among the Jews? Maybe we should ask Jules about this. Jules seems to be our resident expert on Israel."

"It had nothing to do with being Jewish," said Ted. "She was just a wild, slutty drunkard. And she always claimed that *who* she elected to kiss was a completely random decision. Sarah swore that there was nothing premeditated about whom she would hook up with: She claimed that she would just suddenly find her tongue in some unknown bozo's mouth, and it was always random and meaningless. But Tiger and I were skeptical of this. We were skeptical about her story. And the reason we were skeptical was because—inevitably—the random person she kissed was always the best-looking stranger in the room. It was always some guy who played lap-steel guitar or some pole-vaulter from the track team or whoever seemed to be the coolest person available at that particular moment. Tiger and I always accused her of this, and she always denied it. She insisted she smooched haphazardly. This behavior went on for all of the fall quarter and all of the winter quarter: The three of us would party together, and then Sarah would kiss a stranger."

"Did she ever kiss you?" asked Naomi.

"No," said Ted. "That was the thing. She never kissed me or Tiger. We were just friends. There is a word for this."

"Platonic," belched Julia.

"Is that a Yiddish word?" asked Naomi.

"Whatever," said Ted. "But yes. We were *plutonic* friends. But after a while, Tiger and I came up with this plan: We decided to get Sarah as wasted as possible, and then we took her to an architecture party. We knew these pre-architecture majors who were total weirdo geekazoids, and every Saturday they sat around a dorm room and drank Wop."

"Wop?" asked Julia.

"Wop is when you fill a garbage can with whatever alcohol

you can find," Naomi said. "You just pour in a bunch of Everclear and vodka and schnapps and rum, and then you fill up the rest of the garbage can with Kool-Aid or Tang. Sometimes you add fruit, if you have fruit. It's like a communal punch. Sometimes they call it a Hairy Buffalo."

"Exactly," said Ted. "So we're all in this dorm room getting obliterated, and there are simply no hot guys to be found. Everybody in this room looks like a skeleton wearing eyeglasses. Everyone is completely pale and uncomfortable and dressed in a turtleneck sweater. Everybody in that room is still a virgin, probably. And Sarah is *drunk*. I mean, she is a basket case. It's like she's on LSD."

"Wop will do that to you," said Naomi. "That shit is liquid fucknuts."

"Exactly," said Ted. "So this was going to be the ultimate test: Would Sarah still make out with one of these dweebs? If her selection process was *truly* random, whatever these architecture goons looked like should not have been a factor. She still should have kissed one of them."

"But—obviously—she didn't," deduced Julia.

"She didn't," said Ted. "She ended up kissing Tiger Lyons. And that ruined everything."

"So you were in love with her!" exclaimed Naomi. "You were in love with the Canadian Jew. I knew it. I knew that was where this story was going."

"No, I was not in love with her," said Ted. "Honestly, I never found her particularly attractive. She had thick ankles. I never thought of her as a *woman*, you know? But—even so—the moment she made out with Tiger, everything got weird."

"How?" asked Naomi.

"For one thing, there was suddenly this unspoken rivalry between Tiger and me, because it was suddenly obvious that—evidently—he was more handsome than I was, a possible reality that had never occurred to either of us before. It was humiliating. I started to hate my hair and the size of my nose. But that wasn't even the crux of the issue. The larger problem was that Tiger fell in love with Sarah as soon as she kissed him, probably because no woman had ever kissed him before, or at least not so aggressively. He never told us this stuff directly, but it was completely obvious. So now—whenever we went to a party where Sarah got drunk and kissed a stranger, which still happened constantly—Tiger would act all jealous and brooding. It was pretty pathetic. Plus, we still had no idea if our original theory about Sarah was right. I argued that—by kissing Tiger—it proved she wasn't drunkenly kissing strangers *at random*: When left with no other option, she resorted to kissing the hottest person in the vicinity, even if that person was a nonstranger. But Sarah claimed that kissing Tiger *proved* her actions were random, because if her selection process hadn't been arbitrary, and if she had been *consciously* kissing people she was physically attracted to, she likely would have kissed Tiger months before that party, since she obviously would have been attracted to him at an earlier juncture, too. It was kind of a good argument. The point is that we all eventually started to resent each other for different reasons. By the time I quit school the following year, we hardly saw each other. That architecture party was pretty much the end of our three-pronged friendship."

It was time to go home. The car entered an empty intersection. Ted applied the brake, swung the vehicle 180 degrees, and started driving back toward Owl.

"That's a good story," said Naomi. "How come you never told me that story before? We've been drunk about a million times."

"I guess we had never really talked about kissing before," said Ted.

"So what do you think, Jules?" said Naomi. "Do you think that whore was kissing people at random, or do you think she knew what she was doing all along? Personally, I think she knew *exactly* what she was doing."

No response.

"Jules?"

Naomi looked over her left shoulder. Julia was passed out, facedown on the backseat.

They drove the next four hundred yards in silence.

"Ted?"

"Yes?"

"Do you ever wish that Sarah Greenberg would have kissed you instead of Tiger Lyons?"

"Never. I used to, but I haven't for years."

They drove another hundred yards in silence.

"Ted?"

"Yes."

"Sometimes I would like to kiss you."

They drove another hundred feet.

"Naomi."

"Yes?"

"You need to pay closer attention to the stories people tell you about themselves."

They were almost back in Owl. Nothing was different.

DECEMBER 9, 1983

(Horace)

There was not a name for what killed Alma in 1972. Eleven years after her death, there still wasn't. In the future, doctors would begin referring to the disorder as fatal familial insomnia, but Horace would be equally dead before anyone had the chance to explain that to him. As far as he could tell, the problem had been completely straightforward: Alma just quit sleeping. And then she quit acting normal, and then she quit being alive.

It started on Thanksgiving.

"I can't sleep," Alma said. She wasn't even in bed yet. She was just sitting in a living room chair, playing solitaire on a TV tray. But Alma usually fell asleep in her chair at 9:00 p.m., woke up for the local news at 10 o'clock, and then retired to the mattress at 10:30. For Alma, going to sleep was like working out; she liked to warm up first.

"Too much turkey," said Horace, never turning away from the television. "Maybe you ate too much turkey."

"Turkey is supposed to make you sleep," Alma said. "That's what they always say about turkey."

"You'll fall asleep," said Horace. "Just don't think about it."

"Maybe I'll pray a few decades of the rosary," Alma said. She finally fell asleep at 2:00 a.m. It was curious. She hadn't stayed up that late since the 1950s.

This happened more and more; by Christmas, it was happening all the time. It did not matter how tired Alma felt; she could not fall asleep. She started drinking peppermint schnapps with warm cocoa, and then she tried cans of beer. It usually made things worse. The couple began having sex every night, partially out of desperation and partially because she was always going to bed drunk; this improved Horace's demeanor, but it did not have an impact on the insomnia.

"Are you worried about something?" Horace asked every morning. It did not matter what time he awoke; Alma was always sitting at the kitchen table, staring into a cup of decaffeinated coffee, teetering on the precipice of explosive tears.

"No," said Alma. "I'm only worried about not sleeping. That's all I ever worry about anymore."

"Is there something you're not telling me?" he would ask. "I will understand. I don't care what you have done. Just tell me what is on your mind."

"I haven't done anything," she would say. "Nothing is on my mind."

Actually, something *was* on Alma's mind. It was plaque. There was plaque on her thalamus, the region of the brain that regulates sleep. The proteins in her brain were mutating. It was congenital. Her father had had the same disorder, but it was never diagnosed; he hung himself in the barn before anyone noticed.

"We have to take you to the doctor," Horace said in January. "This not sleeping all the time . . . this is not normal."

"Fiddlesticks," moaned Alma. "I am not going to see a doctor because I'm too dumb to fall sleep. How embarrassing! He'd laugh me out of the clinic."

Alma was certain she was responsible for her own sleepless exhaustion. She changed her diet (more fish!) and quit wearing makeup. Nothing changed. She prayed for help, but she started to have a hard time concentrating on any given prayer (even the Hail Mary, which is only forty words). Every day, the universe seemed to shift. The sky would move. She kept seeing gophers and rabbits darting into corners and running through doorways. She could telekinetically melt ice cubes by staring at them. In February, Melba Hereford tried to murder her.

"I think we need to call the police," Alma said at supper.

Amazingly, she could still cook, even though she no longer experienced the sensation of hunger. "Melba tried to kill me today."

"What?" asked Horace.

"Melba tried to kill me."

"Melba Hereford?"

"Yes," said Alma. "I have no idea what got into her. She tried to hit me with her car, and then she chased me around with a butcher knife."

"What are you saying?" Horace pleaded. "Are you listening to yourself? Why would Melba want to kill you?"

"She was frothing at the mouth," said Alma. "I think she has rabies. I tried to call the police when it happened, but the phone wasn't working. She might have cut our phone line with the butcher knife. I'm pretty concerned about this. I think she's a Cuban."

"Where did this happen?"

"Right outside. I was in the garden."

That day, the high temperature had been eleven degrees.

That night, Alma screamed at the television. She thought it was a panda bear.

Horace drove her to the emergency room. The ER doctor did not believe him when he said she had slept only thirty hours over the past thirty days. The doctor said that was impossible. But this is possible. And Horace was actually lying when he said this; during the past thirty days, Alma hadn't slept at all.

You can give sedatives to victims of fatal familial insomnia, but they don't help. Sleeping pills help people *reach* sleep; fatal familial insomnia makes sleep unreachable. The protein in Alma's brain had changed, and it could not be changed back. They prescribed her massive quantities of Valium. Sometimes it did nothing, sometimes it made her vomit and sweat. There was nothing that anyone could do except a) watch her lose weight and b) watch her go insane. Which is precisely what Horace did.

Living with a crazy person is difficult, but living with a crazy person who never sleeps is worse. Like any normal being, Horace still got tired; Horace still needed to go to bed every night. But whenever he tried, he was buried by an avalanche of guilt. He had terrifying dreams that he could not remember. More problematic was the idea of Alma wandering the house alone, bumping into bookshelves and arguing with the sewing machine. They never turned off any lights in any room, ever. They lived in a state of perpetual noon.

"Horace," Alma said in April, "you have to plow the fields. You have to get the crops planted. I did not marry a lazybones."

"I know," said Horace. "Our friends are helping us. We'll get the crop in. Everything is fine. Maybe you should try to lay down for a little while."

"Why are other people planting our wheat? It's our wheat. We invented it. We don't have any quality neighbors. They steal from us. I don't think it's justified. What about the Indians?"

"Please, Alma. Please. Lay down. Just for a little bit."

"We should have children," she said. "We should have twin boys. They could be named Buck and Otto."

"We tried to have children," he said. "We tried."

"We really have a beautiful carpet. I never noticed it before, but we do." In Alma's universe, the living room carpet was made of glass.

"I like it, too," said Horace. "I like it. Maybe you should rest on the couch for a little bit?"

"I'm tired," said Alma.

"I know," said Horace. "I know that you're tired. That's why I think you should lay down. You could lay right down on the carpet."

"Quit trying to seduce me," she said. "I know you've been bringing prostitutes into the basement. I can smell their marijuana cigarettes in the stairwell."

"Alma . . ."

Alma paused. She looked at Horace's chest and squinted her eyes.

"Why is this happening to us?" she asked.

"I don't know," he said, unconsciously inferring that this had been an existential query about why his wife had contracted a hyper-rare sleep disorder that wasn't even supposed to exist. In truth, Alma was asking why both of their bodies were suddenly becoming translucent. But under these specific circumstances, that is probably the same question.

April was the worst month of their lives. May was better, only because Alma became catatonic. She spoke her last words on the morning of May 2: "The soul is a circle. I remember this." From that point onward, she sat silently in a recliner, twenty-four hours a day. It was like living with an emaciated mannequin. Her facial expression suggested bemusement, but it did not change; she would drink water, but she did not eat. For the first two weeks of May, Horace often sat across from Alma and made one-sided conversation; he had heard on the TV that comatose people could sometimes hear loved ones who spoke to them. And while Horace realized that losing the ability to sleep was (technically) the perfect opposite of being in a coma, it still seemed applicable.

"You were the only woman I could have ever married," he would say. "Sometimes I run into other women and all I can think is, What a pill. I think, How awful it must be to be married to that bimbo! Such a marriage would feel like a prison sentence. But I always knew you would be different, Alma. I knew being married to you would be a breeze. You were the only girl who didn't force me to dance. The average gal will pretty much *demand* to get on the dance floor as soon as the band starts swinging, because that's the only reason she went out on the date in the first place: She wanted a dance partner. But you were never like that. You were like, 'Oh, I can take it or leave it. I don't mind just sitting here, drinking punch and people watching.' And that made me *want* to dance with you. You know what I mean? That's why I fell in love with you. You were always so levelheaded."

All the things Horace told his catatonic wife were true. And—as is so often the case in the midst of any tragedy—they were things he would not have told her under nontragic circumstances. He imagined strangers watching his life as if it were a movie; the audience would be amazed by his undying affection. He would be viewed as romantic. But that illusion faded. He found himself repeating the same anecdotes and relying on platitudes. The whole affair started to seem silly: He could not recall a single evening from the previous twenty-five years when he and Alma had sat in the living room and discussed their relationship. Why was he doing it now? He looked at Alma and saw nothing but unsleeping bones. Her vampire pupils stared directly through his translucent torso. Horace was now like the carpet; Horace was made of glass. There was nothing more to do. He angled her recliner toward the television and they watched *Hawaii Five-0.* Horace fell asleep at 11:30, his enormous eyeglasses falling off his face. Alma kept watching until CBS concluded its programming, and then she watched the static.

Horace spent the next three weeks asking himself one question, over and over and over again: "Is it my ethical obligation as a husband to murder my wife?"

Alma's death was reported on June 5. There was no autopsy.

DECEMBER 21, 1983

(Mitch)

Wednesday night was (and is) church night. This has always been the case.

There are no high school sports on Wednesday nights, and there are no choir recitals or FFA meetings or drama rehearsals. On Wednesday night in the Midwest, Catholic kids go to religion class, and the schools schedule life accordingly. Elementary school Catholics go to religion class immediately after school (4:00 p.m.). High school students go after the conclusion of basketball practice (7:30 p.m.). Tonight, the high school members of the Owl CYO (Catholic Youth Organization) sat in the church rectory and discussed the virgin birth and the concept of Jesus being man and God simultaneously. It all seemed reasonable. As a tangent, they also discussed the theory that Jesus was black; this somehow seemed less plausible. When class dismissed at 8:30, Mitch and Zebra did what they always did following CYO: They drove around the countryside in Zebra's silver Dodge pickup, smoking Basic cigarettes and ignoring spirituality completely.

"I think I'm going to nail Miss America," said Zebra. His comment was connected to nothing. This was how they spoke. "Her name is Vanessa Williams, and she is so unbelievably hot. You will not believe how hot this black woman is. I saw her in *People* magazine."

"Why are you reading *People* magazine?"

"My mom gets *People*. It's not terrible. And besides: Vanessa Williams. So hot. She doesn't even look black."

"That's racist," said Mitch. "I think you are being, like . . . pretty racist, I think."

"Why is it racist to say Miss America doesn't look black?"

"I don't know," said Mitch. "I guess because you made it sound like her lack of blackness makes her hotter. I think that counts as racism."

"You are obsessed with black people," said Zebra. "I think you want to be black."

"How does not worrying about the degree of Miss America's blackness—in relation to her alleged hotness—indicate that I want to be black?"

"True or false," responded Zebra. "T or F: You always root for Georgetown."

Mitch was, in fact, obsessed with the Georgetown Hoya basketball program. And that was, in fact, because the Georgetown Hoyas were the blackest people he had ever seen. Mitch's understanding of African-American culture was completely based on how Georgetown played defense. They were the only black people he knew.

"I like their players," said Mitch. "I had a lot of respect for Sleepy Floyd. I also like Michael Graham and Horace Broadnax. They rule ass."

"Exactly," said Zebra. "That proves my point. All those guys are black."

"Well, you love Michael Jordan," said Mitch. "He's black."

"Not really," said Zebra. "Michael Jordan is black the way Vanessa Williams is black."

"T or F," asked Mitch. "You're an imbecile. The answer is T. Also, this music is terrible."

"How can you not love Judas Priest?" asked Zebra.

"Why would I love them?" asked Mitch. "I don't even know who they are."

"Maybe you'd like them more if they were black."

It started to snow. The flakes flew toward the windshield like accelerating stars. It looked the way *Star Wars* portrayed spaceships that were jumping into hyperspace. Zebra flipped his headlights from high beams to low; when it snowed, it was easier to see the road with dimmed headlights. They were on a gravel road, sixteen miles south of Owl. It was a good night. They had more cigarettes than necessary. Smoking feels wonderful if you do it only once a week.

"What do you make of this latest Cubby Candy rumor?" Zebra asked.

"I don't know," said Mitch. "I don't think it can possibly be true."

"That's what I thought," Zebra said, "but I've now heard the story from three different sources. The dude is unhinged."

"I know," said Mitch. "I believe the first part of the story, and maybe the second part. But not the part about the dog."

Four days ago, Cubby Candy drove to Jamestown to wash and wax his Barracuda. That evening, he (allegedly) drove to a bar called the Jackelope and immediately got into a dispute with another patron in the parking lot; Cubby proceeded to beat the stranger senseless. That was the first part of the story. The stranger's horrified girlfriend then rushed into the bar and explained the situation to three members of his posse. The trio (allegedly) went outside and angrily confronted Cubby, and one of them (allegedly) scratched the door of his Barracuda with a house key. This was (allegedly) a poor decision, because Cubby (allegedly) responded by wordlessly grabbing the man's hair and smashing his face against the Barracuda's hood, thereby breaking the hooligan's nose, an orbital bone near his temple, and seven to ten teeth. Cubby then (allegedly) attacked the other two guys simultaneously and obliterated both, (allegedly) breaking a total of three arm bones in the ninety-second melee. That was the second part of the story. The third part of the story was that Cubby (allegedly, and somewhat inexplicably) exited the bloodbath by walking *into* the Jackelope's entrance and consuming five beers at the bar, all by himself. When he exited the establishment two hours later, the brother of the original beaten stranger (who had been phoned by the horrified girlfriend) was waiting next to the 'Cuda with a frothing Doberman pinscher by his side. "You are going to pay for what you did," the brother (allegedly) said. "Serpico is gonna make you bleed, fuckwad." Upon that (alleged) declaration, the brother released Serpico's leash. The hound jumped for the jugular, which was his (alleged) nature. But Serpico didn't make it. Cubby (allegedly) caught the dog by the throat and smashed its snout into the pavement. He (allegedly) squeezed its windpipe with his left hand and punched with his right; he (allegedly) hit Serpico until Serpico (allegedly) stopping twitching.

This was the part of the story Mitch did not believe.

"People have seen the key scratches on the 'Cuda," said Zebra. "Curtis-Fritz has verified that the car was keyed. I'm sure the fact that he had just waxed the vehicle intensified his bloodlust. T or F: That psychopath loves his car? The answer is T."

"I'm not questioning the likelihood of his car being damaged," said Mitch. "And I'm sure somebody got beat up that night. I just don't believe the stuff about the dog. Are we supposed to believe that some guy brought an attack dog to the parking lot and just *waited there* for two hours? What kind of person would do that?"

"True," said Zebra. "T. But that notwithstanding . . . if all this is even semitrue, it's a pretty amazing story. He won a street fight *against a Doberman*! That's like punching a mountain lion in the face. I'm starting to think Candy could defeat Grendel."

"I don't think it's possible," said Mitch. "I don't think any human could win a fight against an animal."

Just as he said this, an amorphous shape zipped across the road, twenty-five feet in front of the pickup. It immediately disappeared on the other side of the road. The shape had been visible for .75 seconds. The shape was extremely fast, brownish in color, and weighed between ten and ten thousand pounds.

"What the fuck?" said Zebra. He slammed on the brakes. The vehicle almost fishtailed. "What the fuck was that?"

"A fox?" Mitch guessed. "A deer? A wildebeest?"

"Let's go," said Zebra. He slammed the truck into park and

reached behind the seat, pulling out the double-barreled shotgun that was always there. They scampered onto the road in front of the vehicle, leaving both of the truck's doors wide open. They stared into the darkness; they saw nothing, except for more darkness.

"That was outrageous," said Zebra. "I want to know what the fuck that was."

"It must have been a fox," said Mitch. "It was quick like a fox. What the hell did you bring the gun for?"

"I don't know," said Zebra. "I guess I'm no Cubby Candy."

"Well, as long as you have it, you might as well shoot it."

"Good point," said Zebra. He raised the barrel of the shotgun toward the moon and fired both shells skyward. The meaningless reports echoed toward God. They sounded massive.

"Nice," said Mitch. "You're an outlaw." They meandered back to the truck, lit new cigarettes, and drove away. Zebra removed *British Steel* from the cassette deck and replaced it with *American Fool.*

"So, here's a question," said Zebra. "You know how we were talking at CYO about the likelihood of Jesus being a black guy?"

"Yes," sighed Mitch.

"Knowing what we know now, and knowing how you feel about the Georgetown Hoyas, I'm curious about something: If Jesus turned out to be black, would that make you want to be a better Christian?"

"I don't know," said Mitch. "Would Jesus be black like Vanessa Williams, or would Jesus be black like Horace Broadnax?"

"Don't make me shoot you," said Zebra.

"You'd never get away with it," said Mitch. "You'd die in prison. T or F?"

It is important to have questionable friends you can trust unconditionally.

DECEMBER 22, 1983

(Julia)

Owl High School was (and is) almost (but not quite) perfectly square. It was four hallways, connected by four right angles: The north-south hallways measured 120 feet and the east-west hallways were 110 feet. The gymnasium was in the interior of the building; the classrooms were on the outside perimeter of the hallways, four doors per hall. If it were possible to tear off the facility's roof and look upon it from the perspective of a blimp, the school would have looked like a brick, surrounded by a tile moat, protected by interlocking cubes. It had the aesthetic character of massive beige Legos.

Every morning from 8:10 a.m. until the first bell at 8:35, certain students walked laps around the halls in a continual loop, half of them moving clockwise and half in the opposite orbit. These certain students tended to be females between the ages of thirteen and sixteen, although the practice was also popular among eighth-grade boys. They would briskly walk in pockets of three or four and gossip, occasionally saying "Hey" to kids walking in the opposite direction; for anyone still waiting to pass driver's education, this was the pedestrian version of driving around town. It had no goal, but it had purpose.

In order to police the undangerous hall walkers, all members of the Owl faculty were expected to stand outside their respective rooms as figureheads of menace, making sure no one did anything disruptive or obscene. Julia's assigned prebell post was twelve feet from John Laidlaw's door; unless one of them was in an exceptionally angry or empty mood, they typically moved a few steps closer, stood alongside each other, and talked about things they did not care about.

"The cattle are restless this morning," said Laidlaw. This was true: Because it was the last day before the beginning of Christmas vacation, everyone was talking louder (and walking faster) than usual. Boys were shoving each other and forcing their laughter.

"Today will be a waste," said Julia. "We might as well send them home at noon."

"We might as well shoot them," said Laidlaw. Julia chuckled at this sentiment, but just barely.

"Going back to Wisconsin for Christmas?" asked Laidlaw.

"True," said Julia. This was like taking a test. "I'm going to get up tomorrow morning at six and drive straight through."

"Worried about the weather?" Meteorologists had forecast snow for the weekend.

"Yes," she said. "That's why I'm going to leave so early. The idea of waking up at six is already making me cry."

"Well, just be careful," said Laidlaw. "And if you do get caught in bad weather, don't leave the vehicle. Always stay inside the car."

"I know," she said. "Truthfully, I'm more concerned about the gridlock through Minneapolis. If it snows, it's going to be a madhouse."

Teenagers continued to walk and talk with maniacal enthusiasm. At the other end of the hallway, a fat ninth grader named Andy stole the hat off a seventh grader's skull and held it in the air like a severed head. When Laidlaw noticed this, he said, "Andy!" The hat was returned. That was all it took.

"Any plans for your last evening in town?" Laidlaw asked Julia.

"I have to wrap some presents," said Julia. "After that, I might go uptown for a drink or two. But nothing exciting. Like I said, I want to be on the road by six thirty or seven. Do you have any plans?"

"No plans," said Laidlaw.

"How come you never go to the bar?" asked Julia. "Don't you drink?"

"I drink," said Laidlaw. "But I don't get much pleasure from it. Besides, my wife runs my life. You know how it goes."

Julia did not respond to this remark. She did not know how it went.

The two teachers stood in silence, comfortable with each other's presence. Mitch Hrlicka walked by with *Nineteen Eighty-Four* in his left hand, trying to ignore both of the authority figures who were watching him. His hair was out of control. There were bags under both his eyes.

"Merry Christmas, Vanna," said Laidlaw. "Are you going to be an elf this year?"

"Probably not," said Mitch. "No."

"You would make a fine elf, Vanna," said Laidlaw. "You could be Sleepy."

"Sleepy was a dwarf," said Mitch.

"So what? Don't you think elves have names?"

Mitch slouched toward Bethlehem.

"I don't understand that kid," said Julia. "He seems nice enough, but he always looks depressed."

"Mitch is a good kid," said Laidlaw. "He's a really good kid, relatively speaking. But he has no sense of humor. That's his problem."

The bell rang.

DECEMBER 28, 1983

(Horace)

His '58 Chevy Apache was still chugging in place when he exited the café, exhaust billowing from its tailpipe in slow motion. He had allowed the pickup to idle for the last two hours; this was standard procedure when the air was fourteen degrees below zero. Everyone in town ran their vehicles continuously on afternoons like today; if you turned the engine off, the liquids inside the engine block would become viscous and immovable. Your vehicle would turn into a metal house. During the coldest snaps, people who owned diesel pickups let the trucks run all night, twenty-four hours a day, never turning back the key for weeks at a time. Diesel fuel burns slowly and is not molecularly designed for arctic conditions. Almost all the vehicles (diesel or otherwise) had extension cords peeping out from under their hoods; this allowed their owners to plug them in overnight. The charge from the current kept the engine block warm and fluid. Once, when he was driving through Indiana, a confused mechanic noticed the extension cord on Horace's Apache and asked him if he drove an electric truck. Horace enjoyed telling this story. He usually told it two or three times a winter.

Horace was wearing an Elmer Fudd hat, leather gloves, a wool scarf, a winter jacket, denim overalls, a sweater, a turtleneck, a flannel shirt, an undershirt, long johns, Red Wing work boots, and two pairs of socks. "It's not so cold today," he thought. "The TV said it would be colder." He opened the door of his Apache, which was (of course) unlocked, because people in Owl don't steal cars, even if they are empty and the keys are in the ignition. The Red Owl grocery store was one block from Harley's

Café, so Horace drove his truck sixty feet and diagonally parked on the opposite side of the street.

He entered the store and reached into his pocket, pulling out the list he had written with a pencil three hours before. The fog on his glasses made it difficult to read, but he knew most of it by memory; he always bought all the same things. It was a list of the old-man food he needed to live, and it was as follows:

- Campbell's tomato soup
- hamburger meat
- sausages (*these were what he called hot dogs*)
- candy
- Folgers crystals
- noodles (*this was what he called Kraft Macaroni & Cheese*)
- fake butter (*this was what he called margarine*)
- cookies
- potatoes
- Elf Krispies (*this was what he called Rice Krispies*)
- whole milk
- Wonder bread
- black licorice (*this was not the same as candy, somehow*)

Horace had now been a food shopper for eleven years of his life, but he remained baffled by the layout of grocery stores. He knew they were designed to confuse people on purpose, and they were supposed to make him buy things he didn't need on impulse. What a ludicrous business model. Who would buy something they didn't need? Horace felt grocers made organizational errors. Why wasn't the cereal aisle next to the milk? Why weren't condoms in the same section as tampons? It didn't matter to him that these weren't necessarily things he needed; it was the principle. Didn't anyone realize that certain products had relationships?

Horace felt stupid pushing a shopping cart around the store.

He felt like a woman, but it was the only way to get everything at once. How typical. The wheels rolled flawlessly, almost as if they were greased. There was no friction with the floor. When he turned the first corner, he almost collided with the Dog Lover. The Dog Lover was carrying a fifty-pound bag of dog food like it was a newborn baby. How typical.

"Pardon me," said Horace. "Didn't see you there. Got ahead of myself. Sorry."

"Yeah," said the Dog Lover. That was all he said.

Horace had just been talking about the Dog Lover at the café. What a troll. Apparently, the Dog Lover had decided not to go home to Minneapolis over Christmas. Instead, he and four of his miscreant friends decided to have a party on Christmas Eve. What kind of outlaw wants to get liquored up on Christmas Eve? Horace could only imagine what kind of motley crew the Dog Lover must associate with in his holiday time. The party started inside the Dog Lover's apartment, but they ran out of booze before 10:00. Somebody pissed in the hallway like an animal. Pissing in public. On Christmas! What were they thinking? They weren't thinking. That was the problem. That's always the problem. Around 11:10, they decided to open up Yoda's and drink all night. Idiots! And—evidently—a few of those fools must have been rope smokers, too, because—evidently—they lit the Christmas tree on fire. *While it was still in the bar.* So just picture the scene: The Christmas tree is now a seven-foot fireball that's standing three feet from the jukebox, and they're all laughing like doper hyenas and cursing the sky and trying to douse the flames with Old Milwaukee, and the room gets smokier than a goddamn Ojibwa sweat lodge. They think this is radical. They think they're protesters. But then the Dog Lover suddenly (or maybe *finally*) realizes he's going to burn the whole tavern to the ground if he's not careful, so he picks up the tree by the trunk and runs outside. That was how the Dog Lover celebrated the birth of Jesus Christ: By running around Main Street with a burning evergreen at 1:15 in the morning, screaming about how he was gonna joust with Santa Claus. What a tragic clown. He was dumber than his dog and five times as mean.

Horace found all the products he needed in ten minutes, except for the licorice. (He consistently forgot the licorice.) As he rolled his cart of old-man food toward the checkout counter, he saw a teenager paying for a can of Rondo and a pack of unfiltered Camel cigarettes. The boy wore a flannel shirt with the sleeves cut off, covering a T-shirt that depicted Kenny Rogers as the Gambler. He wasn't wearing a jacket. His biceps looked like coils of copper wire, swaddled in pleather. He smiled at Horace while waiting for his change.

"Son, you're going to freeze to death," said Horace. "You're going to turn into the damn yeti."

"Lost my jacket," said the kid.

"You must be tough," said Horace. "If I walked outside the way you're dressed, they'd be digging me a grave. No jacket! You must be tough as nails."

"Naw. I'm not tough," said the kid. "You're probably tougher than me."

They laughed.

"You shouldn't smoke cigarettes," said Horace. "Those bastards will kill you alive. I smoked for seventeen years. Never thought I'd quit. Thought I'd kill myself before quitting. Hardest thing I ever did, and the desire never leaves. I'd give you a five-dollar bill for a cigarette right now! You should stop while you're still a young man."

"I know," replied the kid. "But if I didn't smoke, I'd freeze to death."

They laughed again and nodded goodbye. Horace pulled out his checkbook to pay for the old-man food. He thought, Now, that's a helluva pleasant kid.

The kid walked out of the Red Owl and barely noticed the cold. He ignited a cigarette and pulled open the door of his '74 Barracuda. The engine was still running. He had already forgotten the entire conversation.

NEW YEAR'S DAY, 1984

(John Laidlaw)

"No dystopia," he thought when he looked out his living room window. "Still just a topia."

This was (kind of) true: No Thought Police were visible to the naked eye. All he could see was four inches of snow, a street, a sidewalk, an invisible barking dog, and seven empty cans of Old Milwaukee some kids had thrown at his mailbox the night before. It was ten thirty in the morning. It was much warmer than yesterday; it was nine degrees. John Laidlaw tightened the belt of his robe, opened the front door of his little green house, and stepped onto his porch to smoke a cigarette. The air was icy and jagged. It was like walking through a broken mirror.

He lit his cancer stick and sucked it down. The smoke and the cold made him feel better, but he still didn't feel good. There had been a time in his life when nicotine had made him feel great, but now it just stopped him from feeling awful. He was like everybody else. A sedan rolled by; Laidlaw halfheartedly waved at its driver. He recognized the person behind the wheel, but he could not recall the man's name. "I should know that guy," he thought. "I need to become a better member of this community."

John Laidlaw had regrets. He felt bad about his habit of never tipping any waitress he knew he'd never see again. He felt shame over the way he pretended to show concern whenever his wife got sick, fully aware that his only true anxiety was that her germs might infect him, too. John Laidlaw had many, many, many regrets. But—curiously, or perhaps predictably—this litany of regrets did not include the first time he slept with one of his students. That had made total sense at the time, and it still made sense to him now. Yes, she was sixteen, and—yes—adults aren't supposed to have sex with sixteen-year-olds. Yes, yes. He knew this was the conventional wisdom. But—at the time—he had been an unmarried twenty-three-year-old, living in a western North Dakota ghost town that had yet to realize it was built above an oil field. What else was there to do? Had it been the 1940s, he probably would have married the girl. It was (arguably) the best relationship he ever had, at least for the first six weeks: Like all superlative relationships, it was nothing except sex and secrecy. Her name was Jenny, and she was a cat. The girl had balls of lead. She would openly flirt with him in the middle of class, uninterested in the other students' shock; months before they kissed, Laidlaw feared he had already fallen in love with her. He thought about her constantly, and especially when he smoked. Smoking made him amorous and solipsistic. Tobacco injected improbable thoughts into his brain. He started to believe Jenny was wearing jeans with the sole intent of making him suicidal. Laidlaw didn't understand how to manage his lust; devoid of ideas, he assigned essay exams and searched her responses for hidden romantic subtext. Was he simply too stupid to realize she was making fun of him? He did not know. Perhaps. One night he got drunk in his living room and called her on the telephone; her mother answered, so he hung up and masturbated into a sock. He got drunk two nights later and called the house again. This time it was Jenny who picked up the receiver.

"Why are you doing this to me?" he asked.

"Who is this?"

"It's John."

"John?"

"John Laidlaw."

"Mr. Laidlaw?"

"Yes. How are you doing, Jenny? No hot date tonight?"

She vocalized her confusion by laughing uncomfortably.

"How are you doing?" he asked. "Tell me how you are doing. How are you doing?"

"Okay. I'm okay. Why are you calling me?"

"Because you're driving me crazy."

"I'm sorry." She laughed again.

"No, I like it. I like it when you drive me crazy. I want to see you."

"When?"

"Right now."

"Right now? Like, tonight? Like, while it's dark out?"

"Yes."

"Where?"

"Anywhere."

"Are you sure?"

"I'm sure."

That was how it started. Laidlaw was shocked by how easy it was. It was the first time he had ever told a woman to do something and she just *did it.* There was no negotiation; there were no compromises. He declared they were going to start sleeping together, and they did.

He started to enjoy being a teacher.

Over time, relations with Jenny did not work out. It was exhilarating throughout the second semester of her junior year (and even for most of the ensuing summer), but then things started to drag. She was too emotional. He realized he did not love her long before the conclusion of track season. However, what he *did* love was dating someone he wasn't supposed to be dating. He loved making clandestine plans and concocting alibis; he loved the way all their covert meetings were hyper-intense and crazy physical, and he loved the fact that they always had something to talk about (when they would meet again, whom they'd have to deceive in order to make that happen, what cover story they would use if they were caught). Illegally dating a high school student was more challenging than designing football plays and often more rewarding. Laidlaw kept sleeping with Jenny throughout her senior year, months after his interest had evaporated. He was addicted to this life. That April, it was Jenny who actually broke it off. "I don't make you crazy anymore," she said, "and you talk to me like I'm a child." This was true. They both cried, although Jenny cried more.

"I must evolve," decided Laidlaw. "I cannot be this kind of man for the rest of my life." He stopped drinking at home. He decided to begin research for a nonfiction book about the space race, told from the perspective of the Soviets. That June, he started writing beautiful, semi-sincere letters to a woman he had sporadically dated during college. Her name was Sarah. She had majored in nursing. By the following summer, they were married. No one dreams of becoming the wife of an assistant football coach in Williston, North Dakota, but Sarah thought it would be better than being an unmarried nurse in Sisseton, South Dakota. They watched TV and played conservative games of Scrabble, and she could arrange the living room furniture however she desired. She loved (or at least really liked) John, and she liked (and sort of loved) rereading the letters he had mailed her during their summer of sexual seriousness. But Sarah knew something was wrong with him. She had always known this, even during college. His emotions were backward: Whenever he heard good news, he seemed to grimace; whenever something bad happened, it was almost as if his mood improved. When he got angry, he made jokes. Failure made him arrogant. He seemed depressed during intercourse. They eventually had a baby, and John repeatedly told Sarah how much he adored their son—yet whenever he was in the same room with the boy, John always looked bored. He could not relate to a child. For some reason, he always wanted to argue with it.

"Great news," a seemingly downcast John told his wife in 1977. "We are moving to Owl."

"Where?" said Sarah. They had talked about relocating in the past, but only casually.

"Owl," he said. "I have been named the new head football coach at Owl High School. It's a smaller school than Williston, but they have a great football program. They won the Class B state championship five years ago. This, for all practical purposes, is my destination job. I have fulfilled my career dream. This is my dream. My dream has been fulfilled. This is my dream."

"It is?" asked Sarah. For as long as she had known him, John had never mentioned moving to Owl or having dreams.

"It is," he said. "It is my dream. I will finally be the head coach of the high school football team in Owl, North Dakota. You will finally be married to an authentic leader of men. You will not just be married to an offensive coordinator. I will be in control."

Technically, this was all accurate. But Laidlaw was lying completely. The reason John, Sarah, and four-year-old Lawrence Laidlaw were about to leave Williston was because a seventeen-year-old girl named Doris Stahl was—at that very moment—driving to Montana to abort the child he had planted in her gut, a detail everyone in Williston (except Sarah) seemed to suspect. The Williston High superintendent had made Laidlaw's career options very clear; John selected option C, which was the only one that did not involve contacting a lawyer.

For a second time, Laidlaw vowed to live a different kind of existence. Things would be different in Owl, if only because he assumed it would be impossible to sleep with teenagers in a town of eight hundred people without getting caught. He decided to become a normal human, and he assumed that transition would be easy. It wasn't. Being a decent guy was no easier than being a terrible, secretive jackass. He didn't feel less anxious or more content. He still had responsibilities and pressures. Most of the time, being a normal person was harder than the alternative. He preferred being the human he used to be. He started seducing Darcy Busch in the fall of 1980, typically during senior English; Darcy was the kind of short, cute, stocky girl who traditionally dominates gymnastics. He liked her handwriting and her perfume. Darcy was skeptical of John's creepy, abstract advances, but she caved after Christmas break. Laidlaw knew how to wear people down; his livelihood as a football coach was built on that specific gift.

One would think sexual impropriety would not be feasible in a town the size of Owl; everybody knows everything about everyone, all the time. His initial rendezvous with Darcy was communicated through a Byzantine series of codes; he left nothing to chance. His trickery failed absolutely. Almost immediately, he could sense that everyone in the school knew something was going on; the morning after he had seen Darcy pantsless for the first time, the whole community looked at him as though he were a vampire. They could see the blood on his fangs. But he also noticed something else: That recognition didn't seem to matter. *Nobody did anything.* They knew about it, and they whispered about it, and they thought it was terrible. But that was as far as it went. People may have liked him less, but they treated him exactly the same. Compared to Williston, Owl was easy. In fact, he almost missed the rush of risking his future. To compensate, he started taking foolish chances: Darcy got pregnant. When she told him the news, he almost enjoyed the internal panic. "Oh, my God," he thought. "I've finally done it. My life is over." But it wasn't. Two weeks later, Darcy just disappeared. Her parents moved her to Fargo and never spoke of it again. It was so queer: A problem was there, and then it just wasn't. And everybody knew this.

Everybody.

"Did you hear about Darcy Busch?" Sarah asked in bed one night. The question did not sound as pointed as it was.

"I heard she got in trouble," said Laidlaw.

"Do you know who got her in trouble?" asked Sarah. She wasn't stupid.

"Of course I don't," said Laidlaw, feigning sleep, managing

fear. "How would I know who got Darcy Busch pregnant? Who am I?"

"They say she doesn't have a boyfriend," said Sarah. "I've heard that from several sources. Doesn't it seem strange that this would happen to a girl without a boyfriend?"

"Maybe she had a boyfriend nobody knows about," said Laidlaw. "Maybe she got around. Maybe it was an immaculate conception and she's going to give birth to the next Jesus. I have no idea what her story is."

"But you certainly must have heard rumors," said Sarah. "I *know* she was in your class. They certainly must gossip about this around school."

"They probably do," he said, "but hearsay doesn't interest me."

Sarah refused to turn off the light. She kept waiting for her husband to become a different person from the one he actually was.

"What kind of student was she, John?"

"A good one. She always did her work."

Sarah kept waiting.

The results were the same.

"John," she finally said, "if you know anything about this situation, you need to tell me. I'm serious, John. You really need to tell me now. Right now. Right this second."

"What is that supposed to mean?" he asked. "What are you implying?"

"John," she said. "I want to know what happened to Darcy Busch. I want to know if you know what happened."

"I already told you that I have no idea," he said. "And why do you keep using direct address during this conversation? 'John. John. What do you think about this, John. Tell me what you know, John.' Am I on trial? Tell me if I'm on trial."

"I'm sorry," said Sarah.

"Don't worry about other people's problems," he replied.

And with that, the conversation ended, even though neither party fell asleep for at least two hours. It was the last time they would ever discuss such matters.

Laidlaw still thought about that conversation they had in bed; he thought about it a lot. He thought about it while he smoked. What did she want me to say? he always wondered. What would have been the correct answer to those questions? He dropped his cigarette into the snow, briefly hugged himself, and walked back inside. He wondered how long it would be before Sarah asked the same questions about Tina McAndrew. Two weeks? Two days? Two minutes? His answers would have to be the same as they were three years ago. John Laidlaw did not know why he did the things he did. Does anyone?

Back inside, he sat down in his La-Z-Boy and quietly watched Lawrence play with the magnetized racetrack he received during Christmas. Sarah was making waffles in the kitchen. "People will judge me," he thought. "People will look at my life, and they will look at the decisions I have made, and they will always focus on this one specific weakness that I have. This one specific problem will define everything about my character. To so many people, this problem will be the only thing about my life that matters. And that is so unfair. I've done a lot of good things. I'm a great driver. My kid seems like a decent little person. I've read difficult books, and I've understood what they were about. My problem is plain, really: If I wasn't attracted to high school girls, I wouldn't have sex with them. That's the whole dilemma. Is it my fault that I happen to work at a high school? It's not like I selected these women arbitrarily. I liked all of them. How was I supposed to know that this could become a vice? Everybody has a problem. I'm sure my father had a secret problem, and I'm sure my son will have a secret problem. I didn't *decide* to be like this. Nobody *decides* to have a problem. So why is this the only thing about my life that matters?"

He walked across the room and awoke the television.

"What were you doing outside?" Sarah asked from the kitchen. "Were you smoking?"

"I was smoking," he said.

"Again?" she said.

"Yes," he said. "Again, I was smoking."

"Do you want a waffle?"

"No. But thank you."

"Do you have any plans for today?"

"I'm going to watch the Rose Bowl at three thirty, and then I'm going to watch the Orange Bowl tonight."

"Who's playing?"

"UCLA and Illinois. Nebraska and Miami."

"Who do you want to win?" she asked, still in the kitchen.

"I have no rooting interest in either affair," he said. "I just want to watch them."

"I will never understand why you watch games you don't care about," Sarah said.

"Those are the games I enjoy the most," he replied.

JANUARY 5, 1984

(Mitch)

Name: Mitch H.
Class: English III
Date: 1-5-84
Instructor: Mr. Laidlaw

Question 1: Orwell wrote *Nineteen Eighty-Four* as a warning to society. What was he warning society about?

[Why would anyone try to warn society about a problem by writing a book about it? Wouldn't it make more sense to run for president or something? But I suppose Orwell couldn't run for president, being British.]

Orwell wanted to warn us about the government taking away our freedom and turning us into human robots who will believe whatever we are told, even if what we are told is oppressive and cruel in an illegal way.

Question 2: Who is "Winston"? What qualities define his personality? Compare and contrast those qualities with the characteristics of "Julia" and "O'Brien."

[Winston is the main character in the book and Laidlaw loves this book, so Laidlaw must believe he and Winston are fundamentally the same person. That's usually what makes people love any book: They believe the story that they are reading is actually about them. I suppose Laidlaw relates to Winston because they're both sex addicts without much grit. I guess that would make Julia like Tina McAndrew, although probably less hot. O'Brien was the most confusing character; he is clearly supposed to be evil, but I liked him the most. He was able to read Winston's mind. He was kind of like a more skilled Zebra.]

Winston is the main character in the book. He is noble, rebellious, and folds under torture. He hates rats and does not want his face eaten by them. Julia is the woman in the book who he has sex with. O'Brien is like a spy who Winston trusts, but O'Brien is actually not trustworthy and pretty much a spy. He uses the rats on Winston and makes him deny his feelings for Julia. O'Brien also has no first name, which is enigmatic.

Question 3: Who were the Thought Police? What was thoughtcrime? How do these things relate (or not relate) to the class structure of Oceania?

[Maybe Cubby Candy should fight Grendel with rats. If Cubby had a two-rat advantage, he would probably become the favorite. Actually, that seems like the kind of maniacal commando shit Candy would be into: He seems like the type of person who'd quietly walk around with a backpack full of live rats. He'd throw them into his enemies' faces during fistfights. He'd be some kind of rat-throwing supervillain. Grendel would have to swat away the incoming rats like they were helicopters and he was King Kong. Maybe he could catch one in midflight and bite off its head. Or maybe he would ignore them completely and just punch away at the universe, covered in rats and blood and sweat and rat blood. He'd be like a zombie of the apocalypse, oblivious to pain. He'd be like Conan the Barbarian, but with heightened agility.]

The Thought Police were like the KGB of Oceania. They stopped people from committing "thoughtcrime," which was whenever people would secretly think about Big Brother in unflattering ways. This did not impact the class structure of Oceania.

Question 4: Explain "doublethink" and "Newspeak," using examples. How do these concepts symbolize *Nineteen Eighty-Four* as a whole?

[This morning I walked past the new social studies teacher on the way to this class. She looked like shit. She said to me, "How is it going, Mitch?" I said, "Okay." But this is not really true, because she did not specify what "it" was and I did not immediately assume "it" referred to any preexisting situation in my life. I'm sure she didn't have any idea what "it" was either. She just said, "How is *it* going, Mitch," because she wanted to say something aloud in public. Basically, she asked a question she didn't understand, and I gave an affirmative response to that question, even though I did not know what I was responding to. Neither of us cared about what the other person was talking about or how the other person felt. We expressed two ideas that seemed to be interconnected, but neither of them was true. They were just words. They were neither good nor bad. They could have been any words, really.]

Doublethinking is when you have two thoughts at the same time that appear to contradict each other, but you believe both of those thoughts are equally true. This is like "Freedom Is Slavery" or "Sadness Is Funniness." Newspeak is a futuristic language where you eliminate certain words in order to make things more simple ("simpler"), such as saying "boring," "doubleboring," and "doubleplusboring." These concepts symbolize 1984 because they make it possible to believe things that don't make any sense while being unable to explain why those thoughts are problematic, which seems to be the main thing Orwell is worried about.

Question 5: In *Nineteen Eighty-Four,* the government attempts to a) observe the population at all times while b) falsifying the history of Oceania. What was the purpose of these acts?

[What if Tina McAndrew isn't pregnant? Just because everyone thinks they know something doesn't mean it's true. I mean, nobody has seen any baby. There is no proof. It could all be rumor. Maybe Tina is actually in a sanatorium and this "unplanned pregnancy" was the cover story. She wasn't exactly normal. They say she believed unicorns were real animals until, like, the tenth grade. She saw some circus on TV where they glued a horn onto the nose of a Shetland pony, and she refused to question its authenticity. "Why would they lie about something like that?" she supposedly asked. "Maybe they're just an endangered species." There are several people who can verify her belief in unicorns. Taking this into consideration, I suppose it's possible that she fabricated her whole relationship with Laidlaw and then claimed he got her pregnant in hopes of ruining his life. That's not so implausible. Laidlaw deserves to have his life ruined. Then again, if he *didn't* make love to Tina McAndrew, he probably didn't make love to Darcy Busch, either. He probably didn't make love to anyone, except his wife and maybe a few other normal-aged women he dated before getting married. So maybe he doesn't deserve anything.]

If you know what everyone is doing in the present and you dictate what they know (or believe) about the past, you can control the future.

Extra credit: How does the book *Nineteen Eighty-Four* reflect real-life America in the year 1984?

[They're exactly the same, except everything is reversed.]

1984 is very much like the world today, because everyone watches TV and we pay too many taxes. 1984 is also like the Soviet Union in many ways, and Big Brother is like a Communist version of _60 Minutes_ combined with President Reagan, if he were a Nazi. The U.S. is also like Oceania in that we are fighting a continual war where nothing happens. However, we are still a free society, so no major worries.

JANUARY 7, 1984

(Julia)

They were all her friends now.

She knew everything about them.

She could look around the bar, and some of them would always be there, and those who were would always smile back. She was not a man, so they all liked to get drunk and tell her the semi-interesting stories drunks always tell in hopes that women will find them disturbed and sympathetic and vulnerable and desirable.

Bull Calf was her friend. He was scared of things. When he was five, faulty wiring set his family's house on fire in the middle of winter. His parents were not home. His older sister rushed into his bedroom and carried him outside. They stood barefoot in the snow and watched their home burn to the ground. It was a terrible, beautiful experience. Over time, it became difficult for him to differentiate between things that were scary and things that were attractive. This, he assumed, is why meeting women was difficult. When he was in second grade, older kids told Bull Calf that he would end up retarded because of his father; Bull Calf's father thought it was amusing to let his eight-year-old son sip beer and get dizzy. Now that he was thirty-two, Bull Calf had sadly concluded that those children had been correct. He couldn't get an interesting job and he couldn't remember anyone's phone number without writing it down. "If I ever have a baby," he said, "I will never get it drunk."

Koombah was her friend. He liked to talk about isomorphism, although he was not aware that this topic had a name. "Being a farmer is like being an artist," he would say. "It's like being a painter or a sculptor: It doesn't matter how good you are at your job, because you don't have any control over the value of what you're producing. Everything is dictated by demand and climate, and you can't control either of those things. Two people will do the same things in the same way, and one will make a living while the other goes bankrupt. Sometimes I feel like Lou Reed." People said Koombah looked like Rollie Fingers without the handlebar mustache. This meant he didn't look like anyone. "Everyone talks like they're on TV now," he said. "I hate talking to anyone on Monday morning. Every Monday conversation ends up being an interrogation, because everyone watches *60 Minutes* the night before and thinks all their conversations need to be an attack. TV controls the way we think we're supposed to talk. People don't even realize this is happening, but this is happening."

Disco Ball was her friend. He was a married man. He had fallen madly in lust with a twenty-four-year-old woman when he was only nineteen. Their wedding was picturesque and well attended. She was vivacious and loquacious, which made her flirtatious. Words ending in *-ious* are bad for marriages. Her behavior drove Disco Ball toward madness. He constantly accused her of cheating on him; it was all they ever talked about. They would go to lawn parties, and Disco Ball would spend the entire evening tracking her movements, mentally cataloging a checklist of future indictments. He could not stop himself from believing that his wife was having sex with every man she met. He opened her mail and looked through her purse. He asked trick questions about her day-to-day activities and assessed the credibility of her answers. He sometimes hid a tape recorder in the pantry, exited the house for the afternoon, and then checked the machine at night to see if she had made any suspicious phone calls while he was away. Finally, his vivacious, loquacious wife could not take it anymore: She arbitrarily claimed to have slept with the driver of a Schwan's ice cream delivery truck, mostly because it did not seem to matter if she was unfaithful or not. When she confessed this fabrication to Disco Ball, he did not know how to react; he had obsessed over this event for six years, but he'd never rehearsed a response. He always assumed this would be the kind of information he would *find out* (as opposed to being told directly). Seeing no other viable option, he unzipped his pants in the living room and pissed all over his wife's four-hundred-dollar stereo system. She responded by kicking him out of the house and ignoring all the apologetic phone calls he made twice a week. This was three years ago. He didn't understand how to file for a divorce, so they were still legally bound by the state of North Dakota. "Misplaced jealousy," Disco Ball was wont to say. "That's what destroyed my marriage: misplaced jealousy. That, and the urination."

Drelf (the Drunken Elf) was her friend, but it was complicated. The Drelf had problematic, unpopular thoughts he was unafraid to speak aloud. He not-so-secretly despised all the people who made fun of his height, which meant he not-so-secretly despised almost every man he had ever met. When he was in grade school, he wrestled his tormentors and regularly won, sometimes biting their legs and shoulders. During his high school years, he dedicated summer vacations to physical self-improvement, eventually growing into a tenacious wingback who caught forty-four passes in a single season (an Owl school record at the time). While studying agribusiness at North Dakota State, he adopted the persona of pussy hound, sleeping with twenty-four women (a so-called "case of bitches") in less than three years, including one All-American volleyball player who was seven inches taller than he was. He returned to become general manager of the Owl grain elevator and earned forty-nine thousand dollars a year, more money than almost everyone he knew. It did not matter. It did not make him a normal-sized human. He would grow despondent when he was intoxicated, and Julia would tell him that there were many, many things worse than being affluent and five foot four. "I suppose you're right," he would say. "I could be a midget. Or a midget woman."

The Flaw brothers (Ass Jam and Baby Ass Jam) were probably her friends, but she wasn't positive; they didn't drink very much.

Buck Buck was her friend. Buck Buck had a clandestine compulsion: Whenever he sat across from another person, he was possessed by an overwhelming urge to lean forward and kiss them. The gender and age of the individual did not matter; a voice inside his brain kept saying, "Do it. Just do it. See what it's like. See what happens." Buck Buck had never acted upon this urge, but it made him feel very guilty (and sometimes bisexual). One night in December he finally told Julia about this compulsion when Yoda's was almost empty. Julia asked if he was only telling her this because he wanted to kiss her. "I do want to kiss you," he said, "but only because you're no different than anyone else."

Phil Buzkol was her friend. When he was nine, Phil built a snow fort with another boy named Toby Haugen. When it started to get dark, Toby went home. Four hours later, Phil's parents showed up at the Haugens' home. "Do you know where Lil' Phillip is?" they asked. "He never came home for supper." It was now 8:30 p.m. Toby said they had been building snow forts, but that was all he knew. Everyone got flashlights. Toby led a search party back to the spot where they had tried to build an igloo. They found nothing but whiteness and blackness. Somehow, the fort had collapsed. Phil Buzkol Sr. began to panic. He took his shovel and attacked the snow, seemingly at random. Almost immediately, he hit something that was kind of soft and kind of hard. It was his son. The flesh was stiff. The boy's eyes were open. His arms were frozen above his head. They thought he was dead, but he wasn't; his body had reflexively shut down the flow of blood to his extremities in order to keep his heart and brain alive. The fort had collapsed because the snow was dry and porous, which was the same reason stray molecules of oxygen were able to permeate the icy sarcophagus and nestle in his little lungs. His parents rushed him to the hospital. Lil' Phillip did not speak for three days. Everyone feared brain damage. Here again, everyone was wrong. On the fourth day he started speaking and eating, and by the sixth day he was the same nine-year-old boy he had been before. For twenty years, Phil never discussed this incident with anyone. But he talked about it with Julia, because she was a girl. "For a moment, I was pretty fucking worried," Phil said. "It was the scariest thing that had ever happened to me. It was probably the scariest thing that had ever happened to anybody. I'd dug one tunnel horizontally from the side of a snowdrift, and then a second one—vertically, from the top of the drift—that went straight down. The two tunnels intersected. That's where I got stuck. I tried to enter through the vertical tunnel with my arms above my head, but I couldn't make it all the way down and I couldn't back up. That's when the cave-in happened. It was unbelievable. I couldn't believe it. Everything changed so quickly. And then—for maybe two minutes—I thought, 'Fuck you, Toby Haugen. Thanks for killing me.' And then I got scared again, and then I thought about my mom, and then I tried to dig my way out, and then I started to think about my mom again, and then I thought maybe I was just having a dream, and then I felt sleepy. That was the last thing I remember. It was really cold." Julia asked if the event still haunted him. "Oh, not really," he said. "I mean, obviously, yes. But not really. It's mostly just a story I never tell anyone. These things happen to people."

Little Stevie Horse 'n' Phone was her friend. She considered him *cute, enthusiastic, idiotic,* and *sometimes annoying.* He chewed his nails and talked about cryptozoology. "Loch Ness is twenty-three miles long and eight hundred and thirteen feet deep," he told her on multiple evenings. "The water is exceptionally cold. The loch also serves as the storage reservoir for a hydroelectric scheme, the first of its kind in Scotland. Its turbines originally provided power for a nearby mill, but now electricity is generated and supplied to the national grid." Little Stevie was the only person in North Dakota who could lecture about the Loch Ness monster for over an hour without using the word *monster.* "I've seen the Robert Rhines underwater photographs, and I think any rational person would have to conclude that he's probably captured the image of some kind of warm-blooded plesiosaur," he would say. "But then again, who knows for certain? Rhines was a credible aquatic investigator, but he was also a U.S. patent attorney. Maybe he had an agenda. I've seen copies of the CIA documents where Special Ops guys speculate that the creature is the *ghost* of a dinosaur—perhaps some kind of astral projection, or something along those lines—but that doesn't strike me as realistic." Little Stevie Horse 'n' Phone had no idea that he was abnormal. Such a notion did not strike him as realistic.

B.K. (aka Brother Killer) was her friend. Brother Killer liked to talk about Vance Druid. All the boys did this to varying degrees, but B.K. did it almost exclusively. "Vance and I played football together," he said. "I was on the field when he made That Play. I threw a block for him. It was a key block. *Key.* You couldn't see it when they showed it on TV, because my block was out of the frame. The cameraman was an amateur. But I was part of That Play. I was. I was totally part of it. Vance is such a cool guy. You'd never even know he made That Play unless somebody else brought it up. He was always like that. About everything. He never cares about what things are supposed to mean. One time we were all over at the White Indian, and some jackass—this guy named Kent Jones—decides he wants to challenge Vance to a drinking contest. Kent's acting like he's in ninth grade or something. It's embarrassing. But Kent keeps talking about this and talking about this and talking about this, and finally Vance says, 'Okay, fine. Let's have the goddamn contest.' So Kent pulls out two twenty-dollar bills and orders twenty shots of Jäger and sets them up in two rows of ten, and the two guys sit across from each other. The rule is that each man will drink one shot every six minutes. If they're both still alive after an hour, they start over with four shots of Lord Calvert. These are standard rules. So everybody gathers around the table, and somebody says, 'Go.' Kent drinks his shot down and Vance drinks his shot down. And then Vance walks away. Kent says, 'Where are you going?' And Vance says, 'I guess you win. Thanks for the Jäger.' And then Vance sits back down at the bar, orders a Schmidt, and goes back to watching TV. So Kent gets stuck with eighteen shots of Jägermeister, and he just has to sit there and throw back shots all night like a lonely fucking asshole. Brilliant. See what I mean? Vance is such a cool guy. I always love telling that story. Always. It's a classic."

"Valentine was right," Julia said to Naomi, boozy from vodka and befriended by all. "I like it here."

Naomi was lying on her back on the other side of the booth. She was watching the ceiling fan rotate. The ceiling fan wasn't on. The only part of Naomi's body still visible to Julia was her left hand, still wrapped around a drink that remained on the table. Sometimes she would hear Naomi exhale; blue smoke would rise from the void. "You like it here," she repeated. "I'm glad you like it here, Jules."

"This is an easy place to live," Julia said. "Everybody is so nice. Everybody is different, but everybody is the same."

"I'm different," spoke the void. "I'm not the same. Who the fuck are you to say that?"

"That wasn't an insult."

"I know. I'm sorry. I love you." Her hand disappeared from the edge of the table. The cocktail remained.

"I love you, too," said Julia. "We're good friends. I love my good friends."

"Fuckin' A."

"Maybe I'll try to coach volleyball next year."

"What?"

"Volleyball. How hard can it be?"

"What are you talking about? What did you say?"

"Never mind," said Julia.

"I love you, Jules," said Naomi. "We're good friends. Jules. Remember Jules? We're the good friends inside this bar."

"Yeah, I remember," said Jules. "I remember."

JANUARY 11, 1984

(Horace)

When that afternoon's café conversation started at 3:05, the principal topic of debate had been Vice President George Bush—specifically, what he had done (or not done) while in charge of the CIA. However, the discourse slowly evolved into a different question: What was the worst thing any person could do?

The answer—for reasons that were supposed to be self-evident—was operating as a spy. This was what Marvin Windows insisted. Marvin hated deception.

"There should be no trial for anyone accused of treason," he said. "There should be no judge. There should be no jury. Just find the man and kill the man. Point a pistol at the traitor's head and squeeze the trigger until the hammer goes *click*."

"But what if the man is not a spy?" asked Edgar.

"Doesn't matter," said Marvin. "Maybe he's guilty, maybe he isn't. Sometimes we're right, sometimes we're wrong. Justice isn't perfect. But if the penalty for spying was *always* execution, regardless of proof . . . well, you wouldn't have to worry about who was—and who wasn't—a spy. The problem would disappear overnight."

"That's asinine," said Gary Mauch. "You can't shoot people on suspicion. Just think what would happen to our own men over in Moscow and East Berlin and down in Cuba. If we started randomly murdering everyone we thought was a Soviet spy, they'd do the same to our spies."

"They should," said Marvin. "The Russians should freely

execute any and every spy they find. That is completely within their rights."

"You're losing your mind," said Gary. "You're talking like a drunken sow."

"No," said Marvin. "I don't care what country you're from or what you claim to believe: There is nothing worse than a man who pretends to be someone he is not. There is nothing more pathetic. What kind of person builds his life around lying? What kind of person builds trust, solely with the intention of betraying those who trust him most? The desires that motivate a spy are worse than whatever objective he thinks he's fighting for. It's the coward's way. Nothing could be less honorable. It is almost like they *want* to die. They're asking for it. They know they're horseshit."

Horace swallowed a mouthful of wet caffeine and closed his eyes. It was not his practice to disagree with this man; Marvin Windows understood things that he did not. Only Edgar was stupid enough to regularly question his principles. But this time Marvin was dead wrong. Horace could not allow this conjecture to pass without a confrontation.

"That's not really so," said Horace. "I understand what you're saying, but that's not how it is. Take the case of Juan Pujol, for example. Pujol is a decent fella who grows up in Spain during the 1930s, hating the Nazis. He hates the Russians, too. He hates fascists. He wants to be a spy for Britain, but the snooty Brits turn him away. So—in order to become a spy for England—he becomes a spy for Germany. He becomes part of the Nazis' war machine, and he does a lot of quality work for them. He creates something like twenty-seven separate identities. Twenty-seven! But once he's a Nazi insider, he starts delivering misinformation for the Allies. He tells the Nazis that Allied forces are planning to invade the north of France, which prompts them to withhold troops from the beach at Normandy. We all know what happened there. Juan Pujol probably won us the European theater. So here's a man who nearly gets knighted by the British, but he also gets the Iron Cross from Germany. And he deserved both honors. You think they should have killed this guy for being exceptionally good at his job? That's not right."

Two days before, Horace had finished a 452-page book called *Code Name Garbo: The Juan Pujol Story*.

"To hell with that. They should have rekilled him twenty-seven times," said Marvin. "You talk as if this Spaniard was some kind of hero. All he did was lie to people. That was his whole vocation. He could have just as well moved to California to be an actor and drink orange juice. That's all a spy is: an actor. It doesn't take talent to be a liar. It doesn't take guts to be a liar."

"But sometimes it does," replied Horace. "Look at Takeo Yoshikawa. Here's a Jap from Tokyo who knew as much about the U.S. Navy as anyone at Annapolis. He moves to Hawaii in '41 and rents an apartment overlooking Pearl Harbor. Now, bear in mind that this kid is twenty-seven years old. He wanders around Oahu and takes notes on everything. He's like a computer. He rents a single-engine prop plane and flies around the naval base. He fashions a reed into a breathing device so he can swim underwater. A swamp reed! That's what he breathed through! If that happened in a John Wayne movie, you wouldn't believe it. But it happened. He invented that. And this one little man—working completely alone—is the reason the Japs were able to deliver the most devastating blow in American history. And we never even caught him. He destroyed all his data on the day of the attack. He moved back to Japan and opened a candy store. And you know what he got for that? Do you know what his reward was? Nothing. He was ostracized. Once the war was over, the Jap media blamed him for starting it. They blamed him for Nagasaki! He died a despised man, trying to sell Tootsie Rolls to gutless freeloaders. So you tell me, Marvin: You explain to me how Takeo Yoshikawa didn't have brains and guts. You explain to me how Takeo Yoshikawa didn't lead a brilliant, tragic existence."

During the winter of 1982, Horace had read a 369-page biography titled *The Brilliant, Tragic Existence of Takeo Yoshikawa.*

"Listen to this guy," said Bud Haugen. "You're like some kind of Berkeley professor now."

"I have always had an interest in espionage," replied Horace.

It was so goddamn annoying: What did Marvin Windows know about the motives of spies? Maybe their drive was completely internal. Maybe they just liked knowing things. In the context of war, the only people who know the real truth are the spies; they are the only ones who can tell the difference between what's fact and what's fiction. They are the only people with a fixed perspective. Everyone else can only build a reality out of propaganda and conjecture.

Horace could have been one of these people.

Seven years before she stopped sleeping, something appeared on Alma's left areola. It looked like a black ladybug. It wasn't hard, but it also wasn't soft; it was alien. For weeks, they both examined it on a nightly basis. They poked at it with their index fingers. "What do you think it is?" Alma kept asking. "I do not know," Horace replied a few dozen times. He told her to see a doctor. "I'm afraid of what he might tell me," she kept saying. "That is why you need to go," repeated Horace. "Please don't tell anyone about this," she said. "I won't," he replied.

Variations of this conversation happened many, many times. It was their secret dilemma.

Alma eventually saw her doctor on a rainy day in April. The man had no theories; he sent her to a different doctor. That one used a scalpel to slice part of it away; the cutting did not hurt Alma's breast, which seemed like a bad sign. The doctor said he would conduct a battery of tests and would know more in seven to ten days. He did not seem particularly worried, but that signified nothing. The doctor was a stranger. His actions were meaningless.

Horace and Alma worried about those tests, but not in the way that modern people worry: They did not talk about it, nor did they awkwardly avoid the subject on purpose. They just thought about the problem while doing other things. On the eighth day, Horace decided to think about the problem while he fixed the lawn mower (a few inches of bailing twine had become entangled around its blades). "I will be in the shop," he called to Alma as he opened the back door. However, he did not go to the shop and he did not fix the mower; he let the door slam itself shut and quietly walked down the basement stairs. Sometimes he did this on lazy afternoons; sometimes Horace would proclaim that he was going to go outside to do something practical, but then he'd spontaneously elect to slink into the basement and sit on an army cot, alone in the dark, looking at nothing. He had behaved this way his entire life.

It was cool in the basement. It was damp. Basements have predictable climates. Horace was sitting on the cot when the phone rang. He could follow Alma's steps across the living room and into the kitchen. The rest of the house was soundless.

"Hello," she said. He could hear her voice, barely muffled by the floorboards.

There was a pause.

"Yes, this is she." Pause. "Yes." Pause. "Yes." Pause. "Okay, what does that mean?" Long pause. "Oh, it's so good to hear you say that." Pause. "That's what I thought, too. We got all worried over nothing." Pause. "Good, good. Thanks for calling. Thank you. I will. I will." The phone emitted a wounded *ding* when she hung up the receiver.

Horace loved his wife, and he knew that he loved her. But he was still shocked by how wonderful this news made him feel. It was like an injection of morphine. He suddenly realized that he'd had a stomachache for more than a week; he didn't realize this until it instantly evaporated. He felt like he was going to cry or puke or laugh. He began to thank God.

Then he heard something else.

He heard an unexpected, familiar sound: He heard the sound of a finger dragging the numbers on a rotary phone, counterclockwise. He heard that sound seven times in succession. There was another pause. And then he heard this:

"Hey . . . they just called . . . no, just right now . . . it's nothing . . . no, not cancer, not anything . . . they don't really know for certain, but it's nothing to worry about . . . I know . . . I *know,* honestly . . . no, not yet . . . I will . . . okay, I will . . . I will . . . bye-bye." Alma hung up the phone. He heard her footfalls retrace across the house, returning toward the back door. He heard the door open. "Horace," she called toward the shop. "Horace?"

Now, there are men who would have heard this conversation and assumed what might seem apparent; they would have assumed their wife was sleeping with another man. But Horace was not one of those men. Was it *possible* that Alma was having an affair? Oh, it was possible. Anything is possible. Humans have walked on the moon. But it was not *likely,* and he was exceedingly confident of that. It was simply not in her nature. If Alma was having an affair, it would contradict everything he had ever known about who she was and how she lived; as a result, he would have to rethink everything he knew about every person he'd ever met. It was beyond reality. He did not overreact. But Horace had still learned something vital and complex: There was someone else in the world who knew all the things no one else was supposed to know. Clearly, there was someone to whom Alma told everything—perhaps even things she did not tell Horace. There was someone who likely knew details about his life that were profoundly private. There was someone who probably knew how much money he made, and what TV shows made him laugh, and how much he secretly hated his dead father's dead father, and that he was deathly afraid of swooping birds. And he had no idea who this person was. He would never know whom his wife just called on the telephone.

It was troubling.

Yet, still . . . knowing it made him feel so much better. It made him feel smarter. *And knowing it was enough.* Nothing else was required. He did not need to confront Alma, and he did not need other people to recognize that he had been clever enough to deduce this truth.

He could have been Takeo Yoshikawa.

Horace began to walk up the staircase, his face showing nothing. He was a wall of bricks. "I'm down here, Alma," he said. "I was looking for a Vise-Grip. Who was on the telephone?"

He kissed his wife when she told him the good news. He acted surprised.

That was nineteen years ago.

"I don't give a shit about what Honda Fugimoto did at Pearl Harbor," said Marvin. "I'm not impressed by any of that. If he got ostracized back in Japan, it's only because he deserved it. He deserved worse. It doesn't matter whose side you're on. At least the Japanese respect loyalty. Your Jap hero made a living spreading secrets and telling lies. That was his whole identity."

"Secrets are lies," Edgar interjected.

"Yes," said Marvin. "Secrets are lies. Secrets are lies."

"I suppose there's truth in what you say," said Horace. And there was: Secrets *are* lies. But these people didn't understand what that actually meant, and there was no use in trying to explain. He surrendered, but he admitted nothing.

JANUARY 17, 1984

(Mitch)

Nobody looked at Grendel's penis. What was the point? Doing so would have only made them feel like infants.

All twelve of them showered at once, sharing one bottle of Suave shampoo while guzzling complimentary concession-stand Cokes from six-ounce plastic cups. Steam made everything Amazonian. Music that Mitch did not recognize distortedly blared from a thirty-five-dollar JVC ghetto blaster. The first song was futuristic, churchlike, and boring. The second song celebrated the inherent pleasure of jumping. The third song promoted the nation of Panama. It was almost 10 o'clock, and the Owl Lobos had upset the Hankinson Pirates in basketball. Contrary to preseason expectations, Owl was emerging as a hard-court wrecking crew: No one could physically compete with the Power That Was Grendel. Tonight he had scored twenty points, grabbed twenty-four rebounds, and blocked thirteen shots. He terrified people. He could dunk with either hand, and sometimes he did. Vocal members of the community convinced Walter Valentine to install glass backboards in the gymnasium, solely because it was believed Grendel might shatter one. Everyone agreed that such an event would be thrilling.

Grendel did not care about any of this. He was still thinking about football season, and sometimes tits.

Against Hankinson, Mitch had scored nine points while adding five rebounds. On the season, he was averaging 8.9 points and 5.1 rebounds. Mitch didn't over- or underachieve. He preferred playing defense, especially now that they were letting him wear a T-shirt under his jersey, just like Horace Broadnax. Laidlaw was merely the assistant coach for varsity basketball, so he wasn't in a position to control Mitch's life, beyond making fun of his name during practice and accusing him of having a sleeping disorder during English class. The head hoop coach was a new elementary school teacher named Bob Keebler. He wore sunglasses indoors and spoke with a monotone voice, usually about how God and Bobby Knight expected everyone to work harder. Had the juvenile population of Owl not included an illiterate six-foot-eight-inch rebounding cyborg, the Lobos' record would have stood at 2–8; because it did, they were 9–1. Everyone in town thought Bob Keebler was a genius. The only people who disagreed were the twelve players he coached (who thought he was uncreative and impotent) and his assistant John Laidlaw (who thought Keebler resembled cult leader Jim Jones).

Mitch stood next to Grendel in the shower. He could feel the water ricocheting off Grendel's shoulders and landing on his hairless chest. It reminded him that he was weak.

"Good game," Mitch said to Grendel. "You ruled the glass, man. That is your glass. You rule it."

"Fucking refs," mumbled Grendel.

"Who cares about the refs," said Mitch. "We won by twelve. We could have won by twenty."

"The refs didn't call shit," he replied. "If I ever see that one fucker with the mustache, I'm going to rip his neck open and watch him bleed to death. I'm gonna skull-fuck his wife and blast my load through her eye socket."

"Yeah," said Mitch. "Yeah. But still . . . nice game."

"Shut up, Vanna."

Mitch stepped out of the shower and dried himself with a towel that had not been washed since November. Some of the slacker kids who hated extracurricular activities were planning a postgame car party at the apple grove, but Mitch was not going; it was a Tuesday night, and it was five below zero, and drinking beer made him feel insincere and inauthentic. He asked Zebra if he was going to the party.

"Maybe," said Zebra. "Are you going?"

"I don't know," said Mitch. "I'll probably only go if everybody else does. Are you going?"

"I don't know if I'm going. Do you want to go? I'll go if you go."

"I'm not going," said Mitch. "Unless you decide to go." They had a lot of conversations like this.

"Grendel was pretty badass tonight," said Zebra. Somehow, Zebra had managed to score four points despite playing less than one full minute of the game. "Grendel's a white Moses Malone."

"Yeah, whatever," said Mitch. "He's kind of a cockpunch. I don't like that dude. He's not cool. He's the Antichrist."

"The Antichrist? Since when?"

"Since now."

Mitch had not appreciated the way Grendel had said, "Shut up, Vanna." He said *Vanna* exactly the way Laidlaw had always intended. And the moment that happened, something suddenly occurred to him: Why should he be nice to a person just because he happened to be big and fast and aggressive and Antichristlike? Grendel offered nothing to society. To hell with that dude.

"Well, whatever," said Zebra. "But who cares how cool he is? I mean, come on: twenty-four rebounds? Are you kidding me?"

"He's not as good as Jelinski," said Mitch. Todd Jelinski had played for Owl in the late 1970s and had been named to the All-Conference team twice. Last winter he had been killed in an ice-fishing accident.

"Vanna, are you high? Grendel is *way* better than Jelinski. It's not even close. I don't care how dead Jelinski is."

"He's not as good as Jordan Buhr, either." Jordan Buhr was a five-foot-nine-inch guard for Pembina High School, a town four hundred miles from Owl. Buhr was left-handed and averaged forty-one points a night. Mitch had never seen him play, but he'd read about his statistics in a newspaper column by Abe Winter of *The Bismarck Tribune.*

"You're crazy," said Zebra. "Isn't Jordan Buhr supposed to be a dwarf? Grendel would probably eat that kid with gravy."

"If Grendel fought Cubby Candy, Cubby would fuck him up," Mitch said desperately. He did not believe this, but he still said it. Unfortunately, Curtis-Fritz (who was putting on a tie after not playing at all) was eavesdropping on their conversation.

"I knew it!" he yelled. "I fucking *knew it.* Where the fuck is Drug Man? Get his ass in here. I knew it, Vanna, I knew you always secretly agreed with me. I knew it. Cubby Candy would beat Grendel's butt. I agree completely."

The entire locker room could hear this.

Mitch thought about telling Curtis-Fritz to quiet the fuck down, but it was too late. Everybody knew everything, all the time. And now they knew this.

"Who is gonna beat my ass?" asked Grendel. He was drying his hair with a towel that had not been washed since 1982. He was completely nude.

"Cubby Candy," said Curtis-Fritz. "Mitch says Cubby Candy claims he could kick your ass."

"No," said Mitch. He started to feel waves of nervousness creeping out of his stomach, up into his throat and down into his scrotum. "No. No. No. That's not what I said. No. That's wrong."

"Then what the fuck did you say?" asked Grendel. His shoulders appeared to be pulsing in place. Mitch felt like he was standing in front of a cobra. His options seemed limited.

He elected to lie.

"It was nothing," said Mitch. "Cubby Candy *supposedly* said that playing basketball was for queers. And then somebody else said, 'Well, what about Chris Sellers? He plays basketball and he's not queer.' And then Cubby *supposedly* said, 'Well, he's a queer, too.' So—basically—he did not say he could beat you up. He just said you were a homosexual. But I think the discussion was originally about beating up gay people or something, so maybe that's how this rumor got started. But that's all I know about it. Seriously. I was not even there."

Grendel pensively stared at the tile floor, water dripping from his forehead. He looked like a Sasquatch pondering an existential paradox. However, this was not the case, because he eventually just said, "Fuck that guy," and walked back to his locker. He stepped directly into his pants. Grendel never wore underwear.

Crisis averted.

Civilian dressing resumed.

The stereo described the exploits of a socially popular guitarist named Jimmy.

"Is that shit true?" whispered Zebra.

"I have no idea," replied Mitch.

"Do you still want to possibly go to the party?"

"No way." He was now too nervous to be around people who weren't Zebra.

"Cool," Zebra responded. "Me neither." They wordlessly pulled their game-day sweaters over their heads. Before putting on his shoes, Zebra walked over to the ghetto blaster and ejected the cassette. He jammed it into his pants pocket, sans case.

"What were we listening to in there?" said Mitch. "Was that supposed to be acid rock?"

"I just got it," said Zebra. "It's *MCMLXXXIV.*"

"What?"

"*MCMLXXXIV.*"

"You're such a longhair. How long did it take you to memorize that?"

"Almost two hours!"

"What does it mean?"

"*1984,*" said Zebra. "It translates as *1984.*"

"Really?" asked Mitch. "That's weird. Is it about the book we read in class?"

Zebra considered this for seven seconds.

"I don't know," he slowly concluded. "I suppose it must be."

JANUARY 20, 1984

(Julia)

Consumption of gin made her a scarier person than she was. This is not uncommon. It happens to lots of people.

The three of them were sitting by the window: Naomi, Ted, and Julia. Naomi thought she might have contracted strep throat, so she was drinking vodka and orange juice. Ted was only drinking cans of beer, so he was barely buzzing. But Julia was going for the jugular, one glass at a time. Julia was like a Cadillac with a brick on the accelerator, pointed toward the side of a mountain.

On the other side of the window, the snow was magnificent.

It was the best kind of snow to stare at through glass. It was Christmas-card snow: mammoth, ultralight flakes that took decades to reach the ground. The particles were so weightless that any breeze could overtake gravity; as a result, it appeared to be snowing from every direction simultaneously. It was snowing down and it was snowing up.

"Look toward the streetlight," said Naomi. "Isn't that remarkable? It almost looks like a snow globe."

"Well, no shit," said Julia. "That's what snow globes are supposed to look like: falling snow. Did you think that was just a coincidence?"

"Be nice to me," said Naomi. "I have a sore throat."

Ted placed his hand on his right front pocket to make sure his keys were still there. He then felt his right buttock to make sure he still had his wallet. He did this unconsciously sixty or seventy times a day. Ted could not understand why these women drank so much. He understood why *he* drank, but their reasons had to be different. When compared to himself, they seemed both happier and sadder at the same time.

"Did your kids make you sick?" he asked Naomi. "Did they infect you?"

"I doubt it," she said. "I don't see them enough to share any germs. Ricky spends ninety percent of his life in his bedroom. He quarantines himself when he's healthy."

"I noticed that you never talk about your kids anymore," said Ted.

"What would I say? I don't know anything about them. They never talk to me."

"Well, what does Ricky like to do?" asked Ted.

"I honestly have no idea," Naomi responded. "What do seventh-grade boys like to do? I assume he just sits in his room and either reads books or jerks off. Although I think he started stealing my cigarettes, so I guess we have at least one thing in common."

"Does he get along with Butch?" asked Ted. Butch was Naomi's husband. He was a sugar-beet farmer, which meant the government subsidized everything he did, which meant he and Naomi were rich. Not rich compared to the rest of America, but rich compared to the majority of Owl. They were "Owl Rich." They had a satellite dish and an aboveground pool, and sometimes they took family vacations to Florida or the Grand Canyon.

"Butch doesn't say anything about Ricky," said Naomi. "Butch doesn't say anything about anything. He just likes the TV. That's his little friend. That's his little square friend."

The conversation was making Julia bored, and that made her feel less intoxicated. "I am going up to the bar," she said. "What do you want me to get you? More drinks, more drinks, more drinks?"

They both said they wanted nothing. Julia sighed and left the table. The Dog Lover was behind the bar, hands on hips, Labrador by his side. His intentions for the evening were as straightforward as they were diabolical: He wanted to hurt somebody's feelings. That singular desire informed every conversation he had. His dedication to anecdotal cruelty was so sincere that it almost seemed admirable; the Dog Lover was like an antihumanist version of Ralph Nader, except eight inches shorter and less interested in seat-belt technology.

"Gimme a G & T," said Julia. "Please."

"I don't know why you're so intent on getting inebriated," said the Dog Lover nonchalantly. "Your boyfriend isn't coming in tonight."

"Who's my boyfriend?" asked Julia. But she knew who he was referring to.

"Your boyfriend was already here this afternoon," said the Dog Lover. "He said he had plans tonight. He said he had *a previous engagement.* So mysterious! But—then again—who knows? Maybe he's two-timing you. Maybe he knows a boozy school teacher in Wishek, too."

"Just make my drink," she replied. The walls of Yoda's tavern were starting to revolve counterclockwise, but just barely. It reminded her of the summer her family went to Seattle and her dad took her to a restaurant at the top of the Space Needle. What a clean, uninteresting vacation.

"Maybe you should direct your seductive efforts elsewhere," said the Dog Lover. He knew he was going to destroy her; it made him feel like he was on amphetamines. He nodded toward the corner of the bar. "Maybe you should unleash some of your Wisconsin romance on old Woo-Chuck over there. I bet Woo-Chuck played some football back in the sixties. Probably six-man football, back when men were still men, except for the ones who were smart enough to go to Canada instead of Southeast Asia. Isn't that right, Woo-Chuck?"

"Fuck off," said Woo-Chuck. "Fix the woman her drink. Do your job."

"Sorry there, Woo," said the Dog Lover, turning back to Julia. "I guess Woo-Chuck didn't score enough touchdowns for a high-class historian such as yourself. He just shot people in Cambodia. He never made it on the TV like Your Man did."

"Why are you like this?" asked Julia. "What is your problem?"

"You do realize that he's never going to marry you," said the Dog Lover. "He only pays attention to you because you're somebody new. He only talks to you because he's already talked to everybody else a million times. I'm sure you must realize that. You seem relatively intelligent."

These words did not hurt Julia. She knew they were not true. She knew the Dog Lover was simply trying to hurt her, because that was what he did. But it occurred to her that his reason for making this specific attack was (probably) because that *was* what some people in this bar thought about her relationship with Vance. And if *some* people thought that, then *all* people thought that. Because everybody in Owl had the same thoughts about everything.

This was humiliating. It did not matter that it was untrue.

Julia felt the blood inside her head, sliding over and around her skull. Her body was 111 degrees. She looked at the Dog Lover. Half his face was smiling.

"You killed that cat," she said.

"I didn't kill any cats," said the Dog Lover. "Christ, how drunk *are* you?"

"Yes, you did," she said. "I know that you did. For one thing, if you hadn't killed that cat, you wouldn't have responded by saying, 'I didn't kill any cats.' You would have said, 'What the fuck are you talking about?' And for another thing, I know you did it. I just do. I heard you killing it. I heard you."

"Did you just drop acid or something?"

"Shut the fuck up, you fucking sadist. You tortured that cat on Halloween. You and your sick bastard friends."

"I honestly have no idea what you're talking about," said the Dog Lover. "Go sit down and drink yourself to death." He slid the gin in front of her. "Two dollars."

"You're gonna burn in hell for what you did," said Julia. She lost her balance slightly and staggered to her left. It took a moment to regain her composure. "You are going to die alone, you twisted fucking cat murderer."

"Duly noted," said the Dog Lover. "Now leave me alone, hooker."

Julia picked up her glass of gin and tonic. In her hand, it felt like the answer to all her problems. It weighed more than dialogue. Julia threw it as hard as she could, aiming for the forehead of a man standing three feet in front of her. She missed; she had always sucked at softball. The projectile flew past the Dog Lover's left ear, smashing against a Budweiser mirror that hung above the liquor bottles. The mirror became a psychedelic spiderweb. Her eight-ounce highball glass turned into an art project you'd have to keep away from small children. The room instantly smelled like gin and tonic and violence, which transmutes as evergreen trees and ozone and uric acid. Everybody stopped talking. Journey kept coming out of the jukebox. The wheel in the sky kept on turning.

Three seconds passed. They felt longer than the seven months Julia had lived in Owl.

"What did you just do?" asked the Dog Lover. "WHAT THE FUCK DID YOU JUST DO?" He was shaking. Everybody could see this. He was stunned. The Dog Lover finally pointed one finger at Ted, who was unconsciously checking to see if he still had his wallet. "You! Ted! Get this crazy fucking slut out of my bar. Get this crazy fucking slut out of this bar before I break both her fucking arms."

"I'm sorry," said Julia. Jesus, she was so drunk. Had this really happened?

"Shut up," said the Dog Lover. "Quit talking. You're crazy."

Julia felt two masculine hands upon her shoulders. "Let's go," said Ted. He backed her up like a grain truck and directed her toward the door. He pushed forward; eventually her feet moved as she intended. Every step took effort. It was like walking through the kill zone of Everest. Behind her, she could hear Naomi talking to the Dog Lover, saying something along the lines of, "We're really sorry about this, you goddamn pigfucker." Julia fell out the front door with an unfathomable, zombielike slowness; it was as if she were wearing a parachute. She landed on the sidewalk. The fall did not hurt, but she could feel the dry snow on her palms and on her knees. Ted put his hands under her armpits and dragged her vertical. It was a night devoid of dignity.

"He tortured that cat," said Julia. "I know he did. I know it. I heard it dying."

"I'm sure he did," said Ted. "He seems like the kind of bartender who tortures cats."

Main Street was empty. They both stood there, looking at the ground. Julia began to cry drunken, nonspecific tears that symbolized nothing beyond abstract regret. This is not uncommon behavior.

"Are you all right?" Ted asked. "Do you need to make yourself throw up? Sometimes that helps."

"No, I'm okay," said Julia, crying harder. "I just don't . . . I mean . . . I just don't . . . oh, why do I act like this? This is so fucking . . . *juvenile.* What's wrong with me?"

"Nothing is wrong with you, Julia."

"I'm not supposed to act like this anymore. This is unacceptable. I teach things to children. I teach them about geography and George fucking Washington."

"Julia, this is only one night. You're usually a really amusing drunk. A happy drunk. Everybody thinks that."

She cranked her neck backward and woozily looked toward the bulb of the streetlight. The falling flakes were random and without purpose; the snow was drunker than she was.

"I need to change my ways," said Julia. "I can't keep doing these things. I can't keep living like this."

Like all self-destructive creatures, she completely meant these words, but only while she spoke them.

"You can do whatever you want," said Ted. "It doesn't matter. Everybody around here loves you. You're totally normal."

Just as Julia was able to tell that the Dog Lover had been lying, she was equally able to tell that Ted was not.

The door to Yoda's swung open, its glass banging against the outside wall. Naomi charged through the opening like a black rhino with a bad haircut. At moments like these, Naomi was constructed of inertia. "You are a legend now, Jules." She said this in mock admiration, but that did not mean she was kidding. "You are a legend forever. That was, in all probability, the greatest event of my lifetime."

"I'm so embarrassed," said Julia, her tear ducts closing. "I've never done anything like that in my entire life. How much am I going to have to pay for that mirror?"

"Who cares," said Naomi. "Tonight you became a different kind of person. Your life will never be the same. Now make yourself puke so we can finish getting drunk in Ted's heated garage. I have some schnapps in my trunk."

Without hesitation, Julia jammed her middle finger down her esophagus until she gagged. It was the best decision she made all night.

JANUARY 23, 1984

(Horace)

He sat in the dark, drinking a ceramic mug of room-temperature tap water. The TV was on, so the room glowed aqua. Joan Rivers was talking to Charo, making puns about her bosom; it was slightly titillating and completely undignified. Joan was no Johnny Carson. Carson was from Nebraska, and that mattered. Johnny would be back tomorrow.

The living room hadn't changed in twenty-five years, except for the television (replaced by a better model in 1976) and his reading chair (replaced in 1981—he was still getting used to it). There was a wall of books, most of which he had read twice. Two hundred and nine of them were about wars and espionage. Forty were about agriculture. Fifteen were about American history, seven were about horses, three were about college football, and the final fifty-five addressed all remaining facets of existence. There was no fiction; he had not read a novel since high school (*Tom Sawyer*).

Above his davenport was a Terry Redlin painting of two hunters shooting at mallard ducks, moments before twilight. The carpet was abysmal. There were no plants. There was a stack of newspapers, there was a *Time* magazine, there were twenty issues of *Western Horseman,* and there was a *TV Guide.* There was a framed picture of Alma with gloves on her hands and a red handkerchief on her head, working in her garden, smiling (but annoyed that she was being photographed). There was a window that overlooked the yard and his neighbor's ninety-acre field; four months ago, the field had been filled with sunflowers. Now it was filled with moonlight and winter and unplowed dirt.

Horace's pajamas made him clownlike. He was not aware of this.

Sometimes, after the *Tonight Show* ended at 11:35, he would manually turn off the television and his reading light and the floor lamps before returning to his chair. Within minutes his eyes would adjust to the darkness, and he could vaguely see the photo of Alma from across the room. She never got old. Unlike Horace, Alma would have despised growing old. It would have made her apoplectic. She couldn't even wait in line at the post office.

Sometimes Horace felt like she was still watching him, quietly judging his actions. He did not mind this. By dying, she had earned the right to judge him. Late at night, it sometimes felt as if she were still roaming about the house, clichéd and predictable as that might sound. One of the books on his wall was titled *Beyond the Boneyard*. It was a Time-Life book about the Spiritualist movement that had swept America during the middle-nineteenth century. The trend had been so widespread that even President Franklin Pierce held several séances in the White House during the 1850s.

Horace fantasized about holding a séance in his living room.

It was absurd, but he thought about it a lot. He imagined lighting candles and burning incense and wrapping a rosary around his hands, asking Alma if she was there. His eyes would be closed. The room would grow inexplicably cold, but he would be unafraid. Any outsider would see and hear nothing; Horace alone would connect with Alma's ghost. She would communicate with him through telepathy. Her voice would just emerge.

"Horace," she would say from inside his brain. "Why are you doing this?"

This was the point where the fantasy always faded. There was nothing else to fantasize about.

Horace wanted to talk to his wife, but he had no idea what he wanted to say.

Her deadness notwithstanding, he did not want to waste her time.

Joan Rivers said goodnight to her audience. Tomorrow the guests would be Eddie Murphy and Jack Hannah. Joan reiterated that Johnny would be back. Horace lifted himself from the chair, turned off the TV and his reading lamp, and sat back down. He finished his water. His eyes began to adjust to the blackness. He would be seeing Alma soon. He was not drowsy.

JANUARY 26, 1984

(Mitch)

"It's going to happen. I have proof."

"What are you talking about?"

"It's gonna go down."

Zebra was whispering to Mitch, who was listening over his shoulder while trying to remember the difference between sine, cosine, and tangent. They were in trigonometry.

"What are we talking about?"

"Grendel and Candy," said Zebra. "It's going to happen. Apocalypse Rock City."

"What? Seriously? Why?"

"No one knows. But Grendel told Candy he was going to kill him."

"When?"

"Soon."

"When did they agree to this?"

"No one knows," said Zebra. "Last night, probably. Or maybe this morning. Three days ago? No one knows."

"How did Candy react when Grendel threatened to kill him?"

"Apparently, he said: 'Enjoy work, robot.'"

"What does that mean?"

"What does it mean? It means Candy is bonkers. That's what it means."

"I still don't understand," said Mitch. "I don't see how this situation could be upon us."

"Nobody knows why," said Zebra. "Things came together."

* * *

This is what happened:

1) Grendel departed Owl High School after the basketball game against Hankinson. He got into a car with Dudley Stonerock, a cousin of Rockwell's and a recent graduate of Owl who had found employment as an arc welder. They planned to go to Stonerock's rented four-room house to drink a fifth of lime vodka, watch professional wrestling (specifically the Iron Sheik), and speak in short sentences.
2) On the drive over to Stonerock's, Grendel mentioned that someone in the locker room had claimed that Cubby Candy was (apparently) suggesting that Grendel was gay for playing basketball. Stonerock said that this seemed like something Candy would say. Dudley added, "That's fucked-up."
3) Grendel said he did not care about Cubby Candy, but agreed that what he said was fucked-up.
4) Dudley asked, "Are you going to accept that shit?"
5) Grendel didn't initially respond to this, but he realized it was a valid question.

Around 11:20, they climbed back into Stonerock's Camaro and cruised Main, looking for people to ignore. They saw Wendy Black and Allison Crowley parked under the water tower, smoking cigarettes, listening to REO Speedwagon's *Hi Infidelity*, and talking about God. Stonerock pulled up alongside them and manually rolled down his window. He said, "Why aren't you in bed, Witch Tits?" This was what Stonerock called Wendy. She was fifteen.

6) Wendy told Dudley to fuck himself and asked if they had any beer or wine coolers.
7) Dudley asked if anyone cool was driving around Owl. Allison said, "Just your boyfriend."
8) Grendel heard this.
9) Grendel said, "That guy is so dead."

10) The girls did not know what Grendel meant by this, or whom he was supposedly referring to. Allison's remark had been arbitrary and meaningless. She knew nothing of consequence.

Grendel opened the passenger door of the Camaro and walked across the street. "What is he doing?" asked Wendy. Dudley said, "I don't know, but I think I know." Grendel walked over to a tree suffering from Dutch elm disease, its trunk bulbous with a wooden cancer. He punched the tree three times. The lumber splintered. He grabbed the trunk like a child's throat and shook it back and forth, snow and ice falling from its upper branches. He screamed something about liars and fuckwads. Allison laughed so hard she dropped her cigarette. After thirty seconds of public rage, Grendel recrossed the street and pounded both his palms on the hood of Allison's car. "Cubby Candy is a corpse," he said. "Somebody tell that faggot he is going to die."

"We're all going to die," said Wendy.

"But not at the same time," said Grendel.

"Why hate on Cubby?" asked Allison. "He's a loser. But kind of cute. Kind of." Allison didn't have a father.

"He's a dead loser," said Grendel. "I don't care how cute he isn't."

"Why do you keep talking about killing people?" asked Wendy. "It's seems like the only things you ever say always involve somebody getting their brains mashed. You're like a robot."

"He is," said Dudley. "That's some truth. Witch Tits speaks the truth. You're a robot, Grendel."

"Shut your teeth."

"Why are you pissed at me?" asked Stonerock. "Do you disagree, robot?"

"I should kill all of you," Grendel said robotically. "You all deserve to be killed. After I kill Candy, I'm going to kill the rest of you dirtbags, one by one. I will build a pyramid with your dead bodies."

"That sounds like a lot of work, robot," said Wendy. "Enjoy work, robot."

Wendy turned her ignition key forward and drove away. She had a lot of phone calls to make.

Nine days later, the news finally reached Mitch's eardrums during fifth-hour trigonometry. Within the casino of his imagination, he immediately made Grendel a four-to-one favorite, assuming the weather held and Cubby did not have access to rats.

JANUARY 29, 1984

(Julia)

She didn't go to the bar anymore. Instead, she took walks. Julia would put on her mittens and her fake cashmere scarf and sneak down the rear stairwell of her building, terrified of bumping into the Dog Lover living downstairs. She had become a prisoner of war. It was an uneasy existence, perpetuated by awkwardness and remorse. It sucked. Yet the moment she escaped from her rented four-plex prison barracks, her confidence returned in full; she walked with tenacity around the perimeter of Owl, completely alone. Each lap took eighteen minutes; she usually made three of them, unless it grew too dark or too cold. Sometimes she listened to *Kissing to Be Clever* on her Walkman, but the device used up its AA batteries almost instantaneously. Rewinding Boy George cassettes was like smoking clove cigarettes inside an oxygen tent: diminishing returns.

Julia would stride past smallish white houses and pretend she did not notice all the elderly people watching through their picture windows and speculating over how goofy she must be to walk for pleasure on a winter afternoon. (The idea of walking recreationally would not become popular in North Dakota until the summer of 1987.) She could see her breath when she exhaled, but only in wisps; the mercury had hovered above thirty-two for most of the week. She stared straight ahead and dwelled upon the calories she was eliminating, imagining them as spherical units of translucent lard being shoveled into a wood-burning stove by a leprechaun. Whenever she passed her own apartment building, she visualized what the living room looked like without her inside (two-dimensionally, as if it were the stage for a play without actors). She always assumed that the phone was ringing, and that it was Naomi on the other end, and that Naomi was trying to convince her to return to Yoda's. This made her remember why people take up walking: It is because they no longer have anywhere to go.

Vehicles moving in the opposite direction passed her, the drivers nodding upward and raising two fingers off the steering wheel to gesticulate their hellos. She could see the sun disappearing when she walked toward the west, its orange light turning the distant leafless trees into bipedal allosaurus skeletons. Sometimes Owl could be a scary place, she thought. She also thought about the bar, and the people she had not seen for a week, and how unnaturally long that week had seemed, and what it would be like if Vance Druid suddenly pulled up alongside her in his Silverado pickup and tried to make conversation. She mentally scripted the dialogue they would exchange and the things they might discuss. It would be a pleasant, plausible interaction.

And then it happened, almost exactly as she had imagined.

"Why are you walking?" Vance asked after rolling down the driver's-side window, his engine still chugging. "Where are you going?"

"I'm not going anywhere," said Julia. "I'm just walking for the sake of walking."

"That's different," said Vance. "You have been MIA this week. You didn't even come out on Friday. What did you do instead? Were you reading a magazine or something?"

"I can't go back there," she said. "I can't go to the bar anymore."

"That's what Naomi told me," he replied, "but I disagree."

"I pretty much lost my mind the last time I was in Yoda's."

"That's what Naomi told me," he replied, "but I disagree."

"I'm too ashamed to show my face back there. It was mortifying. I can't believe I did that."

"It was one glass. You threw one glass," said Vance. "Everybody throws at least one glass in their life."

"I don't. Although I guess I did."

"Can't you just go to a different bar? There are plenty of bars in town. Yoda's isn't even the best one."

"That's not the point," Julia said. "The bar is not the point. That's not the problem."

Julia could hear the stereo inside Vance's pickup, even though he had turned it down to chat. She recognized the song: it was "Waiting on a Friend." She noticed that Vance still did not look directly at her when he spoke. Maybe that was something he couldn't control. She wondered if she liked him less than she originally believed.

"So, what are you doing tonight?" asked Julia. "It's Sunday. The bars are closed."

"I'm just driving around. Nothing to do today. I didn't feel like watching the Pro Bowl."

The pickup truck continued to idle. Nobody said anything for what seemed like a long time, but it was only a few seconds. How do sober people talk? That was a hard thing to remember.

"Well, I have four beers in my fridge," said Julia. "Do you want to come over and hang out for a little while?"

"I would do that," said Vance. "But four beers isn't very many."

"You can have three of them," she said. "I only want one."

"That sounds reasonable. Jump in here and we'll cruise over."

"Oh, no need for a ride," said Julia. She pointed north. "I live right there." Her apartment was three blocks away. She could see her living room window.

"I know where you live," said Vance. "Get in the truck. You don't need to walk. Quit acting like a hippie."

Julia walked around the front of the vehicle and climbed

aboard the Silverado, smiling and sighing. It was an eighteen-second ride.

• • •

BEVERAGE I: Because this is the first evening Julia has entertained a male guest since arriving in North Dakota, the two of them initially discuss the apartment. Vance mentions that it looks modern. Julia tries to straighten up while they talk, as if this unmarried buffalo farmer might care about the aesthetic alignment of magazines. Julia asks Vance what his home looks like. He says he can't remember. He asks where she purchased her movie posters. She says, "Spencer Gifts."

BEVERAGE II: Julia flips on the television. They watch a thirty-second news break; Ronald Reagan has officially announced his decision to seek a second term. "What do you think of the president?" asks Julia. "He seems to be doing an okay job," replies Vance. "He's certainly an upgrade from Mr. Peanut. I never trusted that guy, or his sweaters. Never. What kind of president listens to the Allman Brothers?" Julia asks Vance if he considers himself a Republican or a Democrat. He snorts. She understands what this means. They decide to listen to music instead; she slides *Can't Buy a Thrill* into the stereo and presses the oversized play button with her thumb. She doesn't own any Stones cassettes. She used to have a copy of *Big Hits (High Tide and Green Grass)*, but one of her college roommates left it in the sun.

BEVERAGE III: After fetching his third beer from the kitchen, Julia elects to sit on the couch next to Vance; prior to this decision, she had been sitting in an adjacent chair. Julia was now 90 percent sure she was attracted to this man and 49 percent positive he was attracted to her. Vance was 100 percent attracted to her, but he thought there was only a 33 percent chance she was interested in him (20 percent of that coming via the original invitation). She played with her hair, which (according to her magazines) was supposed to serve as a romantic signal. This confused Vance; it made him think Julia was uncomfortable. They talked about different breeds of dogs, and why the Dog Lover was a despicable human, and how they both hated the Winter Olympics.

They were out of beer.

"What do we do now?" asked Vance. This was not innuendo; he really had no idea what they should do next. He was not at ease in this situation.

"I don't know," said Julia. "I guess we'll just have to talk, unless there's a movie on channel four."

"I would like to keep talking," he said. "You're an interesting talker."

Julia was in control. She could tell.

"Well, I have one idea," she said. "Do you want to get high?"

This was a gamble.

"What?"

"Do you want to get high?"

"By taking drugs?"

"Not drugs. Just pot," said Julia. "Have you never smoked pot before? Not even during college?"

"No. Never. No. I had friends who did, but they were all pathetic burnout stoner failures."

"Oh," she said, blushing imperceptibly. "I'm sorry I brought it up. I didn't know. We don't have to."

"But—what will it do to me?" he asked. "Is it just like being really drunk?"

"Actually, it's completely different."

They looked at each other. Julia could feel her heart pounding inside her chest, because she knew what was going to happen next. She was in control of everything. Vance shrugged and smiled.

"Let me get my thesaurus," she said. He did not know if this was supposed to be some kind of drug slang, but he did not care.

• • •

—How will I know if this is working?

—Because you'll start asking that specific question a whole bunch of times.

—No, you don't understand what I'm asking. I mean, "How will I know the difference between how my mind works right now and the way my mind works normally?"

—Your question is the answer to that question.

—Maybe so. You know, I had no idea you were stockpiling narcotics here.

—That would be an exaggeration. This is my entire stockpile. You are holding my entire stockpile as we speak, and it is on fire.

—Where did you get this? I heard that you can buy marijuana at this record store in Fargo. It's called Mother's Records. You are supposed to find the Doobie Brothers album *Toulouse Street,* pay for it at the counter, and then tell the salesclerk you want your change in dimes.

—That's probably not totally true. This is just weed I kept from Wisconsin. It's old. This is nostalgia pot. It harkens back to a previous age. The Bronze Age.

—Were you one of those druggies during college?

—Sort of. Yes.

—Really. That's shocking. I'm shocked. I didn't think girls were ever like that.

—Only the cool ones. And the lazy, fat ones. Sometimes we would get high and watch made-for-TV movies, and sometimes we would just sit around and see how high we could be. We spent a lot of time talking about being high, and comparing our level of highness to previous dope-smoking occasions. That's a big part of it. The main thing you talk about while doing drugs is doing drugs.

—You know, I really, really like this apartment. You've done an excellent job with the placement of the furniture. Everything is set at a right angle. It's like we're playing Battleship.

—Thank you very much.

—Julia, I am extremely thirsty. Is this to be expected, or is something wrong with my esophagus?

—That's normal. You're normal. Would you like a glass of ice water or skim milk or Nestle Quik?

—Maybe. I don't know. Not yet. Let's not get crazy. Let's keep talking, as was our plan. Let's talk about something controversial.

—I shy away from controversy. It's like calling someone a powder monkey.

—A powder monkey?

—You know what I mean. You should never make fun of a man with a limp, because—eventually—your taunts will grow more vociferous and you'll slowly find yourself saying things like, "Nice limp, powder monkey." That's horrible. It's common sense, Vance. It's just good sportsmanship.

—What are you talking about? Are we secretly on television right now?

—Cool out. Be cool, Bison Man. That was an inside joke.

—I don't get it.

—That's because you're not far enough inside. But as long as we're on this subject—or any subject, really—can I ask you a North Dakota question?

—Absolutely.

—What the fuck is Medora?

—Medora? Medora is a town.

—Yes. So they tell me.

—It's west of Bismarck. It's in the Badlands.

—Yes. Yes, that's what I've come to discover. But why does everyone *know* about this town? I looked it up in the atlas, and the atlas said it had a population of one hundred people. Yet Medora is something we're supposed to cover this semester in Our State. Why am I supposed to teach eighth graders about the significance of some one-hundred-person village I've never heard of before?

—Because Medora is a famous place.

—That's what everybody keeps telling me. But how the fuck can it be famous if it only has one hundred citizens?

—Medora is a town that was founded by a French millionaire named Marquis de Morès in the late 1800s. He named the town after his wife. Medora was his wife's name. He built a mansion out there and he started a meat-packing plant, and he hated the Jews. I think he once challenged Theodore Roosevelt to a pistol duel, although that's probably a lie. Today, Medora is where tourists from Nebraska go for the weekend. They come to tour the mansion he built for his non-Jewish wife. Everybody knows this.

—How is that possible? How can this be something everybody knows?

—I'm not sure. I've never thought about it before. When you live around here, that is just something you become aware of.

—Fuck. *Fuck.* I'll never get used to that. I'll never get used to all the things that everyone in this town seems to consider common knowledge. Everyone knows the same stuff, and I can't understand why. There's no pattern. It's so weird.

—It's not so weird. I don't think it has anything to do with this town, Julia. What I have come to realize is that totally different people are still basically the same. I mean, everyone I've ever known who majored in criminal justice and became a cop started out as an adolescent criminal. The kind of fifteen-year-old kid who wants to bring a shotgun to school and shoot his teacher can become a twenty-two-year-old war hero under slightly different circumstances. I mean, Gordon Kahl was a war hero, and look how that turned out. It's not just Owl. I think all people have all the same feelings, more or less. And feelings and thoughts are pretty much the same thing, more or less.

—I would say less than more. How high are you?

—Why are you asking?

—Because my feelings aren't *anything* like my thoughts. They seem completely disconnected. That's probably why I miss smoking pot: It makes my thoughts match my feelings.

—That's weird. That's a weird problem.

—Do you have any weird problems?

—I don't have problems, weird or otherwise.

—You seem like you have problems. Sometimes I see you drinking at the bar, all alone, ignoring all the people who want to be your friends. And I think to myself, "This man is depressed. This man must have weird problems." I'm paraphrasing myself here.

—Oh, I'm certainly depressed. But not because of any *problems*.

—Then what makes you depressed?

—What difference would that make? You seem to think there is a big distinction between *knowing things* and *not knowing things*. There isn't. There's a difference, but it's negligible. Like, I knew about Medora, and you didn't. But what does that mean, really? What does it indicate?

—Well, you still seem like a really nice guy. I'm sorry you're depressed. That sucks.

—You're depressed, too.

—Actually, I don't think I am. I don't think I've been depressed for a long time. I think I used to be depressed, but not anymore.

—No, you're depressed. You just don't realize it, because you're a drug addict. Also, do you still have access to that ice water? Because that would be wonderful.

• • •

"What time is it?" he asked.

"Ten thirty," she said.

"You're kidding me. I figured it was two a.m." Vance stood up. "I should be getting home. I have things to do in the morning. But thanks for having me over. This was a real experience."

He searched around for his winter jacket, finally locating it on the floor behind the couch. It was difficult to slide the buttons through their holes.

"It was," said Julia. Her legs and shoulders felt thick, like slabs of beef. She didn't want to get up from the couch, so she didn't. "It was an experience. It was nice to talk when no one else was around. I feel like there are all these people in town who I see all the time, but I don't really know them at all. Or someone will see *me* and know *me* and they'll wave hello, but I won't even be sure who they're supposed to be. So . . . yeah. Talking. It was stellar. Let's do it again."

"We will," said Vance. He looked at her on the sofa and started walking backward toward the door. This Is When You Are Supposed To Kiss Her, he thought to himself. This Is When Normal People Try To Kiss Other Normal People. It should not have been a problem. He was an accidental, unoriginal football legend. He was the coolest person in town, and nobody could disagree. But he still could not act. "We will," he said again, and then he opened the door and disappeared into the hall.

He Wanted To Kiss Me, she thought.

But He Was Nervous. I Made Him Nervous, Somehow.

Julia looked at the ashtray that sat upon the glass coffee table and at the roach that remained from the stoning; perhaps one eighth of an inch was still unsmoked. "There are two kinds of people in this world," she said aloud. Sometimes she talked to herself when she was high; she imagined that her friends from college could watch her actions on a hidden camera. She did not audibly speak the rest of the platitude, but the two kinds of people Julia split the world into were as follows: People who said, "This joint is cashed," and people who said, "Well, let me try." Julia placed herself in the second category, although she wondered if that made her an optimist or a pothead.

The tip of her left thumb blistered and charred white, just like old times.

JANUARY 31, 1984

(Horace)

He printed his name and address in block letters because that was how you were supposed to do it. His printing was small. He inscribed his Social Security number and found himself amazed that he could still remember most of Alma's (it was 202–98-something-something-12). He was amazed by this memory every year. He put an "x" in the box that said "single." He looked at the chicken-shaped clock above his sink. It was almost midnight.

Last May, he sold his non-working 1969 John Deere auger to the Flaw brothers for $120. They must have been pretty desperate for an auger. He wasn't sure if selling an auger counted as Business Income (line 12) or Farm Income (line 18). It felt more like business, so that's what he went with. The government would barely care about an auger, anyway. The only thing the IRS would care about was the half section of land he still owned: 320 acres of sandy loam that he rented to Jake Druid for thirty-nine dollars an acre. The Druids used it to raise alfalfa, which was turned into hay, which was fed to the bison. By extension, Horace was sustaining the existence of the American buffalo, a noble creature of sweeping symbolism; he was supporting the notion of government without even trying. He wrote the digits $12,480 into line 17. He made his eight as two tiny circles, one on top of the other. Line 21 asked for "other income." He declared nineteen dollars, just to be safe (he didn't know if gambling revenue counted). He merged all these lines and numbers with an adding machine. He subtracted the standard deduction for a widower. He licked his fingers and paged through the brownish index of the IRS booklet to establish his tax liability, which was $212. He used a fountain pen with blue ink to write a check on his kitchen table for the appropriate amount. He had no W-2s or 1099s to attach. He inserted his check and the tax return into an envelope, adhered a twenty-cent stamp, and walked out to his mailbox. The sky was (of course) very dark, but he (of course) knew the way. From the bottom step of the porch, it was exactly one hundred steps to the mailbox. *Exactly* one hundred. The logistic perfection of that distance deepened his faith in God. It was beyond coincidence. He placed the letter inside the box and lifted the flag. His sense of relief was immediate. He had looked forward to this act since Christmas.

It was important to do these things. It was important to pay one's taxes, even if the government was wrong and the money would be wasted on drug addicts and boat people and Minuteman ICBM missiles. The state did not ask for much; the state only asked for a little money. And what was money? It was merely a temptation to commit wrong. Rich people weren't happy. They were generally miserable and usually confused. Most of the time they didn't even realize they were rich; almost without exception, they wrongly viewed themselves as middle-class. But there's no such thing as middle-class. The middle class does not exist. If you believe you are part of the middle class, it just means you're rich and insecure or poor and misinformed. Horace understood this. That bastard Chester Grimes had taught him that having money was without value (and that the wanting of money was even worse). What had that extra ten thousand dollars done for Gordon Kahl? It got him shot. It got his dog assassinated. It made him an icon to idiots like Edgar Camaro. Pay your taxes and don't ask why. How hard was that to understand?

FEBRUARY 3, 1984

(Cubby Candy)

Who am I even talking to? I suppose it doesn't matter. What I say won't change anything. Still, I want you to know that I had nothing to do with this, which probably doesn't surprise you. I don't even know the guy. He's tall: That's all I know. He plays football and basketball and throws the javelin. He doesn't like to communicate. Somebody said he listens to that live Ted Nugent album a lot, but I don't know if that's true. I don't care what happens to him.

This kind of thing always happens to me. How can things backfire when you haven't done *anything*? Everything explodes in my face; it doesn't matter what I have or haven't done. Whenever I tried to be nice to people, they hated me. Teachers would say, 'Just ignore those kids.' But that never worked. That made things worse; everybody assumed I was fucking retarded. I remember when I was in third grade: All these older kids would chase me around on their BMX bikes. They would chase me all over town, screaming at me, making fun of my name, making those Indian whooping sounds. They said we were playing *Planet of the Apes,* and they were the apes. I didn't have a bike, so I would just try to run away. It sucked. I'm not fast. I have short legs. After three weeks of that shit, I realized it was easier to slow down and let them ride up alongside me, because then I could just grab them by the hair and rip them to the pavement. It was my best option. I only did it because there was no better alternative. But ten years later, that's all anybody remembers about that summer: All they remember is Cyrus Cobb splitting his head open on the sidewalk and living in the hospital until school started. They don't remember *Planet of the Apes* or the rules of the game; they honestly want to believe I randomly attacked a bike-riding fifth grader and smashed his head against the sidewalk for no good reason. Which, I suppose, is fine with me. They can believe that. I hated that kid. I hate kids named Cyrus. Smashing his skull wasn't my decision, but I have no remorse.

Every time I get involved in some kind of incident, people always want to know the reason why. 'Why did you throw your desk through the window, Cubby? Why did you try to grab that policeman's gun, Cubby? Why did you vandalize the moose head inside the VFW?' I know why they ask these questions. They ask them because they assume I will be unable to provide any answers, and that will (somehow) prove their point. It will (somehow) illustrate the stupidity of my actions. But they are wrong. All of those acts were completely justified at the time. All of them.

My father deserves to die. I want him to die, and I will dance on his grave when he does. But at least he understands these things. When I was younger, he used to kick the shit out of me, and—of course—I would ask him *why* he did that. His sadism seemed to materialize out of an empty void. I could never predict when he was going to hit me. So I would ask him why. Sometimes he would say things like, 'Because you stole beer' or 'Because you made your mother cry.' But not always. Sometimes he would say things like, 'End of the world' or 'Quit speaking German.' For a long time, those responses confused me. People on television always talk about how kids blame themselves for being abused, but I rarely felt that way; my day-to-day existence seemed completely unrelated to my father's punching. That disconnection drove me crazy. I would have preferred to blame myself.

When I was thirteen or fourteen, my dad came home from the Oasis Wheel extra wasted, and he crawled behind the couch and started crying and apologizing for all the times he hit me, which is the kind of shit pathetic old drunks always do. Even at the time, I knew it was bullshit. I knew he would hit me again. I knew he would probably hit me tomorrow. But he really wanted to talk about his problems, so we talked. I eventually asked him what he meant when he said, 'End of the world.' I wasn't sure if he'd even remember saying that. But he did remember. He said, 'Well, you know how it is when you're driving on the interstate and all the exit signs have numbers? If you read the numbers, they turn into letters. And if you string the letters together, they make foreign words. And the words control your car. You don't even have to steer. It steers itself, like a sea turtle. But then you eventually see the letter *Z*, and that always means the same thing: the end of the world. *Z* is what you see at the end of the world.' He sounded totally normal when he said this, or at least not abnormally wasted. It was probably the best conversation we ever had.

I still hate my father, and I will always hate him. If I could get away with strangling him in his sleep, I would certainly consider it. But his explanation about the letter *Z* made a lot of sense to me. For some reason, my dad had to punch me because he thought the world was ending. Or maybe he had to punch me to *stop* the world from ending, or to *make it* end. Whatever. Doesn't matter. He was using his best judgment. What else can a person do? I threw my biology desk through a window because I was angry at the wood. Wood makes me angry, sometimes. The *idea* of wood. I can't tell if it's alive or dead. But I know I could never explain that concept to anyone else, and I don't care if other people understand what I mean or even if they have the same feelings. I never care about those things. Never. So I did what I did. I have no remorse.

I've had so much preposterous shit happen in my lifetime. I used to think my life was normal, but now I know it's been big-time fucked-up. The fact that my grandpa was in love with me was fucked-up. The fact that I had to wear the same pair of tennis shoes *for four years* was fucked-up. The fact that my mom cries all day is fucked-up, although now I realize she cries because she *always* knew our lives were fucked and that I would probably figure that out eventually. Sometimes she'd be too depressed to cook, so I'd eat a bowl of Bac-Os for supper. It didn't seem that different from eating cold bacon. It was okay. But when I casually mentioned this to Curtis-Fritz, it blew his mind. He told everybody at school that I ate Bac-Os for supper. That was when I started to understand that things were very, very different for me. My life had been prefucked. If it wasn't for my car, I don't know what I'd have to live for.

Am I good at fighting? Yes. I'm amazingly good at fighting. Amazingly good. Everyone knows this. It's probably the only thing everyone knows about me. Now, do I *enjoy* fighting? Sometimes. People ask me that question all the time, and I generally say yes. But I don't know if I really mean it; fighting doesn't seem good or bad to me. I suppose it's nice to be recognized for my success. I like the confusion of hitting and of being hit. When normal people go someplace where poor people live, they worry about getting attacked. I want to be attacked. I want someone to attack me. It's comforting. It doesn't seem fun or unfun, because I know I can't lose. It's almost like playing tic-tac-toe against a computer.

There are only three qualities required for successful fighting. I have them all, and I have them to the highest possible degree. The first is a high threshold for pain. Most people surrender the moment they start to ache or bleed; I only feel pain in retrospect, so this is not a problem. The second quality is commitment. What are you willing to do to win a fight? Most people think there are *rules* to fighting, even when it's a street fight. There are certain things they won't do: They won't kick someone who's already on the ground. They won't throw a bottle. They won't bite a wrist. People who follow such rules are not committed to fighting. I, however, am fully committed, all the time.

The third quality is motive. Why are you fighting? What are you trying to achieve? This, I suspect, is the true key to my unstoppability: I never have a motive.

If someone is fighting over a woman, there will come a point when his head is being slammed against a car door and he'll start to think, You know, she's really not worth it. If someone starts a fight because you ashed a cigarette on his pants, there will come a point when his lungs are collapsing and he will think, I never really liked those pants anyway. He will weigh his motive against the violence, and he will quit. People never care about things as much as they claim, or as much as they would like to pretend to themselves. But I am able to separate my desires from my circumstances. Something ignites inside my brain, and I can feel fresh blood flowing down my spine and into my hands, and I see everything in black and white. This is literally true; when I fight, I am color-blind. I have no idea why this happens, but it happens. I stop caring about being alive, or about being a human, or about anything from the past or anything about the future. I don't care what happens or who wins or who lives or who doesn't. I am without motive.

It's a sizeable advantage.

I could never explain these things, and I could never write them down. This is how I imagine saying them, were I a writer or an actor or a totally different kind of person. If I tried to speak them aloud, I would probably sound as stupid and insane as my asshole father talking about the letter *Z* and the end of the world. But I know these things are true, and so does everybody else in Owl. And it fascinates them. *I fascinate them.* I know this is true. They all pretend like they hate me, but they don't. Nobody hates or loves anyone except themselves. Fighting is just the thing I do. Last week I was putting gas in the 'Cuda. These two girls I kind of know pull up alongside and say, 'So when are you going to fight Grendel?' And I was like, 'Who?' And they were like, 'Chris Sellers.' And I was like, 'You mean the tall kid?' And they were like, 'Yeah, he says he's gonna murder you.' And I was like, 'Why?' And they were like, 'Because he says you're a pussy who's been talking shit behind his back. He says he's wanted to kick your ass for the last three years.' And I was like, 'That's interesting.' And they were like, 'Yeah, we'll see how interested you are on Saturday.' And I was like, 'Yeah, I guess we will.'

So I guess we will.

FEBRUARY 4, 1984

2:44 P.M.

(Mitch)

(Julia)

(Horace)

When Mitch arrived at the apple grove, there were already nine people sitting on the hoods of their vehicles, drinking Coors Light. Julia was still inside the Jamestown Pamida store, contemplating the purchase of a beanbag. Horace was rereading *The Best and the Brightest,* which he viewed as biased. Mitch got out of his car and failed to catch the beer immediately thrown in his direction. Julia decided that beanbags were too expensive. Horace could feel the sun on his neck through the window. Somebody asked Mitch what the temperature was, and he knew the answer. Julia revolved a tower of sunglasses and wondered how much was too much to pay for something she would almost certainly lose. Horace crossed his legs and remembered watching the Checkers speech on ABC. Somebody asked Mitch if he still thought Grendel was going to win the fight. Julia paid for her items and pushed them out of the store in a shopping cart, amazed by how unseasonably warm the air was. Horace turned a page, quickly. Mitch explained his latest theory, which was that Grendel would defeat Candy by landing timely punches to his solar plexus and temples. Julia threw her right arm across the Honda's passenger seat and pulled out of her parking space, listening to a radio tribute to the music of Karen Carpenter, who had died exactly one year before. Horace turned another page. Mitch tried not to look at Tami Jorgen's confrontational nipples, despite that fact that she was wearing only a yellow T-shirt in forty-degree weather. Julia listened to the song "Superstar" at an unnecessarily high volume, partially because she thought it would be funny if someone could witness her doing this when she was all alone in the car. Horace imagined himself in a room with David Halberstam, arguing about the context of Laos. Mitch wondered if Cubby would show up before or after Grendel, and if either of them would appear as nervous as he always felt for no reason. Julia listened to an a cappella version of "(They Long to Be) Close to You" and wondered if any of her Mormon roommates had been bulimic. Horace fantasized about the heat and wetness of a Southeast Asian jungle he would never visit. Mitch pretended to drink his beer while listening to other people's lies. Julia slid her Civic into the left lane of the interstate and pushed the accelerator to the floor, flying past elderly farmers in seed caps who did not question the validity of a fifty-five-miles-per-hour speed limit. Horace glanced at the clock and realized he would not make it to Harley's Café until after 3:00 p.m., but that was nothing to worry about; his colleagues would still be there. Mitch watched the other teenagers arrive at the apple grove and wondered if this was how it felt before prizefights at Madison Square Garden. Julia listened to the happy sadness of "Goodbye to Love" and decided she would just call Vance and ask him to go bowling, because what was the worst that could happen? Horace used a one-dollar bill as a bookmark and decided it was time to comb his hair and get ready for coffee. Mitch could not believe how excited he was about the possibility of watching two people fight each other for no reason. Julia stared at the line on the highway and let herself be hypnotized. Horace put on his hat and walked out the front door, choosing to leave it unlocked for the eight thousandth consecutive day. Mitch lay back on the hood of somebody else's cherry-red sedan and watched high-altitude cirrus clouds rush across the sky at speeds that contradicted the warm windlessness of the reality he assumed he was experiencing.

Jesus, it was so nice out!

FEBRUARY 4, 1984
3:11 P.M.

(Mitch)

Somebody said, "He's here." He was. He was Cubby. He was sitting in his car, alone. Had he actually arrived before everyone else? Had he been here since noon? Maybe. Nobody had noticed, somehow.

Zebra arrived with Ainge and Curtis-Fritz. They all climbed out of the same vehicle at the same time, like freelance circus employees. Mitch wondered why they had been hanging out together without him; it's not like it hurt his feelings, but—still. Weird. Why hadn't they asked him? Did they often spend time together without him? Had they spent another afternoon arguing over which idiot from which band should attempt a solo project that would sound exactly like the terrible group he was already in? Perhaps. They did that sometimes. There would always be cultural gaps between Mitch and his peers. He knew this. They weren't like him at all.

"Is this really on?" asked Zebra. He was not the first person to pose this query. "Vanna, what are the odds that this fight will actually happen? Fifty-fifty?"

"Forty percent," said Mitch.

A pickup door slammed. Somebody said, "Aw, shit." A full can of beer flew through the air and hit a tree. All of these events were connected.

"Sixty percent," said Mitch.

Grendel stomped into the clearing of the apple grove, effortlessly embodying everyone's preconceived notion of grassroots terror. Here it was. This was it. This was The Fight. Mitch could not believe it was actually happening.

He also could not believe how clichéd it seemed.

Grendel began removing his letterman's jacket, very deliberately. This almost made Mitch laugh aloud. Was he really *taking off his coat* to fight? Would he also dramatically pound his right fist into the palm of his left hand? Did Grendel think this was being televised? The other teenagers started to form a large circle around Grendel, murmuring their excitement like extras in a gladiator movie. Mitch felt like an idiot. He could not believe he used to lie in bed and imagine this very situation, analyzing its tendencies and potentialities. It now seemed wasteful. There was nothing organic about what he was about to watch. It was no different than watching an episode of *Happy Days,* except with swearing.

"Where the fuck is he?" asked Grendel. It sounded like he was reading from a script.

"Here," said Cubby. He was standing outside of his car now. He didn't have a jacket to take off. His T-shirt promoted Waylon Jennings. He staggered into the human circle, his shoulders hunched and his head down. This was all so fake. Mitch, still on the hood of somebody else's car, looked back toward the sky. It had turned gray. *Symbolic,* he thought. This time he actually did laugh, but only a little. With mild surprise, he noticed that he could see his breath in the air, which had not been the case just seconds before. How did it get so cold so fast? Curious. He jumped off the hood and took his place on the perimeter of the circle. This was stupid and this was formulaic, but this was his life. He had to watch this fight in order to make it real, just as he had needed to make it happen in the first place. He was a central figure.

"I am going to fuck you up," Grendel said to Cubby. "You think your shit doesn't stink, but you are wrong. It does."

"Okay," said Cubby. He was not smiling or frowning. He looked like he was thinking about something else entirely. His eyes would not focus. He looked like a dog with rabies. He needed to shave.

"Shut the fuck up," said Grendel. "Don't talk to me."

"Okay," said Cubby.

"What did I just tell you?"

"I don't know. Okay? I couldn't hear you."

"You fucking heard me."

"Okay. What did you say?"

"Fuck you!"

"Okay. Okay."

"Quit saying that word, you gay retarded dirtbag faggot."

"Okay. Okay!"

"Fuck this. You're dead."

Grendel took half a step in Candy's direction. Somebody gasped.

Candy screamed. It was not a scream of fear. He was not afraid. He was the person he was supposed to be. The sound rushed out of his mouth. His lungs were like a fog machine.

And then everything was white.

And then everyone fell down.

FEBRUARY 4, 1984

3:12 P.M.

( )

People always want to know what it was like. Well, this is what it was like:

It was like being hit by something heavy and flat and wide. And vast. And *fast.*

It was like a massive human hand sweeping across a relief map of North Dakota, knocking cars off the highway and cattle off their hooves.

It was like falling asleep on a beach near Diamond Head and waking up inside an industrial meat freezer.

It was like standing eight inches from a moving freight train, which is how people typically describe the sound of tornadoes. So it was like standing next to a freight train, during a tornado.

It was like keeping your eyes open while submerging your head in a fifty-gallon drum of white latex paint.

It was like being inside the film footage from the atomic-bomb tests off the Bikini Atoll that would later be used in MTV videos by white New York hip-hop artists.

It was like being swept forty feet below sea level by a twenty-five-foot wave, when all compass directions become interchangeable and there is no difference between up or down.

It was like inhaling frozen granules of cocaine and glass, but not being able to expel them.

It was like standing up very quickly and hitting the back of your head against an oak beam that had materialized out of nothingness.

It was like filling the nozzle of a hair dryer with dry ice, holding it one centimeter from your retina, and plugging it into an electrical socket.

It was like suddenly remembering that you'd completely forgotten to do something very, very important.

It was like being Helen Keller, in Greenland, naked.

It was like being with everyone, and then being with no one.

FEBRUARY 4, 1984

3:13 P.M.

(Julia)

She was twenty-nine miles southeast of Jamestown, driving west at sixty-seven miles per hour, headed toward a blizzard moving south by southeast at eighty-two miles per hour.

Her future was a math problem.

The woman on the radio cut off the end of "It's Going to Take Some Time" to inform listeners that they should not be driving anywhere. "What is she yammering on about?" wondered Julia. "Look at the sky. It's gorgeous. Look at the sky."

FEBRUARY 4, 1984

3:14 P.M.

(Horace)

He shifted his pickup into reverse and made a three-point turn in the front yard. He drove down his driveway at fifteen miles per hour and turned right on County Road 17. It was two miles over gravel to the highway, and then it was one more mile to town. He shifted from first gear to second gear to third. He had made it a quarter mile from home; he could still see his house in the passenger-side mirror. He pushed in the clutch and the road disappeared. His vehicle was no longer moving in the direction the wheels were turning. He was sliding into the ditch. Drive it straight down, he thought. The ditch was steep. He did not want to roll it. He cranked the steering wheel all the way to the right and drove down the incline, blindly and directly. He was jostled about the cab, but not violently. He came to a stop at the bottom. He could not believe what the wind sounded like. It made all the windows shake. He could feel it through the glass.

He could not open the driver's-side door; the wind was forcing it shut. He slid across the bench seat and opened the other one. He poked out his head, squinted into the wind, saw nothing, felt terrified. He tried to slam the door shut, but the wind kept it open. He had to pull it with both hands. It closed, but just barely. He wasn't sure if it latched.

This was really bad.

He peered at his fuel gauge. The tank was almost empty, so he turned off the engine. He reached under the seat and pulled out a green army blanket, an empty tin coffee can, a candle, wooden matches, a flashlight, and two Snickers bars from 1975. He placed the candle inside the can, lit it with a match, and aligned the can on the floorboards. He could feel the warmth immediately. Horace wrapped the blanket around his legs and waited for the storm to subside. "Important to be prepared," he thought. "To a certain extent, I am prepared for this." He tried not to look back at his fuel gauge, but he could not help himself.

FEBRUARY 4, 1984
3:15 P.M.

(Mitch)

Everything was gone now. Everything was white and thick. Mitch was on his hands and knees and—for a moment—did not know why. He wondered if perhaps something had exploded inside his brain; perhaps he was having an aneurysm. But that notion did not last long. "This is snow," he calmly concluded. "It's blizzarding." It was different from other blizzards he had experienced, certainly, and it was the first time he had ever been knocked to the ground by the movement of air. But it was still only snow. No cause for alarm. He turned his head toward Zebra to comment on the intensity of the wind. Zebra was no longer there, or at least he could not see him. He looked in the opposite direction and—again—saw nothing. He slowly stood up, bracing himself against a wind that did not seem possible. He looked in (what he believed to be) the direction of his car, but he saw nothing. He held his hand six inches in front of his face; he knew his hand was there, yet he could see not it. Whenever people try to describe especially intense blizzards, it's common for them to say, "I couldn't see my hand in front of my face." This, of course, is almost never true. This is an expression. But now he was looking at his hand, and it was literally in front of his face, and he could not see it.

This was really something!

Here was Mitch's problem: The apple grove was not really a *grove*, per se; that was merely the nomenclature among the kids. The apple grove was just two parallel belts of apple trees, forty feet apart. If you were between the lines of trees, you were hidden from the adjacent county roads (and, by extension, the local cops who drove upon them), which was why teenagers went there to drink. However, it was open to the world at its north and south ends. As such, the apple grove was a wind tunnel. It was almost as if the trees had been planted by engineers from NASA, solely for the purposes of testing wind shear (and possibly for killing high school kids who had wanted to watch a fistfight).

So this was the situation. The situation was this: Mitch had to get inside his car, or inside somebody else's car, or inside anything that contained qualities of "insideness." He knew he could not be more than seventy-five feet from where he'd parked his vehicle, although he suddenly found himself unsure how far (or near) seventy-five feet truly was. He tried to imagine two and a half first downs, but that didn't help at all. Had Mitch been a confident person, he would have turned into the wind and walked thirty steps while veering slightly left, because that is where he imagined his car to be sitting (and where, in fact, it was). Had Mitch realized the true gravity of his circumstance, he might have crawled toward the east or the west and collected his wits among the apple trees, as they would have provided rudimentary shelter. But Mitch was not confident, and Mitch was not aware of what was happening. Instead he tried to follow (what he believed to be) the vague voices of his schoolmates, several of whom were screaming and freaking out. But the subzero wind had shifted their shrieks. It was carrying their voices to the south, so Mitch walked in a southbound direction. And since he was walking with the wind at his back, he was not as nervous as he should have been; the wind was excruciatingly cold, but physically reassuring. It pushed him along. It allowed him to walk faster. But he could not see where he was going and he could not tell how far he had gone, and he walked straight out of the opening at the south end of the grove, into a plowed field, away from everyone he knew.

FEBRUARY 4, 1984
3:58 P.M.

(Julia)

I have struck the underpass, she thought. I have driven into a wall of concrete, and now I'm dead. They always claim you see white when you die, although normally in the form of light. Perhaps this is the afterlife. Is this possible?

No.

Julia had no idea what had just happened to her; it had happened faster than anything had ever happened to her before. She was driving, she glanced at the stereo, she looked back at the road, there was no road, and then she was flying through the air. Her Honda Civic had been picked six inches off the road and tossed like a baby thrown from a carriage. The landing was hard, then motionless. Her vehicle was still running, but the engine was whining like a wounded boar. She did not know if she had been thrown off the highway to her right (which would place her in a field) or if she had been thrown off the highway to her left (which would place her in the median). It was impossible to tell or remember. She released her seat belt and turned off the radio. She shook in place for two minutes, listening to wind that didn't sound like wind.

This was really terrifying.

Julia pulled on her gloves and decided to walk toward the road, assuming she could deduce which direction that was. Her hands were still shaking, so it took a long time. She finally opened the door and tried to walk; the elements knocked her back inside. The cold was unrealistically palpable; it was like having salicylic acid thrown in her face. She pulled off her right glove and touched her left cheek. Her fear increased. There was no way her skin should feel that frozen, that fast.

Remain calm, she thought. Get back in the car. Think calm thoughts. Think about friendly animals. Think about cows, chewing on cud and mooing.

Stay in the car. That is the key. *Stay in the car, no matter what.* That is how people live.

FEBRUARY 4, 1984
4:40 P.M.

(Horace)

This wasn't the worst blizzard of all time. Horace knew that much. It couldn't be. Absolutely not. Not even close. Who could ever forget the March blizzard of '66? That lasted three days. The snowdrifts were as high as telephone poles. You could walk over the high wires. And even that was minor compared to 1888, when the so-called Children's Blizzard killed five hundred people across the upper Midwest, most of them kids walking home from one-room schoolhouses. When viewed against the expanse of history, this storm was not so terrible.

But still.

This wind!

That was his concern: the wind. Its ferocity was extraterrestrial. It did not wax and wane. He kept trying to recall any other situation where he had felt (or heard) wind like this before, and he couldn't remember a moment that was the least bit similar. Horace had lived his entire life in the windiest region of North America, yet he still possessed the capacity to be surprised by air.

When he first lit the candle in the coffee can, Horace had been startled by how much warmth it immediately provided; now that the temperature in the cab had normalized, he was equally disillusioned by how impotent the flame seemed. He would need to run the heater, at least for a few minutes. Horace turned the ignition key forward, slid across the seat, and (again) opened the passenger door. He stepped out into the maelstrom and walked toward the back of the truck, guiding himself along the pickup's box with his right hand. He had to make sure the exhaust pipe was not blocked by snow; this was a vitally important detail. If the pipe was clogged, he could die in his sleep. Seeing that the pipe was clean, he guided himself back inside the vehicle. This process should have taken thirty seconds, but it took four minutes. It was like walking on K2. When Horace finally reclosed the passenger door, he exhaled deeply, almost erotically. He wasn't exhausted, but he felt like he was. He leaned forward and put his face in front of the heating vents. The warm air smelled like a fried cat.

Against his will, Horace found himself glancing back at his fuel gauge compulsively, ten or eleven times a minute, stupidly hoping it would mysteriously indicate that his tank was full. "Idiot," he thought to himself. "Never drive in winter with less than half a tank of fuel. Even a child knows that. Idiot." He only allowed himself to run the heater for five minutes. He had to be judicious.

There is no way the wind can blow like this all night, he thought. That was unthinkable. A wind this powerful could not sustain itself over time. Unless, of course, everything Horace had come to understand about wind was incorrect. And that was possible. Two hours ago, he had not believed a wind this intense could even exist. That being the case, how could he assume to know how long it could (or couldn't) last?

He thought about Harley's Café and wondered if the other boys were trapped inside its walls, drinking coffee and talking about memorable storms of the past forty years. If they were, they'd undoubtedly assume Horace had been smart enough to stay at home; they would assume he'd heard about the Alberta Clipper on the TV and played things close to the vest. He had such awful, ironic luck. Everyone in Owl knew everything about everyone, but they couldn't know that Horace was sitting in a ditch, looking at his gas gauge, listening to a wind he could not fathom, and dreaming about the dead wife and nonexistent children who were not wondering where he was.

FEBRUARY 4, 1984

5:15 P.M.

(Mitch)

This is just like that story, he thought. It's like that story we read two years ago in English about the man who walked the old Yukon trail. "It certainly was cold." That was the line Mitch remembered most, along with the part about the man wanting to kill his dog in hopes of warming his hands inside its carcass. Mr. Laidlaw claimed the story was about mankind's lack of humility and our unwillingness to respect the awesome power of nature. He also said it was about rejection of government, which is why people were walking the old Yukon trail in the first place. That same semester, they read "The Most Dangerous Game," a story about Burmese tiger traps. It's peculiar what you remember when you're not trying.

Jesus. It certainly *was* cold. How could it be this cold? Girls had been wearing T-shirts today. They had been wearing T-shirts outside. What happened? What made this happen? Just like in the story, Mitch spit to see if he could hear his saliva crackle in midair, freezing before it hit the ground. He heard nothing. He saw nothing. He could not even see his own spit, much less hear it crackle. It had been two hours since he had seen any color except white. For a while, he tried to turn 180 degrees and walk back to where he had come from, but he kept overcompensating; he kept turning 270 degrees and drifting farther to the east. After four attempts, he started to realize that every move he made was making things worse.

You know, I might die today, he thought.

But then he changed his mind.

"I am still cold," he told himself. "As long as I am cold, I am alive." Everybody knew this. Everyone knew that as long as you can *feel* the cold, it's not killing you. The time to start worrying is when you start to feel warm. "Walk straight." He wasn't saying these things aloud, but he could hear them inside his skull. "If you walk in a straight line, you will eventually hit something. You will hit a farmhouse, or you will hit a car, or you will hit a grain bin. Everything ends somewhere. You do not have to see the end in order to know that it is there." He was surprised that he spoke to himself in platitudes during this type of situation, but maybe these types of situations were why platitudes existed. "You want to be a quarterback. Well, be a quarterback. Be a leader. Lead yourself. If you can't lead yourself, you can't expect anyone else to follow." This, of course, was bullshit: Walking through a blizzard had no relationship to playing football, and 90 percent of Mitch's brain understood that completely. He was reflexively echoing the irrational sentiments of a man he hated. What the fuck did *leadership* even mean? Wasn't it simply a word people used to reconcile any kind of charisma that was impossible to otherwise explain?

Probably.

But right now, within the arctic blankness of his circumstance, that intellectual reality did not matter. In fact, it was an anchor. Which is why the core of Mitch's brain—the 10 percent that had made him realize the likelihood of his own death—demanded that he ignore what he knew to be true in order to embrace what he had been told by others. It was the only way.

"Walk straight. Prove you want to live. Come on, Vanna. *Vanna!* Are you sleepy, Vanna? Are you freezing to death? Are you snow-blind and confused and desperate? Maybe you *want* to die, Vanna. Maybe you think dying would be fun. Maybe you don't care. Come on, Vanna. *Vanna!* Prove you want to live."

He said these things to himself, and he believed them.
He was a warrior.
But he was walking toward nothing.

FEBRUARY 4, 1984

7:02 P.M.

(Julia)

For a while, the little stoner girl from Wisconsin regretted her decision not to buy any magazines when she was back at Pamida. It would have been nice to look at words and pictures; it would have made her less anxious. But now it was dark. Her regret became meaningless. She drank two warm cans of Tab and opened a box of Dolly Madison Zingers she'd impulsively purchased upon noticing they were only ninety-nine cents. Considering her present situation, that had been a brilliant move: There was nothing to do now except sit in the dark eating spongy fingers of yellow cake while listening to DJs on the radio explain how apocalyptic the current meteorological conditions apparently were. The fiberglass of her Japanese two-seater shuddered with every gust. She could not turn up the radio loud enough to block out the wind, even when she switched over to Q-98 and found some AC/DC.

Her suffocating fear was now entirely gone; it had been replaced by boredom, and by the expectation of greater boredom in the near future. Now that night had fallen, Julia knew no one would be coming to rescue her until daybreak, unless the storm stopped completely and the highway department released the plows. She would have to wait. It would be a long night. Still, things could be worse: At least she drove a Honda. Julia didn't know much about cars (including her own), but she knew at least one thing: She knew that Hondas got incredible gas mileage.

Everybody always noted that, including her mechanic. Her engine could easily idle all night. She wouldn't freeze. She'd just have to sit and do nothing for nine hours, which (actually) wasn't that different from her job.

At worst, this entrapment would give her something to talk about with Naomi and Ted, and maybe even with Vance. Maybe Vance would find her blizzard anecdote amusing and meaningful. "What did you spend your time thinking about?" he might ask. And perhaps that would be a leading question, solely posed to deduce whether she had been thinking about him. But Julia would (of course) be too coy for such obviousness, instead responding with something along the lines of "Oh, I mostly just thought about art." To which Vance would say, "Art? I question that." To which Julia would say, "Oh, there is a lot about me you don't know, Mister Druid." Their flirting would be hardcore. As their dialogue grew deeper, she would admit that she had been very scared for the first hour or so, and she'd paint a chilling verbal portrait of the storm's ferocity. Her description would be so emotive that Vance would immediately feel closer to her, which would prompt him to tell Julia about a situation where he had been scared. Maybe it would be a story about something that had happened to him during kindergarten; maybe a dog had chased him up a tree and trapped him there for hours, and—years later—he can still recall that paralyzing fear whenever he sees a German shepherd or notices a child sitting inside a tree house. He would tell this anecdote in a humorous and self-deprecating manner, but it would elucidate many of his deeper qualities and motives. Moreover, Vance would fully realize that his (seemingly innocuous) story completely explained who he really was and how he viewed the world, which is why he'd specifically choose to tell it to Julia in the middle of a casual exchange that would not be remotely casual.

Maybe I don't need a relationship at all, she thought. Maybe thinking about these conversations was just as good as having them. She could sit in her Honda in the dark and experience whatever kind of life she wanted. Sometimes you think, Hey, maybe there's something else out there. But there really isn't. This is what being alive feels like, you know? The place doesn't matter. You just live.

FEBRUARY 4, 1984

8:00 P.M.

(Horace)

We all have to make decisions. We don't know if they're right or wrong until later. Gordon Kahl made a decision to shoot and kill federal marshals over taxes. Horace would have never made that choice. He knew that. After the murders, Kahl fled across the country alone, leaving a distraught wife and a critically wounded child back in North Dakota. Faced with a similar state of affairs, Horace might have done the same, but he wasn't sure. In the end, Kahl elected to be burned alive before surrendering. Horace liked to believe he would have done the same thing, but—here again—he could not be positive. We all believe that we are a certain kind of person, but we never know until we do something that proves otherwise, or until we die.

His pickup was running out of fuel.

The engine was knocking. It was operating on fumes. Every time Horace turned off the motor to conserve the remnants of gasoline, he feared it would be impossible to restart.

It was dark out. It was very dark out.

The wind was not decreasing.

Sometimes the howl would momentarily relax, but then it would gust and explode all over again. Even inside the cab, he could feel the Canadian air biting through the driver's-side window, dragging the interior temperature lower and lower and lower.

A candle inside a coffee tin cannot solve your problems.

If only he knew when this blizzard might subside; a rudimentary weather report would solve so many problems. For the first time in his life, Horace wished that his pickup had a radio. For years, he had viewed the introduction of car radios as a laughable innovation—a needless luxury for people who were too shallow to concentrate on the process of driving. Car radios were for insurance salesmen and con artists and orange-juice drinkers. He refused to install one in anything he drove, and he had actively removed the one that had come standard with this truck, solely on principle.

What a fool I was, he thought.

I deserve this.

My life, my fault.

So here were his choices, and he had only two: He could stay in the truck and possibly (probably) freeze, or he could try to walk back to his house through the blizzard and either live or (absolutely, irrefutably, undeniably) die in the open country. He was only a quarter mile from his home. Four hundred and forty yards. High school boys could run that distance in under a minute. Plus, he knew where he was. It was a walk he believed he could make blindfolded (and that detail was important, because that's how it would be). However, he also knew that the biggest error any traveler could commit during a whiteout was to leave the safety of his car. Everybody knew this; it was another one of those things everybody knew. If Horace died in the storm and his corpse was found on the road, all the boys at Harley's would say, "What the hell was he thinking? Why did he leave his truck? Didn't he know you're never supposed to do that?" It would be a humiliating legacy. And he would never be able to live it down, because he would already be dead.

I should stay put, he thought. Maybe I have more fuel than I think.

Then again, maybe I don't. Maybe this pickup truck is my metal casket.

But—still again—maybe I don't even *need* to run the heater. Pioneers lived through blizzards, and all they had were sod houses. Sioux Indians lived in rawhide tents. I'm tough. I've lived through worse than this. I'm tough enough to spend one cold night anywhere.

But—then again—maybe I'm not.

Maybe I never was.

After seventy-three years on earth, Horace was amazed by how little he knew about himself.

We all have to make decisions. They are more arbitrary than most of us will ever admit. Horace picked up the flashlight, turned on the bulb, and exited the vehicle through the passenger-side door. He forced himself to ignore the multitude of invisible ice needles poking against his cheeks. He pointed the lamp in the direction of his home. The light was useless; it allowed him to see a tiny circle of moving whiteness within a blanket of motionless black. He struggled up the ditch and onto the road, and he began walking in (what he believed to be) the direction of his driveway. He had drafted himself.

FEBRUARY 4, 1984

8:12 P.M.

(Mitch)

It's hard being wrong. It's hard being wrong about what you think you can do, and it's hard being wrong about who you are. People who are wrong during particularly important moments inevitably spend the rest of their lives trying to explain how their wrongness was paradoxically correct, or—at the very least—why their wrongness "felt right at the time," which is very, very different from being authentically correct.

We do this because it is impossible to live happily when your life is defined by a mistake.

Yet this is how it goes. Always.

We are remembered for the totality of our accomplishments, but we are defined by the singularity of our greatest failure. It does not matter what you have been right about, and it does not matter how often that rightness is validated by others. We are what we cannot do.

Mitch could walk no farther.

He could not feel his feet, or his hands, or his legs, or his face. He didn't feel cold or warm. There were no more feelings. He was blood and lumber. He couldn't remember things; he had insane, non-sequitur thoughts about polar bears and Tina McAndrew's lips and surgeons extracting the lungs from his cadaver. The wind no longer sounded terrifying. It sounded like one of those heavy-metal cassettes Zebra would play in the car. Was this what Zebra meant when he said certain kinds of music sounded "heavy"? Maybe. Maybe this wind was how ZZ Top sounded to Zebra.

Mitch had regrets. Not as many as Mr. Laidlaw, but enough.

He should have spent more time with his sister. He should have asked her more questions about her life and her friends. He should have gotten her a better Christmas present, like a telephone or a wristwatch. Now there would be nobody to throw her the football. That had been his responsibility. She was the most naturally gifted wide receiver in North Dakota history, but nobody would ever remind her of that again. Over time, she would forget how incredible she was. He had let her down.

He should have talked to his parents more. He should have talked to them in general.

There were so many questions he had never asked himself. If playing football made him so unhappy, why had he cared so much about being good at it? Wasn't it cosmically unfair that some people were able to love ZZ Top, but he couldn't even like them? How did he really feel about his friends? How did they really feel about him? Would they cry at his funeral, or would they just sit there and think about themselves? Had he unconsciously planned on living in Owl for the rest of his life?

It dawned on him that he was going to die a virgin. Did that make his death sadder?

Well, he thought, at least I'm dying while I still want to live.

He dropped to his knees. Even though the denim was frozen stiff, he could feel the snow through his pants.

I could just lie down, he thought.

Lying down would make me feel better, he thought. Everyone always says that about freezing. Everyone says it's the easiest way to go. You just fall asleep.

But Mitch did not do this.

He did not lie down. He stayed on his knees, and he kept his eyes open. He could not stand up, but he could still remain vertical. He crossed his arms and waited.

"I will sleep when I'm dead," he thought. "I will sleep when I'm dead." And this is what he continued thinking, until it was true.

FEBRUARY 4, 1984

8:18 P.M.

(Julia)

Here are things you need to do when trapped inside a car during a blizzard:

1) Stay inside the vehicle.
2) Remain calm.
3) Periodically examine your exhaust pipe, making sure that it is not blocked by snow.
4) Roll down a window (that is not directly facing the wind) one to two inches.

Here are things Julia did when trapped inside her car during this blizzard:

1) She stayed inside the vehicle.
2) She remained calm.

Carbon monoxide is a colorless, odorless, tasteless gas that derives from the incomplete combustion of fossil fuels and from volcanic eruptions.

These are the symptoms of carbon-monoxide poisoning:

1) headache
2) depression
3) nausea

4) tachycardia (a rapid beating of the heart)
5) confusion
6) unconsciousness
7) death

This is how Julia rationalized the experience of quietly dying:

1) "My eyes hurt. The dry air is making me ill. My car needs a humidifier."
2) "Sitting alone is so boring. Who would want to live like this? Why did I come here? I guess this is how it goes."
3) "Warm Tab tastes crappy. It's like carbonated hemlock."
4) "Am I in love?"
5) "It's all so wonky: I live in a town where everybody supposedly knows everyone else, yet I've never spoken to half the people who supposedly know everything about me. I see them on the street, but don't even know their names. How is living in Owl any different from living in Hong Kong or Mexico City or Prague? Is every place essentially identical?"
6) "I think I will shut my eyes and wait until the morning. I will listen to the radio and the wind and have nice dreams. I am tired. This is not so bad. I needed a break."
7) —–

The red plastic phone inside her apartment continued to ring, unanswered.

FEBRUARY 4, 1984

8:19 P.M.

(Horace)

He had taken five steps down the road when the wind tore the eyeglasses off his face. They helicoptered into the blackness, far gone and irretrievable. He didn't even notice until it had already happened. Normally, such an event would have thrown Horace into a panic: He was extremely nearsighted, and—more to the point—glasses were expensive and difficult to replace. (He would have to find someone to drive him to the eye doctor in Jamestown, which was always a hassle.) If you are a person who has worn glasses for most of your life, you grow to love them as much as you love your nose or your teeth or your ears; the thought of losing them is petrifying, embarrassing, and omnipresent. But the loss did not bother him tonight. Tonight his eyeglasses were irrelevant. There was nothing to see. This was probably better.

"Maybe I should run," he thought. "Maybe if I jog and sprint for three or four minutes, my momentum will take me to the driveway. Besides, running would accelerate my circulation. I'd feel warmer." This, of course, was insanity. And Horace knew it; he was merely brainstorming with himself. Horace knew that if he started to run, he would undoubtedly veer off course and fall into the ditch. He also might have a heart attack, since he could barely remember the last time he had run anywhere. He chased a stray dog out of his yard during the fall of '77; that was the last time he had tried to run, and the attempt had not been successful. It was terrible being old. No. He would not run. No. Running would kill him faster than the blizzard. His only hope was to shine the flashlight forward and follow its light, even though the light illuminated nothing. He needed to walk in a straight line and hug the left shoulder of the road. If he did exactly that, he'd eventually hit his mailbox, and then he would be halfway home.

He placed his odds of survival at one in six.

The wind was like a jackhammer, except when it gusted; then it became a sledgehammer, driven by God and Dave Kingman. The sporadic hammer gales would briefly knock him off balance, intermittently forcing Horace to stop and crouch in order to stay on his feet. His progress was slothlike. The ultrafine snow filled his lungs whenever he inhaled, paralyzing the walls of his nostrils and jolting him awake. It was like drinking one hundred cups of frozen coffee. He had never been more conscious of being conscious. This was a bad sign.

"Pray," he told himself. And he did, but not in the way he intended. Somewhere inside his brain, Horace repeated the Hail Mary over and over and over again. But he ignored the words completely, almost as if he were being broadcast over the radio in Italian. It was just rote repetition, which is what memorized prayers are for. This is why we force children to memorize prayers—it's so they can be effortlessly repeated while the cerebellum deals with more pressing problems.

I could have lived anywhere, he thought.

That notion had never occurred to Horace before, or at least not with such overwhelming clarity. It was something he had (of course) always realized, but he had never completely believed it; it was so obviously plausible that it was utterly impossible. He could have lived anywhere. Everything about his life could have been different. He could have moved to Tulsa after high school and worked in the oil fields; he would have married a different woman and had a bunch of children. He'd have a Southern accent and a darker skin tone. He also could have stayed in Owl until he married Alma, but then convinced her to relocate to Minneapolis. She was flexible about that sort of thing. They could have opened a restaurant or a funeral home. He also could have married Alma, stayed in Owl until she died, and then taken the insurance money to Alaska, where twenty-five thousand dollars would have lasted fifteen years. He could have joined the Army during peacetime, even though that always seemed superfluous. But who knows? Maybe he would have become the one general who knew how to win in Vietnam. It would have been so unthinkably easy to become a different person. Even if he just sold the farm and moved into one of those new apartments in Owl—which a lot of people advised him to do after the funeral—everything would be different. He would be watching *Fantasy Island* right now, lying comfortably beneath a dead woman's quilt. Why had he refused to consider living any other life?

But this (of course) wasn't an authentic question.

He knew why.

When Horace hit his mailbox, he thought it was a car. He thought it had hit *him*. How was such a collision possible? How could he aim a flashlight at a chest-high metal box and still not see that it was there? This blizzard was not merely ferocious; it had now become sarcastic. It mocked him. He found himself hugging the mailbox without shame. It felt like a pillar of dry ice: The aluminum was so cold, it was hot. Horace looked back toward his pickup. Nothing. It could have been parked three hundred miles away. He looked up the road in the opposite direction. More nothing. He looked down at his boots. He couldn't see them. Maybe they were there. Maybe his feet were inside. Jesus, this was beyond the pale. If he survived, would he even be able to explain what the experience had been like? Would anyone even believe him?

It did not matter.

One hundred steps. There were one hundred steps between the box and the porch. *Exactly* one hundred. There was no way this was a coincidence. If you divided the specific distance of the driveway by the hyper-specific gait of Horace's thirty-four-and-a-half-inch stride, it unreasonably manifested itself as the most perfect of round, whole numbers. If there was a reason for anything, there must be a reason for that. He looked at the chasm where his house was supposed to be. It was the first time he had ever looked at his house without seeing it. It better be there, he thought. There would be no guides. The gravel driveway was flush with the lawn, so there was no ditch to follow. He would just have to trust himself. And that was not so easy. In fact, it was getting harder every second.

He released the mailbox from his bear hug and took the opening step. "One," he said. He took another. "Two." This was going well. "Three. Four. Five." As long as he did not miss the house completely, he could absolutely do this. "Nineteen. Twenty. Twenty-one." He was invincible. His memory was without flaw. But then the sledgehammer returned, and it struck him on the shoulder blades. Horace went down. He got up as quickly as he could. It struck him again; again he went down. He waited for the ungodly howl to abate. It did not. The noise sustained itself like a machine. Things were different now. The sledgehammer was no longer the wind when it gusted; now it was the wind all the time.

Somehow, the storm had intensified.

Horace lay facedown on the ground, shocked that this turn of events had even been possible. It was almost amusing. This was more than bad luck; this was existential scorn. He was forty-four steps from surviving, but he could not stand up. He was going to die in his driveway. He would be a laughingstock. No one would forget about this. Everybody would know.

He started to crawl.

At first he felt like an infant, which is how most adults feel when forced to move on all fours. "This is how I came into the world, and this is how I will leave," he thought. "Seventy-three years and nothing has changed." His existence was frozen. The air inside his lungs was cold enough to store pork chops. His limbs were probably dead already; he could no longer feel them ache. He would crawl until he couldn't crawl, and that would be it. He would perish like a baby, helpless and alone. That would be the story of his life.

And then he hit wood.

There was a flat wooden board right in front of his face. He could barely see it, but he recognized it immediately.

His right hand was on the first step of his porch.

He was there.

Somehow, the distance had been less than he remembered.

He reached over to the wooden handrail and pulled himself up. Three steps up, then the doorknob. Suddenly he was inside. Inside! Is there any better place? The furnace was off, but the kitchen still felt like the bowels of a volcano. The stillness was disturbing. He took off his boots, struggling with his hands of stone. He turned on the kitchen faucet and jammed purple fingers beneath warm water. It stung. The pain was magnificent. He flipped on the overheard light. It was so much fun to look at all the things he owned. He did not care that everything in the room looked fuzzy and distorted. He walked into the bedroom and turned on another light. Everything was in its right place. He peeled off his winter clothing until he was almost naked, recovering his body with a terry-cloth robe and fresh wool socks. The house was silent, except for an exterior wind that no longer mattered. He passed by the bathroom and turned on another light; before he slept, he would take a forty-minute shower. The house would become a sauna. Back in the kitchen, he opened a can of tomato soup and poured it into a saucepan, cooking it rapidly over a high blue flame. He did not mind waiting for it to cook. He loved watching it. When it was nearly boiling, he poured saltine crackers directly into the pot and moved it onto the counter. He began boiling water for coffee, fantasizing about how it would feel inside his mouth, down his throat, inside his stomach. He peppered the soup heavily and attacked it like a murderer, shoveling massive spoonfuls of thick red slime into his jowls. Trails of hot soup rolled down his chin, splattering like gunshots upon the tile floor. He was still standing up. He didn't need a chair. Horace glanced back at the water on the stove and saw that it was starting to bubble. He was five minutes from coffee. It was the greatest goddamn night of his life.

FEBRUARY 11, 1984

Storm victim excelled on sports field, in community

by Bruce Montrose
Bismarck Tribune

While all 20 area deaths from last week's killer blizzard can technically be classified as individual tragedies, no town was hit harder than Owl. The sleepy central North Dakota community lost a stunning six residents to the storm's wrath, including a teacher and four high school students. Among those students was Chris Sellers, arguably the best athlete in Lobo history.

But he was far more than just an athlete.

"Once in a lifetime, you come across a person like Chris," Owl head football coach John Laidlaw said. "He was the most dominating football player I ever coached. Lots of people know that. What people don't know is that he was probably a better person than he was a player. We're all still in shock here. He was the consummate quiet leader."

Sellers was socializing with friends in a remote area outside of Owl when the storm struck last Saturday. Listed at six foot eight and 255 pounds, Sellers was a force of nature, comparable to the storm that eventually killed him: He set school and state records for quarterback sacks in 1983, recording a mind-boggling 23 sacks in nine regular season games. He was equally skilled on the basketball floor; prior to his death from exposure, Sellers was averaging 28 points, 17.5 rebounds and nearly six blocked shots a night for the upstart Owl cagers (13–2, ranked #9 in the most recent Class B poll).

"From a basketball perspective, Chris will be impossible to replace," said Owl basketball coach Bob Keebler. "But what I will remember even more than his rebounding is the way he always showed concern for his teammates, even those who did not have much to offer the program."

Sellers, who had collegiate scholarship interest from Nebraska, Minnesota and

see **Owl Standout,**
continued on page **C11**

ACKNOWLEDGMENTS

This book exists because of Brant Rumble and Daniel Greenberg. I would also like to express thanks to Susan Moldow and Nan Graham for their long-standing support.

Melissa Maerz, Bob Ethington, Rob Sheffield, Alex Pappademas, Greg Korte, Patrick Condon, Michael Weinreb, David Giffels, Eric Nuzum, Jim and Amy Carlile, Chad Hansen, and Dennis Sperle all read early versions of this manuscript and helped me immensely.

This book could not have been written without my wonderful mother and father, Laura and Tom, Bill and Nan, Susan and David, Teresa and Steve, Paul and Mary Anne, Rachel and Matt, and all of their respective kids. I'd also like to thank Adelaide Wodarz for driving me to baseball practice in 1982 and being a nice person.

I must also express specific gratitude to James Corcoran, whose book *Bitter Harvest* was the central resource for at least one chapter of this book.

TOMORROW RARELY KNOWS

1 It was the 1990s and I was twenty, so we had arguments like this: What, ultimately, is more plausible—time travel, or the invention of a liquid metal with the capacity to think? You will not be surprised that *Terminator 2* was central to our dialogue. There were a lot of debates over this movie. The details of the narrative never made sense. Why, for example, did Edward Furlong tell Arnold that he should quip, "Hasta la vista, baby," whenever he killed people? Wasn't this kid supposed to like *Use Your Illusion II* more than *Lōc-ed After Dark*? It was a problem. But not as much of a problem as the concept of humans (and machines) moving through time, even when compared to the likelihood of a pool of sentient mercury that could morph itself into a cop or a steel spike or a brick wall or an actor who would eventually disappoint watchers of *The X-Files*. My thesis at the time (and to this day) was that the impossibility of time travel is a cornerstone of reality: We cannot move forward or backward through time, even if the principles of general relativity and time dilation suggest that this is possible. Some say that time is like water that flows around us (like a stone in the river) and some say we flow *with* time (like a twig floating on the surface of the water). My sense of the world tells me otherwise. I believe that time is like a train, with men hanging out in front of the engine and off the back of the caboose; the man in front is laying down new tracks the moment before the train touches them, and the man in the caboose is tearing up the rails the moment they are passed. There is no linear continuation: The past disappears, the future is unimagined, and the present is ephemeral. It cannot be traversed. So even though the prospect of liquid thinking metal is insane and idiotic, it's still more viable than time travel. I don't know if the thinking metal of tomorrow will have the potential to find employment as assassins, but I do know that—if this somehow happens—those liquid metal killing machines will be locked into whatever moment they happen to inhabit.

It would be wonderful if someone proved me wrong about this. Wonderful. Wonderful, and sad.

2 I read H. G. Wells's *The Time Machine* in 1984. It became my favorite novel for the next two years, but solely for textual reasons: I saw no metaphorical meaning in the narrative. It was nothing except plot, because I was a fucking sixth grader. I reread *The Time Machine* as a thirty-six-year-old in 2008, and it was (predictably) a wholly different novel that now seemed fixated on archaic views about labor relations and class dynamics, narrated by a protagonist who is completely unlikable. That is a trend with much of Wells's sci-fi writing from this period; I reread *The Invisible Man* around the same time, a book that now seems maniacally occupied with illustrating how the invisible man was an asshole.

Part of the weirdness surrounding my reinvestigation of *The Time Machine* was because my paperback copy included a new afterword (written by Paul Youngquist) that described Wells as an egomaniac who attacked every person he encountered throughout his entire lifetime, often contradicting whatever previous attack he had made only days before. He publicly responded to all perceived slights levied against him, constantly sparring with his nemesis Henry James and once sending an angry, scatological letter to George Orwell (written after Orwell had seemingly given him a compliment). He really hated Winston Churchill, too. H. G. Wells managed to write four million words of fiction and eight million words of journalism over the course of his lifetime, but modern audiences remember him exclusively for his first four sci-fi novels (and they don't remember him that fondly). He is not a truly canonical writer and maybe not even a great one. However, his influence remains massive. Like the tone of Keith Richards's guitar or Snidely Whiplash's mustache, Wells defined a universal cliché—and that is just about the rarest thing any artist can do.

The cliché that Wells popularized was not the fictional notion of time travel, because that had been around since the eighteenth century (the oldest is probably a 1733 Irish novel by Samuel Madden called *Memoirs of the Twentieth Century*). Mark Twain reversed the premise in 1889's *A Connecticut Yankee in King Arthur's Court*. There's even an 1892 novel called *Golf in the Year 2000* that predicts the advent of televised sports. But in all of those examples, time travel just sort of happens inexplicably—a person exists in one moment, and then they're transposed to another. The meaningful cliché Wells introduced was *the machine,* and that changed everything. Prior to the advent of Wells's imaginary instrument, traveling through time generally meant the central character was *lost* in time, which wasn't dramatically different from being lost geographically. But a machine gave the protagonist agency. The time traveler was now moving forward or backward on purpose; consequently, the time traveler now needed a motive for doing so. And that question, I suspect, is the core reason why narratives about time travel are almost always interesting, no matter how often the same basic story is retold and repackaged: If time travel *was* possible, why would we want to do it?

Now, I will concede that there's an inherent goofballedness in debating the ethics of an action that is impossible. It probably isn't that different than trying to figure out if leprechauns have high cholesterol. But all philosophical questions are ultimately like this—by necessity, they deal with hypotheticals that are unfeasible. Real-world problems are inevitably too unique and too situational; people will always see any real-world problem through the prism of their own personal experience. The only massive ideas everyone can discuss rationally are big ideas that don't specifically apply to anyone, which is why a debate over the ethics of time travel is worthwhile: No one has any personal investment whatsoever. It's *only* theoretical. Which means no one has any reason to lie.

2A Fictionalized motives of time travel generally operate like this: Characters go back in time to fix a mistake or change the conditions of the present (this is like *Back to The Future*). Characters go forward in time for personal gain (this is like the gambling subplot[1] of *Back to the Future Part II*). Jack the Ripper uses H. G. Wells's time machine to kill citizens of the seventies in *Time After Time*, but this was an isolated (and poorly acted) rampage. Obviously, there is always the issue of scientific inquiry with any movement through time, but that motive matters less; if a time traveler's purpose is simply to learn things that are unknown, it doesn't make moving through time any different than exploring Skull Island or going to Mars. My interest is with the explicit benefits of being transported to a different moment in existence—what that would mean morally and how the traveler's goals (whatever they may be) could be implemented successfully.

Here's a question I like to ask people when I'm 5/8 drunk: Let's say you had the ability to make a very brief phone call into your own past. You are (somehow) given the opportunity to phone yourself as a teenager; in short, you will be able to communicate with the fifteen-year-old version of You. However, you will only get to talk to your former self *for fifteen seconds*. As such, there's no way you will able to explain who you are, where or when you're calling from, or what any of this lunacy is supposed to signify. You will only be able to give the

---

1. This subplot refers to the actions of a character named Biff (Thomas F. Wilson) who steals a sports almanac from the future in order to gamble on predetermined sporting events in the present. There's a popular urban legend about this plot point involving the Florida Marlin baseball team: In the film, Biff supposedly bets on a Florida baseball team to win the World Series in 1997, which actually happened. The amazing part is that *Back to the Future Part II* was released in 1989, four years before the Florida Marlins even had a Major League franchise. Unfortunately, this legend is completely false. The reference in the movie is actually a joke about the futility of the Chicago Cubs that somehow got intertwined with another reference to a (fictional) MLB opponent from Miami whose logo was a Gator. I realize that by mentioning the inaccuracy of this urban legend, I will probably just perpetuate its erroneous existence. But that's generally how urban legends work.

younger version of yourself a fleeting, abstract message of unclear origin.

What would you say to yourself during these fifteen seconds?

From a sociological standpoint, what I find most interesting about this query is the way it inevitably splits between gender lines: Women usually advise themselves *not* to do something they now regret (i.e., "Don't sleep with Corey McDonald, no matter how much he pressures you"), while men almost always instruct themselves to do something they *failed* to attempt (i.e., "Punch Corey McDonald in the face, you gutless coward"). But from a more practical standpoint, the thing I've come to realize is that virtually no one has any idea how to utilize such an opportunity, even if it were possible. If you can't directly explain that you're talking from the future, any prescient message becomes worthless. All advice comes across like a drunk dialer reading a fortune cookie. One person answered my question by claiming he would tell the 1985 incarnation of himself to, "Invest in Google." That sounds smart, but I can't imagine a phrase that would have been more useless to me as a teenager in 1985. I would have spent the entire evening wondering how it would be possible to invest money into the number 1 with a hundred zeros behind it.

It doesn't matter what you can do if you don't know why you're doing it.

2B I've now typed fifteen hundred words about time travel, which means I've reached the point where everything becomes a problem for everybody. This is the point where we need to address the philosophical dilemmas imbedded in any casual discussions about time travel, real or imagined. And there are *a lot* of them. And I don't understand about 64 percent of them. And the 36 percent I do understand are pretty elementary to everyone including the substantial chunk of consumers who are very high and watching Anna Faris movies while they read this. But here we go! I will start with the most unavoidable eight:

1) **If you change any detail about the past, you might accidentally destroy everything in present-day existence.** This is why every movie about time travel makes a big, obvious point about not bringing anything from the present back in time, often illustrated by forcing the fictionalized time traveler to travel nude. If you went back to 60,000 B.C. with a toolbox and absentmindedly left the vise grip behind, it's entirely possible that the world would technologically advance at an exponential rate and destroy itself by the sixteenth century.[2] Or so I'm told.

2) **If you went back in time to accomplish a specific goal (and you succeeded at this goal), there would be no reason for you to have traveled back in time in the first place.** Let's say you built a time machine in hopes of murdering the proverbial "Baby Hitler" in 1889. Committing that murder would mean the Holocaust never happened. And that would mean you'd have no motive for going back in time in the first place, because the tyrannical Hitler—the one you despise—would not exist. In other words, any goal achieved through time travel would eliminate the necessity of the traveler needing to travel. In his fictional (and pathologically grotesque) oral history *Rant*, author Chuck Palahniuk refers to this impasse as The Godfather Paradox: "The idea that if one could travel backward in time, one could kill one's own ancestor, eliminating the possibility said time traveler would ever be born—and thus could never have lived to travel back and commit the murder." The solution to this paradox (according to Palahniuk) is the theory of splintered alternative realities, where all possible trajectories happen autonomously and simultaneously (sort of how Richard Linklater describes *The Wizard of Oz* to an uninterested cab driver in the opening sequence of *Slacker*). However, this solution is actually more insane than the original problem. The only modern narrative that handles the conundrum semi-successfully is Richard Kelly's *Donnie Darko*, where schizophrenic heartthrob Jake

---

2. For whatever the reason, I've always assumed vise grips would be extremely exhilarating for Neanderthals.

Gyllenhaal uses a portal to move back in time twelve days, thereby allowing himself to die in an accident he had previously avoided. By removing himself from the equation, he never meets his new girlfriend, which keeps her from dying in a car accident that was his fault. More important, his decision to die early stops his adolescence from becoming symbolized by the music of Tears for Fears.

3) **A loop in time eliminates the origin of things that already exist.** This is something called "The Bootstrap Paradox" (in reference to the Robert Heinlein story "By His Bootstraps"). It's probably best described by David Toomey, the author of a book called *The New Time Travelers* (which appears to be a principal influence on Season 5 of *Lost*). Toomey uses *Hamlet* as an example: Let's suppose Toomey found a copy of *Hamlet* in a used-book store, built a time machine, traveled back to 1601, and gave the book to William Shakespeare. Shakespeare then copies the play in his own handwriting and claims he made it up. It's recopied and republished countless times for hundreds of years, eventually ending up in the bookstore where Toomey shops. So who wrote the play? Shakespeare obviously didn't. Another example occurs near the end of *Back to the Future*: Michael J. Fox performs "Johnny B. Goode" at the school dance and the tune is transmitted over the telephone to Chuck Berry[3] (who presumably stole it). In this reality, where does the song come from? Who gets the songwriting royalties?

---

3. Semi-unrelated (but semi-interesting) footnote to this paradox: Before Fox plays "Johnny B. Goode," he tells his audience, "This is an oldie—well, this is an oldie from where I come from." Chuck Berry recorded "Johnny B. Goode" in 1958; *Back to the Future* was made in 1985, so the gap is twenty-seven years. I'm writing this essay in 2009, which means the gap between 1985 and today is twenty-four years. That's almost the same amount of time. Yet nobody would ever refer to *Back to the Future* as an "oldie," even if he or she were born in the 1990s. What seems to be happening is a dramatic increase in cultural memory: As culture accelerates, the distance between historical events feels smaller. The gap between 2010 and 2000 will seem far less than the gap between 1980 and 1970, which already seemed far less than the gap between 1960 and 1950. This, I suppose, is society's own version of time travel (assuming the trend continues for eternity).

4) **You'd possibly kill everybody by sneezing.** Depending on how far you went back in time, there would be a significant risk of infecting the entire worldwide population with an illness that mankind has spent the last few centuries building immunities against. Unless, of course, you happened to contract smallpox immediately upon arrival—then *you'd* die.

5) **You already exist in the recent past.** This is the most glaring problem and the one everybody intuitively understands—if you went back to yesterday, you would still be there, standing next to yourself. The consequence of this existential condition is both straightforward and unexplainable. Moreover . . .

6) **Before you attempted to travel back in time, you'd already know if it worked.** Using the example from Problem # 5, imagine that you built a time machine on Thursday. You decide to use the machine on Saturday in order to travel back to Friday afternoon. If this worked, you would already see yourself on Friday. But what would then happen if you (and the Future You) destroyed your time machine on Friday night? How would the Future You be around to assist with the destroying?

7) **Unless all of time was happening simultaneously within multiple realities, memories and artifacts would mysteriously change.** The members of Steely Dan (Donald Fagen and Walter Becker) met at Bard College in 1967, when Fagen overheard Becker playing guitar in a café. This meeting has been recounted many times in interviews, and the fact that they were both at Bard College (located in Annandale-on-Hudson) is central to songs like "My Old School." But what if Fagen built a time machine in 1980 and went back to find Becker in 1966, when he was still a high school student in Manhattan? What would happen to their shared personal memories that first meeting in Annandale? And if they had both immediately moved to Los Angles upon Becker's graduation, how could the song "My Old School" exist (and what would it be about)?

8) **The past has happened, and it can only happen *the way it happened.*** This, I suppose, is debatable. But not by Bruce Willis. In Terry Gilliam's *12 Monkeys,* Willis goes back in time to confront an insane Brad Pitt before Pitt releases a virus that's destined to kill five billion people and drive the rest of society into hiding (as it turns out, Pitt is merely trying to release a bunch of giraffes from the Philadelphia Zoo, which is only slightly more confusing than the presence of Madeleine Stowe in this movie). What's distinctive about *12 Monkeys* is that the reason Willis is sent back in time is not to stop this catastrophe from happening, but merely to locate a primitive version of the virus so that scientists can combat the existing problem in the distant future (where the remnants of mankind have been to forced to take refuge underground). Willis can travel through time, but he can't change anything or save anyone. "How can I save you?" he rhetorically asks the white-clad dolts who question his sudden appearance in the year 1990. "This already happened. No one can save you." *12 Monkeys* makes a lot of references to the "Cassandra Complex" (named for a Greek myth about a young woman's inability to convince others that her futuristic warnings are accurate), but it's mostly about predestination—in *12 Monkeys,* the assumption is that anyone who travels into the past will do exactly what history dictates. Nothing can be altered. What this implies is that everything about life (including the unforeseen future) is concrete and predetermined. There is no free will. So if you've seen *12 Monkeys* more than twice, you're probably a Calvinist.

These are just a handful of the (nonscientific) problems with going backward in time. As far as I can tell, there really aren't any causality problems with going forward in time—in terms of risk, jumping to the year 2077 isn't that different than moving to suburban Bangladesh or hiding in your basement for five decades. Time would still move forward on its regular trajectory, no differently than if you were temporarily (or permanently) dead. Your participation in life doesn't matter to time. This is part of the reason that futurists tend to believe traveling forward in time is more possible than the alternative—it involves fewer problems. But regardless of the direction you move, the *central* problem is still there: Why do it? What's the *best* reason for exploding the parameters of reality?

With the possible exception of eating a dinosaur, I don't think there is one.

3 "Even back when I was writing really bad short stories in college," a (then) thirty-four-year-old Shane Carruth said in an interview with himself, "I always thought the time machine is the device that's missed most. Without even saying it out loud, that's the thing people want the most: The ability to take whatever it is that went wrong and fix it."

Carruth was the writer, director, producer, and costar of the 2004 independent film *Primer,* the finest movie about time travel I've ever seen. The reason *Primer* is the best (despite its scant seventy-eight-minute run time and $7000 budget) is because it's the most realistic—which, I will grant, is a peculiar reason for advocating a piece of science fiction. But the plausibility of *Primer* is why it's so memorable. It's not that the time machine in *Primer* seems more authentic; it's that the time travelers themselves seem more believable. They talk and act (and *think*) like the kind of people who might accidentally figure out how to move through time, which is why it's the best depiction we have of the ethical quandaries that would emerge from such a discovery.

Here's the basic outline of *Primer*: It opens with four identically dressed computer engineers sitting around a table in a nondescript American community (*Primer* was shot around Dallas, but the setting is like the world of Neil LaBute's *In the Company of Men*—it's a city without character that could literally be anywhere). They speak a dense, clipped version of English that is filled with technical jargon; it's mostly indecipherable, but that somehow makes it better. They wear ties and white shirts all the time (even when they're removing a catalytic converter from a car to steal the palladium), and they have no interests outside of superconductivity and NCAA basketball. The two brightest engineers—Abe (David Sullivan) and Aaron (Carruth)—eventually realize they have assembled a box that can move objects backward through a thirteen-hundred-minute loop in time. Without telling anyone else, they build two larger versions of the (staunchly unglamorous) box that can transport them to the previous day.[4] Their initial motive is solely financial—they go back a day, drive to the local library, and buy stocks over the Internet which they know will increase in value over the next twenty-four hours. They try to do nothing else of consequence (at least at first). They just sit in a hotel room and wait. "I tried to isolate myself," Abe says when describing his first journey into the past. "I closed the windows, I unplugged everything—the phone, the TV, and clock radio. I didn't want to take the chance of seeing someone I knew, or of seeing something on the news . . . I mean, if we're dealing with causality, and I don't even know for sure . . . I took myself out of the equation."

If this sounds simple, I can assure you that it is not. *Primer* is hopelessly confusing and grows more and more byzantine as it unravels (I've watched it seven or eight times and I still don't totally know how it works). Characters begin to secretly use the time machine for personal reasons and they begin multiplying themselves across time. But because these symmetrical iterations are (inevitably) copies of other copies, the system starts to hemorrhage—Abe and Aaron find themselves bleeding from their ears and struggling with handwriting. When confusing events start to happen in the present, they can't tell if those events are the manifestations of decisions one of them will

4. This is too difficult to explain in a footnote, but one of Carruth's strength as a fake science writer is how he deals with the *geography* of time travel, an issue most writers never even consider. Here, in short, is the problem: If you could instantly travel one hour back in time, you would (theoretically) re-materialize in the exact same place from which you left. That's how the machine works in the original *Time Machine*. However, the world would have rotated since the hour you're traveling back to, so you would actually rematerialize in a totally different spot on the globe. *Primer* manages to work around this problem, although I honestly don't see the solution as much as I understand the dilemma.

eventually make in the future. At one point, no one (not Abe, Aaron, or even the viewer) is able to understand what's happening. The story does not end in a clear disaster, but with a hazy, open-ended scenario that might be worse.

What's significant about the two dudes in *Primer* is how they initially disregard the ethical questions surrounding time travel; as pure scientists, they only consider the practical obstacles of the endeavor. Even when they decide to go back and change the past of other people, their only concern is how this can still work within the framework they're manipulating. They're geniuses, but they're ethical Helen Kellers. When they're traveling back for financial purposes, they discount their personal role in the success of the stocks they trade; since stocks increase in value whenever people buy them, they are retroactively inflating the value of whatever commodities they select (not by much, but enough to alter the future). When Abe and Aaron start traveling back in time to change their own pasts, they attempt to stoically ignore the horrifying reality they've created: Their sense of self—their very *definition* of self—is suddenly irrelevant. If you go back in time today and meet the person who will become you tomorrow, which of those two people is actually you? The short answer is, "both." But once you realize that the short answer is "both," the long answer becomes "neither." If you exist in two places, you don't exist at all.

According to the director, *Primer* is a movie about the relationship between risk and trust. This is true. But it also makes a concrete point about the potential purpose of time travel—it's too important to use only for money, but too dangerous to use for anything else.

1A I used to have a fantasy about reliving my entire life with my present-day mind. I thought this fantasy was unique to me, but it turns out that this is very common; many people enjoy imagining what it would be like to reinhabit their past with the knowledge they've acquired through experience. I imagine bizarre things I would have said to teachers in junior high. I think about women I would have pursued and stories I could have written better and about how interesting it would have been to be a genius four-year-old. At its nucleus, this is a fantasy about never having to learn anything. The defining line from Frank Herbert's *Dune* argues that the mystery of life "is not a question to be answered but a reality to be experienced." My fantasy offers the opposite. Nothing would be experienced. Nothing would feel new or unknown or jarring. It's a fantasy for people who want to solve life's mysteries without having to do the work.

I am one of those people.

The desire to move through time is electrifying and rational, but it's a desire of weakness. The real reason I want to travel through time is because I'm a defeatist person. The cynical egomaniac in Wells's original novel leaves the present because he has contempt for the humanity of his present world, but he never considers changing anything about his own role in that life (which would obviously be easier). Instead, he elects to bolt 800,000 years into the future, blindly hoping that things will have improved for him. It's a bad plan. Charlton Heston's character in *Planet of the Apes*[5] tries something similar; he hates mankind, so he volunteers to explore space, only to crash back on a postapocalyptic earth where poorly dressed orangutans employ Robert's Rules of Order. This is a consistent theme in stories about traveling to the future: Things are always worse when you get there. And I suspect this is because the kind of writer who's intrigued by the notion of moving forward in time can't see beyond their own pessimism about being alive. People who want to travel through time are both (a) unhappy and (b) unwilling to compromise anything about who they are. They would rather change every element of society *except* themselves.

This is how I feel.

---

5. I realize *Planet of the Apes* isn't technically about time travel. Time moves at its normal rate while the humans are in suspended animation. But for the purposes of the fictional people involved, there is no difference: They leave from and return to the same geographic country. The only difference is the calendar.

This is also why my longstanding desire to build a time machine is not just hopeless, but devoid of merit. It has nothing to do with time. I don't think it ever does (for me, H. G. Wells, Shane Carruth, or for anyone else). It takes a flexible mind to imagine how time travel might work, but only an inflexible spirit would want to do so. It's the desire of the depressed and lazy.

On side two of the Beach Boys' *Pet Sounds,* Brian Wilson laments that he "just wasn't made for these times" ("these times" being 1966). He probably wasn't. But he also didn't want to be. I assume Wilson would have preferred to deal with the possibility of thinking liquid metal before he would accept the invisible, nonnegotiable shackles of the present tense. Which—sadly, and quite fortunately—is the only tense any of us will ever have.